BEAUTY'S CURSED BEAST

A BEAUTY AND THE BEAST RETELLING

THE CURSED BEAUTY SERIES
BOOK TWO

MARY E. TWOMEY

MARY E. TWOMEY, LLC

BEAUTY'S CURSED BEAST

A Cursed Beauty Novel
Book Two

By

Mary E. Twomey

COPYRIGHT

DEDICATION

For my dad,
who took me to Beauty and the Beast 3D when it came out in
theaters, Disney on Ice's Beauty and the Beast, the off-
Broadway musical show of Beauty and the Beast, and bought
me a Beauty and the Beast snow globe just to make me smile.

It did, and you do.

UNEXPECTED GUEST

"You shouldn't have a Pulse!" Audra exclaimed as she set the tea tray down on the stand. There were so many people milling about; she wanted to guard the delicate china cups, lest yet another of them chip. They were down to two-hundred-forty-four, which was barely enough for the crowd Adam had packed into the castle. Though, to be fair, they preferred shot glasses to tea cups.

Adam laughed at his housekeeper, his eyes dancing with mirth. "You're only saying that because you got stuck with putting people at ease as your Pulse. Mine's actually useful."

Audra leaned over and flicked his nose, just as she'd done when he was a little boy stuck in fits of petulance. "Yes. If only *you* were useful, as well." She was only half-joking, but she squinted her eyes at him all the same. "If you hadn't been gifted with the ability to persuade people as your Pulse, you wouldn't have a dime to your name."

"Oh, Audra. Persuasion is such an ugly summary of what I do. I merely strip away a layer of inhibition so they can see themselves and their options clearly. People love to be coaxed into doing things they'd otherwise be too scared to enjoy. Look at her up there. Isn't she a beauty?" He motioned to the mid-twenties woman who was dancing on the stage, stripping off one piece of clothing slowly for the viewers. "Now, if I used my Pulse on you, there's no way you'd end up on the stage doing a striptease for my friends, because you know who you are and what you want, which isn't that."

Audra shuddered. "Oh, my boy. These people aren't your friends."

Adam took a canape from her tray. "This girl wanted, in some buried part of her, to be up there doing exactly that. I just gave her a nudge."

"I believe that's the same logic used by drug-dealing scum."

"Oh, you." Adam batted his hand at the maid who could easily pass for his mother, and had served that function on many occasions when his own mother was away on her many social engagements. Now that his parents were deceased, Audra was one of the few chances he had at a conscience.

Just then, two guests came up to Audra to kiss her

goodbye. Rory and Henry had been regular fixtures in the castle since they'd been children, but ever since Adam had taken the reins of the family fortune, they'd started leaving his parties earlier and earlier. "Goodnight, Audra," Henry said, kissing her wrinkled cheek that still possessed a bit of plump to it.

Adam frowned at his two best friends. "You're leaving already? Come on. It's my birthday! You can stay in your bedroom here."

Rory sank into Adam, her head resting on his chest. She looked dainty and frail in his thick arms, but he was always gentle with her. She was only fourteen, and by far the youngest in the castle. "I thought about that, but there are people up there making babies in my sheets. I think I'll just go home with Henry."

"You could always join them, you know." When his joke didn't garner a giggle from his best friends, but only stiff looks of disapproval, Adam released her with a frown of displeasure. "You never stay for the whole party anymore."

Rory glanced up at the stage, frowning at the impromptu strip show. "Can you blame me? This isn't exactly a proud moment for women."

Henry's arm coiled around her, as if to shield his friend from the debauchery. Though Henry was eighteen, he was much too old for parties like that, and took it upon himself to stay by Rory's side the entire night.

Adam frowned at Henry. "And you? What's your

excuse for passing up on good whisky on my twentieth birthday?"

Henry shrugged, his blond hair still perfectly intact after the evening of dancing and mingling. "You know I can't be seen at events that devolve into this. My father wouldn't approve."

Adam scoffed with too much attitude to be overlooked. He'd started to do that more and more after the death of his parents. "Tell King Hubert that his son needs the royal scepter removed from his ass."

Henry tilted his head to the side, as if to silently ask if that's what Adam truly wanted to say. He paused, and Adam's bravado shrank marginally. Henry sighed heavily, and then brought Adam in for a hug. "I love you, even when you're an arrogant prick who forgets everything about the people he loves."

When the men released each other, Henry donned a wide grin for Audra. He always treated her as if the maternal affection she beamed was meant only for him. She pinched his cheeks to fill in the holes growing up without a mother had left on the boy. "Do stop by the kitchen on your way out. I made those cookies you like. Chef Bouche put them on top of the microwave."

Though Henry commanded many a room with his tall, built and handsome stature, he turned into a boy for her, bouncing on his toes with excitement at the doting. "Really? Did you put the peanut butter chips inside?"

Audra scoffed. "I'd like to know who you think you're

talking to. I would never cheat my boy out of anything." She pulled him in for a hug and kissed his cheek. Instead of releasing him, she stole a moment to whisper in his ear, "Don't give up on Adam. He needs you."

Henry softened, savoring the hug that turned him from man into mischievous boy. "Never." Then he turned to Adam with a forced smile. "Happy birthday. I must say, that's the most unique wall-hanging I've ever seen." Henry's eyes darted to the large printout hanging directly across from the front door, so it was the first thing one saw when they entered.

The banished and feared former queen of Avondale, Malaura, had taken to sending Adam letters in secret, hoping to entice him to join her league of outcasts. The offers turned to love letters, one of which Adam had blown up and hung in the foyer for all to see. It was a shock for each guest when they entered, giving them guilty giggles at the scandal that Avondale's Most Eligible Bachelor was handsome enough to turn even the wicked ex-queen into a blushing schoolgirl.

Adam's grin widened as he glanced up at the poster with bravado. "Why, thank you. You should've seen the one I wrote her in return. Some of my raciest poetry to date."

Henry rubbed the nape of his neck. "Are you sure it's wise to string along someone as powerful and vindictive as my Aunt Malaura?"

Adam rolled his eyes and pulled Rory into his arms,

kissing her atop her straight, raven hair. Rory said nothing of the blatant poke at Malaura, and snuggled into Adam's side, closing her eyes as if she sorely missed her friend, even though she was currently holding onto him. "Happy birthday, Adam."

Audra's nose crinkled in distaste when the only two guests she enjoyed exited the party. "Your mother would be ashamed of you, Adam. Your father had that stage built for your violin performances, and this is what you use it for now?"

Adam's smile froze on his face at mention of his deceased parents, but it didn't fade. His expression twisted with a haughtiness he wore when challenged with integrity. "The violin doesn't amuse me. But this?" He leaned against the gold wallpaper that gilded the ballroom in a veneer of wealth and beauty. "*This* amuses me. Besides, I'm not strong enough to force anyone to do anything. All I did was strip her of her fear." He waggled his eyebrows at Audra. "She did the rest of the stripping all on her own."

Audra bit back her scoff of disgust, and set to pouring tea for the guests who wouldn't have noticed if she'd opted for the good tea. She'd selected the sub-par garbage from a bag instead, and no one said a thing. Most of them were drunk, as they were at all of Adam's monthly soirees. "Enjoy the cesspool you've created for yourself."

"I always do." Adam took the teacup and sipped the

hot beverage with a sneer of distaste that she'd used the cheap stuff. "This is rubbish, and you know it." Still, he downed the cup, much to Audra's amusement.

"I'm glad you hated it. I laced your cup with a laxative."

Adam's thick chestnut eyebrows rose in alarm. He was highly desired due partially to his stunning chiseled looks, and partially because he'd inherited the largest fortune in history, along with taking over his father's profitable mortgage company. Though, he could've won the title on looks alone.

He eyed his tea cup skeptically. "You did what?"

"I'm tired of cleaning up bras from your floor. At least this way, there'll be no women coming after you for child support if you get careless. You'll spend your night in the bathroom, not the bedroom."

Adam glowered at her and placed his teacup on the tray. "You don't have to worry about things like that."

Audra patted his cheek, softening at his smile. "I always worry about you, you stupid, stupid boy."

Adam grudgingly kissed her cheek, and left her to join the others, who were hollering at the woman on the stage. She was down to her underwear and bra, which usually meant that it was nearing on midnight.

Audra yawned, but kept on her job, cleaning up the empty bottles and plates as she went. She caught Lucien's eye across the way, and the two exchanged a sad smile. Lucien's Pulse was that he could increase your happiness with a simple touch. He could have been put to great use in a nursing home or a preschool, but he was posted in the castle, shaking the hands of everyone as they walked inside. No matter what misgivings they'd had on their way in, the partiers left their caution at the door, smiling at the Pulse of happiness they were given upon entry.

Lucien sauntered over to her with a slight wickedness to his smirk that gave Audra a hint of a giggle. Though he was twenty years her junior, he always made it a point to dote on her. Even without Pulsing happiness into her, Lucien had a way about him that made everyone glad. His hips moved in a tango as he caught her up in a dance that made her feel young and enchanting, rather than the constant mother who, it seemed, would never be finished raising the man-child they'd all been entrusted to watch over.

"You look like you could use a little dance," Lucien pressed his torso to hers to coax a tango out of her. He was exactly her height of five-foot-ten, but had a longer nose than her modest one, and the ability to make a joke out of anything.

Audra kept up easily with the steps he slowed for her. "Oh, Lucien. I only dance for you."

Lucien had the kind of deportment that made everyone want to be his friend. While Adam had been blessed with stunning handsomeness (a gift from his far humbler father), Lucien had a smile that touched his eyes, and transcended mere superficial pleasantries. He looked into Audra's gaze and saw the sadness in the makeshift matriarch. "You're disappointed in our young man?"

"I don't want to be. I just can't shake how hurt his parents would be if they saw all this waste. Adam didn't used to be like this. He's barely turned twenty, and he's been given the wealth of a small country, and too much freedom without the life experience he needs to be able to handle it all."

"He's not going to run the company into the ground. He's like his father – brilliant eye for business. He just needs to get his head about him." Lucien looked as if he was about to say more, but the doorbell rang, which was his cue. He stopped the tango with an apologetic tilt to his head, resuming the duty that was truly beneath his talents.

"Mind your post," Bosworth chided Lucien, coming down from the stairs in his military jacket, which had fit him far better a decade ago. That was before Adam's father had offered him a salary he couldn't refuse. Bosworth checked his pocket watch and frowned. "The storm is getting more troublesome out there, and the guests are tracking mud into the foyer. See that Vivienne mops it up." Bosworth's pooched belly was sucked in, but it hardly made a difference to the strained buttons on the brown and red jacket. As head of the household staff, he made it his job to see to everyone else performing to Adam's satisfaction, no matter how depraved the parties became.

Lucien wasn't put off by Bosworth's haughty scolding,

but blew the man a kiss, as he often did to throw Bosworth off his game. "Whatever you say, you old tease."

When Lucien opened the door, it wasn't one of the many twenty-and-thirty-somethings all dolled up for a night of debauchery at Adam's infamous parties. His eyebrows rose at the wrinkled old woman with a long nose and gnarled fingers. She wore a black cloak with the hood pulled over her head, shrouding her eyes in shadow. "The rain's really coming down out there. My car got stuck in the mud half a mile away, and you're the first house I've seen. Can I trouble you to make a phone call?"

"Of course, young lady. Come on in." Lucien doted on older women by referring to them as "young" ladies, which always garnered him a smile. He reveled not in using his Pulse, but in drawing out happiness in others without the use of magic. "Oh, it's really coming down out there. Here, let's get you into a chair and put a hot cup of tea in your hands."

The woman smiled at him, and took his arm as she trembled from the chill.

Adam stumbled out with two women, both drunk and cackling at something "hilarious" Adam had said. When the man of the house saw the old woman, he stopped short. "Go on up without me, girls. I've a matter to see to." He narrowed his eyes at Lucien, who pretended not to see the disapproval. "What is this?"

Lucien straightened, his deportment fitting in nicely with the polish of the marble floors and the dust-free golden sconces that bespoke of good breeding. "This is a woman, and her car broke down. She's coming in to warm up while I ring for someone to assist."

"We have a dress code," Adam reminded his attendant, his chest puffing out to show off the expensive three-piece suit he wore. Though Adam was tall, muscular and built for chopping down trees, he'd been bred for real estate and taking over small companies. The tailor-made jacket was unbuttoned, but the blue vest beneath still made him look dapper and powerful. "She can wait in the stables. I don't need the guests seeing a sopping old crone standing in my foyer."

Lucien balked at his boss, whom he'd taught to ride horses and instructed on many a dance lesson. Now that Adam was an adult, Lucien wasn't "Uncle Lou", but rather the servant who was expected to obey at the cost of kindness. "Adam, surely you don't mean that. She's not bothering anyone."

Adam didn't act as if he cared when his guests disapproved, but his frown was more prominent when Rory, Henry, Audra, and now Lucien tried to control his behavior. "This is my home, and you're my servant, are you not?"

Lucien's jaw stiffened in time with his posture. "I don't think you understand the difference between a servant and a slave."

"I don't think you understand the difference between a paycheck and unemployment." Adam clicked his fingers at the old woman, not bothering with manners. "Out you go."

Lucien reeled backwards, breathless, as the old woman threw off her cloak, straightening her posture to reveal her true self. In seconds, her wrinkles smoothed, the signature royal blonde hue chased away the gray in her hair, she grew several inches in height, and her face shifted from an old hag to a beautiful woman in her fifties with an imperious look about her.

Adam gasped, and started in on a string of apologies when he recognized the woman as none other than the elusive ousted queen who'd cursed Rory as a baby. "Malaura?" Adam glanced behind him guiltily as his crass treatment of her private love letters to him framed his frozen form like a spotlight of doom.

Dread washed over Adam's features and he fell to his knees, knowing it wouldn't bode well for him to run at this point. She hadn't been seen in years, but whenever there were reported sightings, someone had walked away with a curse, if they'd managed to walk away at all.

"Run, Adam!" Lucien shouted, and then turned and darted into the ballroom to end the party and shoo everyone out through the back exit.

Adam was trembling under her intense scrutiny, humbling his posture so that he looked nothing like the haughty heir to the Fontaine fortune.

The sorceress looked down her suddenly slender nose and shook her head. "I've heard rumors of your pride, but never would've guessed the son of Moira and Peter Fontaine would've grown into such an arrogant prat. How I adored you from afar, but up close?" She glanced up at the private love letter she'd sent him, and a flicker of true hurt dashed across her pinched features. "Up close, you're quite disappointing. Beautiful, but utterly vapid."

"Malaura, I can explain."

She began to circle him, her black dress dragging out behind her. "Moira and Peter wouldn't have wanted this lifestyle for their boy. Your parents never sponsored my more interesting projects back when I sat on the throne, but I respected their firm command of their capitalistic empire nonetheless. They were good people who raised you far better than this." She tutted him, and then reached down to tap a pointy red fingernail under his chin to lift his head. "You're even more stunning than in your pictures." She bent over and caught his earlobe between her teeth and tugged, laughing at his shudder. "I prefer my toys to be pretty, and you're by far the most beautiful man I've ever seen. How I would love to take you home with me. Oh, the things I could teach a virile student like your-self." Her tongue darted out to wet her crimson lips as she studied his squirming.

"I'm nowhere near as accomplished as your last student. I would be a disappointment to you!" Everyone in the kingdom knew that Remus Johnstone had been her most treasured student. Rory's uncle had gray eyes that held many secrets, but he never spoke of his time in

Malaura's study, back when she'd ruled Avondale, and he'd been the gifted boy everyone was jealous of for catching the eye of the queen.

Now that her gaze rested on Adam, he squirmed as if that might scrape her attention off of him and cast it elsewhere.

She stroked Adam's arm, and he let out a whimper, his lips parted and trembling with terror. It was widely known that Malaura's Pulse was that she could touch a person and mirror their own Pulse. He felt her shooting his own ability of Persuasion and stripping away of inhibitions into him. "Tell me you'll come away with me and be my toy. I would take such care to train you properly. It's been so long since I've had a pupil worthy of my talents."

"No!" he blurted without filter, since his caution was gone. She'd meant to use his gift to convince him to run away with her, but it backfired, making him speak more honestly than his fear would normally permit. "You're disgusting! Even if you hadn't cursed Rory, I would never run away with you. Look at me, and then look at yourself! Your touch makes my skin crawl. I am not so desperate that I would give myself over to someone so plain as you." Adam shook his head and tried to rid himself of the Pulse he feared might cost him his life. He began to sweat through his suit. "Don't listen to a word I say! Take any room in the castle you like. Stay as long as you need. Only don't curse me!"

Malaura's red painted lips were drawn in a tight line. "Why would you assume you're in need of a curse?"

"I know your mind. Everyone knows Rory won't see her twenty-fifth birthday because of you."

Of all things, the woman laughed. "You do as you please without thinking of the consequences. Me, on the other hand, I only think of the consequences. What is the consequence of letting such selfishness carry on like this? What is the consequence of allowing such spoiled behavior to be idolized by the public?" Then she leaned in. "What is the consequence of letting you go for some other woman to enjoy your loveliness? Eyes that striking and a face that handsome should only be focused on me. If not me, then no one shall have you."

Adam swallowed and closed his eyes, lacing his fingers behind his head. "Please don't kill me."

"Silly boy. If I killed you, then how would you suffer for rejecting me and making me look like a fool by showing off my letters? I want you to live a long time regretting all we could have had together."

"No. No, please!"

She knelt before him and opened her fist, producing a handful of gold dust. Then she gripped the back of his head and forced his mouth upon hers, chortling through his blatant disgust, as if she enjoyed his distress. The moment she released him, she blew the gold dust into his face, smiling as he choked and coughed.

Adam sat back on his heels, still wiping the gold dust from his face. "What did you do to me?"

"Your insides will match your outsides now – horrifying as I've witnessed them to be."

An alarm rang through the house, and Adam guessed that Lucien had set off the fire alarm to get everyone out quicker. He rubbed the gold dust from his face, but recoiled, shouting with distress at the sight of his hands. "What are you doing to me? Make it stop!"

Brown hair sprouted from the backs of his hands, growing thick enough to make his pampered fingers appear animalistic. He felt around on his face, and found that his upper lip was now puffy, and his eyebrows were bushy and unruly.

The sorceress pressed her finger to his lips. "You'll remain ghastly like this until the last petal falls from this rose," she explained as she opened her fist again. This time, a perfect red bud bloomed out from the center of her palm. "You'll live ten more years like this while the slowly rose blooms. Then you'll join the Lupine tribe on your thirtieth birthday when the last petal falls. If I can't have you, I'll make it so that no one wants you."

Panicked, Adam shook his head, murmuring for her to reconsider.

Malaura remained firm in her judgment. "Our world has no place for selfishness like yours. You'll pay for your sins, and then you'll join the outcasts, roaming Avondale as a wolf until you die."

Audra burst into the foyer, eyes wild and arms raised to attack. Despite the danger, she was ready to risk it all to save Adam. "No! You'll not hurt my boy like this. His foolishness began when his parents died. This isn't who he'll always be."

The sorceress arose with a smile. "I'll hurt you all like this, unless you step aside."

Audra dropped to her knees and held Adam, who wailed into her shoulder, clawing at his hands in confusion. Instead of arguing with the woman, Audra closed her eyes and began a chant of her own, her arms shaking with determination that outweighed her fear. Though she'd been cast in the role of servant, she'd sat in on every one of Adam's lessons when he was schooled in the art of magic.

Then Lucien and Bosworth came forward, murmuring the same counter-curse in hopes of saving the boy they'd been entrusted to watch over. The other servants ran to Adam's aid, adding girth to the spell that needed to somehow be more powerful than the curse of the elite sorceress.

Malaura's head tilted back as she let out a hearty cackle. "Oh, how funny you are to try and counter a curse of mine. Only Remus was powerful enough to come up against me all those years ago, and that's only because I trained him. Enjoy the feeling of failure. In fact, for your petulance, I'll grant you with a curse of your own. The Lupine has no use for you all, but you'll be trapped until Adam turns, and then you'll be nothing."

She waved her hand over the foyer, and her voice grew louder as the servants collapsed, one by one as more of them ran forward to try and save the master of the house.

Adam saw precious little through the gold dust and the tears that marred his vision, but when he finally was able to look around, the sorceress had vanished, and the servants who loved him were nowhere to be seen.

2

UNWELCOME VISITORS

"This is a business, not a charity. If you can't make your payments, you shouldn't have signed the mortgage."

"But Mr. Fontaine, we just need more time. We've paid on schedule for fifteen years, and never missed a payment."

"Until the past six months. You've been late or short for half a year now." Adam sat back in his grand leather chair and eyed the next late contract on his massive mahogany desk. His mind was already onto the next task; he'd lost his patience for pleading long ago. He'd never be caught sounding as pathetic as the people who called his office daily for an extension on their loans. "I've been more than patient. You have until the end of the month, and then we'll start the eviction process."

"But, sir!"

Adam hung up on the caller, as he'd done four times that morning already.

"That was rude," chided Audra. She slid slowly into his office atop a tea tray, using her magic to control its trajectory. Though she'd lost her arms and legs long ago, she managed to move around the castle easily enough in the form of a teapot.

Adam glared at her bone china face. "That was business. Something you will never understand."

Audra's china base clicked as she teetered toward him, hopping from her tea tray to his desk. "I understand well enough. You've gone from unpleasant to downright surly ever since Rory stopped coming to visit."

Adam's fist tightened on his pen. "Don't pretend that you know what it's like to be me."

"Are you having a laugh? I'm one of the few who understands completely what it's like to be you. I'm confined to the castle even more than you are. You won't leave because of vanity's sake. I *can't* leave, for fear of people stepping on me and throwing me out with the garbage." Then her tone softened with the maternal coo she couldn't help. "Maybe Rory will come today. It's the first of the month, after all."

"I don't care if she comes. She's probably off with her new husband, boring each other to tears. Henry will be by later, and that's that."

Audra shot him a pained look that shone through on the white teapot with pink rose embellishments, a few of the golden swirl designs shaping themselves into eyes and a thin mouth. All the servants had suffered for their failed attempt at a counter-curse. They'd been turned into common household objects with voices only Adam could hear. He'd tried in the beginning to convince doctors and friends that the servants had become the objects, but no one believed him. Even Rory and Henry had offered up sad smiles and pacifying head-nods. He was labeled mentally ill by doctor after doctor – hearing voices that, according to everyone else, simply weren't there.

It had taken slashing mortgage rates to the bare minimum to keep his company afloat, ensuring clients didn't jump ship on him. That actually turned into a brilliant business move, making the company the most stable of all its competitors, despite its unstable owner.

Adam was deformed now, and as much as people like to claim it's what inside that counts, his new outward appearance had people looking the other way instead of leaning in to listen and help. With the loss of his looks and a diagnosis of major depressive disorder with psychosis, he had only his servants to keep him company. Henry and Rory had stopped by once a month to try to get him out of the castle for nine years, but after Adam let his pride keep him from going to Rory when she'd been in need earlier that year, she'd finally turned her back on him, as well.

Now there was only Henry. Adam knew they were only keeping on with these visits because Henry was a decent person, not because either of them enjoyed each other's company anymore. No one came to visit, scared of the man whose chestnut hair now looked closer to fur, and covered his shoulders, chest, back, legs, arms, and cheeks. His once commanding physique was now a beacon for a body that was still man, but was slowly turning to beast, with a puffy upper lip that made his expressions appear animalistic.

Audra tipped her spout after summoning a teacup to sit on the desk. She poured Adam a steaming cup of Earl Grey and righted herself. "You should call Rory and apologize."

Adam scoffed at the suggestion both of them knew was futile for her to suggest. "You should mind your own business."

"That girl *is* my business. She was a good friend to you. You need people in your life, Adam."

"What do I need people for when I've got a talking teapot who prattles on incessantly?"

Audra glowered at him and huffed as she leapt back onto her tray, scooting it toward the exit as the doorbell rang. "That'll be Henry. Best put on a smile."

Adam snarled, knowing that when he bothered with a grin, his fangs were too visible. "I'm busy."

"You're bossy. Those are two different things. You'll come down and greet your only friend, Adam."

Adam grumbled, but ultimately obeyed. He stomped through the dusty, unlit hallway and moved down the doublewide staircase that had once been grand. The gold fixtures had long since lost their shimmer, the air was thick with cobwebs and dust, and it had been ages since anyone had run a vacuum. None of his servants could manage an appliance of that size, so some of the chores had been left to Adam, who couldn't have cared less.

When he threw open the door, his eyes immediately scanned to the side of Henry and behind him, searching for Rory. When she wasn't there, his shoulders fell, frustrated that he'd been foolish enough to hope she'd forgiven him. Worse was that he actually hoped for the clemency, which was almost as bad as admitting aloud he'd been wrong – something he had no intention of doing. "Hey," he greeted Henry, and then turned around without pretense of a handshake or hug.

Prince Henry had been bred for politics since birth and didn't let his offense show at the lack of cordial greeting. He didn't come to visit Adam on the first of the month to get friendship from him, but to offer it, since Adam was so deprived of the stuff. "Good morning, Adam. I can see you put on your Sunday best for me."

Adam glanced down, cringing that he was still in his pajamas. Worst was that he couldn't remember how long it had been since he'd worn anything else, or even bothered to shower. "Only the best for the Prince of Avondale. What's new in the land of all the beautiful people?"

Henry tried not to take offense at the compliment that was meant as a jab. Adam's curse had left him with a puffy, scarred and hairy face that had swiftly dethroned him as

Avondale's most eligible bachelor. Prince Henry wore that spotlight now, especially since Rory, whom Henry had been betrothed to since her birth, was now married to Cordray Phillips – the man she'd fallen in love with. Prince Henry had never loved Rory as anything more than a sister and best friend, so he was thrilled for them. He'd stood up for her as her Maid of Honor at her wedding, proclaiming to all the eligible maidens in the land that there was no chance he would end up with the Chancellor's daughter he'd been promised to. The female fervor for him had tripled since then.

Henry sneezed three times at the thick layer of dust that only seemed to multiply over the years. It wasn't just the rugs that stank of man feet, but the stench had permeated the walls as well, making the whole place something to wrinkle your nose at. "Father's starting to put on the pressure of marriage, but lucky for him, I'm married to Avondale."

"Sounds tedious. King Hubert should know you're not built for settling down."

"That's what I told him. It went over about as well as you can imagine." Henry followed Adam into the kitchen, which was the only room they ever ventured to in the past year. Everything else was too dusty, and filled with neglect. Plus, Adam was touchy about the objects in his castle. It would have been helpful to his claims for mental health if the teapot was able to move on its own when Henry was around, but the objects only moved for Adam, making him seem unbalanced even to his very best of friends.

Adam was patient while Henry talked about the state of the kingdom. There was a big controversy over whether or not Lethals should be able to roam about freely, or if they should be forced to take a pill that would mute all of their powers, thus making them safer to be around.

Adam cared little about it all, since his Pulse wasn't lethal. The only person in his life now was Henry, so he nodded when expected, and gave grunts of derision when it seemed appropriate. Rory's new husband was a Lethal, so Adam pretended to care, in hopes it might make it back to her that he was civil. He thought it foolish that she'd chosen to fall in love with a Lethal. Cordray could electrocute anyone with a simple touch. He wore gloves and secretly had to take a double dose of the 30-day Pulse-muting pill to keep from killing her by accident, but the threat of her sudden death was very real. It was love that drove her to largely ignore the danger.

When a knock sounded at the door, Adam straightened, and immediately chided himself for the hopefulness that rose in his chest. If Rory decided to come back and forgive him, that meant there would be two people in his life who would notice when he was gone from the bipedal world.

"Are you expecting someone?" Henry asked, his eyebrows raising in surprise.

Adam stood from his stool and moved toward the foyer. "No. Only you and Rory."

"Rory and Cord are out of town, raising funds for her Foundation."

Adam frowned. "I'm the largest sponsor for the Johnstone Foundation. Has she truly gone through all the money I donated?"

Henry kept a pleasant expression in place, but his tone lowered to sadness. "She's preparing, in case the fight between the two of you grows to the point that you pull your funding."

Frowning, Adam took a step back, affronted. "I wouldn't do that to her. It's important work she does, funding the education of literacy and basic education so the government doesn't have to."

Henry shrugged. "A lot depends on her making sure the Foundation runs smoothly. She's just hedging her bets." Henry jumped onto a different topic to lighten the mood. "Her husband's a trip. Can't stand the corporate world, but will follow our girl anywhere."

Adam didn't respond. He went to the door and thrust it open, squinting into the sunlight that violated his pupils. "What?"

A mumbly man with salt-and-pepper hair had his hat in his hands, his wrinkled fingers twisting the knit cap nervously. It was positively icy outside, but Adam didn't offer for him to step inside. "G-g-good afternoon, Mr. Fontaine. I w-w-was w-w-wondering if I might have a word with you. See, I hold a mortgage with your firm, and..."

Adam's puffy upper lip curled. "Do you have a working phone?"

"Yes, sir. I do, but..."

"Then I don't see any reason why you're bothering me. Call the main office with complaints. I don't handle things like that."

"There seems to be a problem with the paperwork, and no one can help me. I'm sorry, I'm doing this all wrong. I'm Fabrice." He paused as if waiting for a hello, but then rushed onward when it was clear no greeting was coming. "It's my mortgage. I'm late for the second month now, but the sheriff..."

Adam ran his hand over his face, tracking each deformity to be certain he still had ample reason to be cross with the world. "You people are getting more zealous every day. I mean, coming to my home?"

The man had a roundish structure to his face, but his cheeks were sunken in from malnourishment. He had bags under his eyes, and his fingers were covered with torn knit gloves. His old jeans bore a rip across the knee, letting just enough of the chill into his pants that he shivered uncontrollably. "I've tried your mortgage hotline, Mr. Fontaine, but I'm not getting anywhere with them. We're two months late, and..."

Adam's eyebrows pulled together as he fisted the side of the door to lean against it. He opened his mouth to speak, but just as he did, the howl of a wolf sounded in the distance. Adam stiffened at the warning. The pack was always coming around, reminding him that they were there – that they were his future. He'd angered them quite a few times over the years by setting traps to keep them off his property, so the howl was meant to remind him of his doom. Once he was one of them, he would not be welcomed into their pack.

A cloud of anger replaced any curiosity that might have occurred. "It takes six months before the eviction process starts, not two. I suggest you bother the office then, and not my home."

Just when Adam was about to close the door, the old man held up his hands and did something so shocking, Adam merely gaped at him. Fabrice got down on his creaky knees on the snow-covered porch and clasped his hands in supplication. It was clear he feared the wolves by the dodgy glances over his shoulder, but his worry over losing his home was even greater than that. "There's an eviction notice posted on my front door, but according to our contract, we still have four months to make up the late payments. When I called Sheriff Aston, he said he was expediting our eviction."

Adam's nostrils flared, but Henry had heard enough. He pushed past his friend and helped the man off his knees, leading him into the foyer. "What's this about the local law making its own rules? Do you have proof of this?"

Fabrice's wide, watery eyes took in the man who helped him inside. Henry was taller in person, and Fabrice looked small and stooped with the cold. Everyone had watched the young prince grow into the political leader beside his great father, King Hubert. "Prince Henry?"

Henry flashed one of his dazzling grins, Pulsing a touch of congeniality into Fabrice, so as to put the man at ease. Such was his Pulse, but when paired with his charming demeanor, one might guess that he scarcely needed magic to draw out amiability in people. "Adam, get your client here a blanket or something. Start up the fireplace. He's frozen!"

Fabrice's teeth were chattering, and his joints were rigid with a deep-set arthritis that was exacerbated by the cold. The snow had started to fall only a week ago, but already Mother Nature was making her claims on the last vestiges of autumn. "I'm sorry. I don't want to b-b-be a b-b-bother. I just can't lose my home. I'm one year away from paying it off. I can't lose it this close to the end."

Henry patted Fabrice's arm. "Of course not. Adam will pull up your contract and see to it all right now. He wouldn't want you to get torn apart by wolves. The Lupine can get quite hungry this time of year."

Adam opened his mouth to argue, but instead he stomped off in the direction of his office up the stairs. When Fabrice made to follow, Adam whirled on him. "You'll not tail me and snoop around my home. You'll stay right here, and try not to get my floors all messed up. I've got my mud stains exactly how I like them."

Fabrice looked down at his shoes that were in the last stages of decay, and grimaced with an apologetic bow of his head. "I'm so sorry, Mr. Fontaine. Thank you for looking into my case. I didn't know what else to do."

"You can start with never bothering me with this kind of thing again."

"Yes, sir." Though Fabrice was easily several decades older than Adam, he didn't hesitate to pay respect. He stood in the foyer, his clothes cold and wet as he shivered.

HENRY'S EYES TIGHTENED AROUND THE EDGES AS HE watched his friend's ascent up the wide and winding staircase. When he turned to Fabrice, his smile was in full swing. "You'll have to forgive him. He left his company manners in his other castle."

Fabrice held up his hands and shook his head. "Oh, no offense taken. I'm a stranger, showing up uninvited. I'd be cross, too."

Henry didn't quite believe Fabrice was capable of such a thing as surliness. Fabrice had a congeniality to him that rivaled Santa Claus, and a lightness to his obviously burdened shoulders that reminded Henry of his own father, years ago before the kingdom was perched so precariously with too much division.

Henry offered to take the man's useless coat. It was too thin and wet to offer any sort of warmth. Just holding it over his arm gave Henry a chill. "Would you like a cup of tea while we wait?"

Fabrice's eyes lit up, and he rubbed his hands together. "I wouldn't say no to that. The Prince of Avondale offering me a cup of tea? My daughter won't believe it."

"Then you might have to lie and tell her it was the best tea you've ever had. I'm honestly not sure what Adam's got in his cupboards."

Henry led Fabrice to the kitchen, apologizing for the state of the dusty and neglected home. He fished through the cupboards, which he hadn't done in weeks. His heart sank when three of them were empty, and actually had a few spiders taking up residence where the spices and canned goods should've been. The fourth cupboard made Henry bite his lip to hold his reaction inside. Where the oatmeal and breakfast fixings should have been were several boxes of dry dog food.

Henry's heart sank, and he shut the door quickly, hoping Fabrice hadn't seen that there was dog food, but no dog. Rory had been the one who'd made sure he was eating human food, but she'd stopped coming by earlier that year. Guilt flooded Henry as he donned the politician son's smile for Fabrice. How long had Adam been living off of dog food? Had he truly given up all semblances of a normal life? There was nearly half a year before his thirtieth birthday.

The fifth cupboard had fixings for tea, though not many. Henry pulled down a teacup and ran water in the kettle, heating it on the stove. He searched around for the teapot, but couldn't find it. He hoped that meant that Adam had at least been drinking something civilized.

"Here we are," Henry said when the kettle whistled a few minutes later. "I'm sorry there's not food to offer you. Adam's a bit swamped with work, and hasn't had time to go to the store recently."

Fabrice waved off the apology. "My cupboards are every bit as scant. These are lean times. I just didn't think they'd fallen on Mr. Fontaine, as well. Do you really think he can get this squared away?"

"If it's as you say it is, I don't see why not."

"That's hope I'll hold tight in my pocket, then. My daughter, I... She does so much to take care of so many people. We can't lose our home. I'm not saying we don't deserve a reprimand, but the contract should be looked at when the alternative is throwing a man and his daughter out on the streets."

"Of course. What do you do, Fabrice?"

"I'm a clockmaker," he said proudly. "I make all sorts of trinkets, too. Right now, I'm working on a record player."

"Restoring it?"

"Improving it," he declared with a twinkle in his eye. He warmed his hands with the cup of steaming tea and sighed contentedly when feeling crept back into his extremities. "When I'm finished, it'll play music while taking each song and synthesizing a painting based on the notes, instruments and rhythm."

Henry took a seat at the counter and leaned back appreciatively. "You're making art out of music? Making art out of art?"

Fabrice batted his hand dismissively. "No one cares about that, but I like it. I've won awards for my music boxes. Those, people like. Anything too off the beaten path scares the public, so that invention is just for my daughter."

"She likes music?"

Fabrice nodded sadly. "She suffered from a high fever and an infection when she was just a baby. It took half her hearing in her right ear. She can hear well enough – no one even notices her leaning in – but sometimes music misses the beat for her. I thought she should be able to see music the way we hear it."

Henry picked up his teacup and blew on it, enchanted with the sweet old man. "How old is she?"

"Twenty-seven. Though she's always been an old soul. Takes care of me well enough."

Henry was enjoying his visit with Fabrice so much that he was taken aback by Adam's grim presence in the entry-way. "Did you want some tea, Adam? I was just getting to know Fabrice here."

"You should go," Adam said with a menace to his tone.

Fabrice set down his cup, his lips pursed before he

spoke. "I can't go until the matter about my home is settled. I'm sure you can understand that."

Adam shook his head. "Not you. Henry, you should leave. You don't want to be involved in this."

Henry set his cup down with a heaviness that suggested he was either tired of Adam or humanity in general. "What is it?"

Adam didn't elaborate, only stood sideways and motioned to the foyer.

Henry bowed his head to Fabrice, and moved toward the front door with a tight frown, not bothering to hold back his frustration with his friend's lack of civility. Adam would not be moved, though, and practically shoved his last remaining friend out the front door and locked it.

When Adam moved back into the kitchen to tower over Fabrice, he did nothing to stifle his imposing presence. Adam was tall. Six and a half feet would be intimidating on anyone, but with his beastly features and snarl that seemed nearly permanent, it was no wonder that Fabrice shook and took a step back.

"Did you think I wouldn't find out about the warrant?"

Fabrice's mostly white eyebrows pulled together in confusion. "What warrant?"

"The one on you for public disturbance. I phoned the sheriff, and Gabe himself said that you were to be detained here until he could come take you in."

Despite the anger radiating off Adam, Fabrice did his best to stand tall. "I've never been charged with anything of the sort. Sheriff Aston wants something from me, and he's making my life miserable until I give it to him."

Adam cleared the gap between them and coiled his beefy fingers around Fabrice's shoulder with all the inevitability of a boa constrictor. He jerked the old man forward, not caring if Fabrice was capable of keeping up with his swift footsteps and long strides. "Tell me the rest from your cell. If you think this place is dingy, wait until you see my dungeon."

3

A WORD FROM THE SHERIFF

The creaky old thing hadn't been used in at least a decade, and even then, it hadn't been for the traditional purpose most would associate with dungeons. Adam's gaze flitted over the first cell, where he recalled engaging in raucous sex with a woman whose name he couldn't recall. He remembered the fire in her eyes when she'd asked about his dungeon, and her wild screams of ecstasy when she got to fulfill her daring fantasy. Before then, Adam supposed his great-great-grandfather had used the space for its intended purpose.

The brass two-foot tall candelabra Adam carried lit the way, its tiny licks of flames casting shadows that made Fabrice jump with trepidation. Though Fabrice didn't fight him, Adam didn't lessen his jerky movements as he shoved the old man into the dank, cold cell. The grating sound of the door swinging shut set both men's teeth on edge. "You should know better than to pull one over on me."

With arthritic fingers, Fabrice held tight to the bars as he brought himself to his feet. "Please, Mr. Fontaine. Sheriff Aston does stuff like this all the time. He's angry that I won't give him what he wants, so he abuses his power to try and twist me."

"Save your stories for someone who cares."

"*You* should care!" Fabrice cried out when Adam turned his back. "You should care because it's your business that suffers. The sheriff makes up fines and takes money we don't have. Then we're late on paying our mortgage to you. If it doesn't affect your conscience, then you should at least be upset that he's gouging your bottom line. How many homes have you foreclosed on in the past year in the West Village?"

Adam paused, and turned his chin to glance at Fabrice over his shoulder. "Too many. But I always abide by the contracts. I wouldn't force an eviction on your home if you were only two months late. No sheriff would enforce it if I did."

Fabrice nodded, now that it seemed they were finally getting somewhere. "Yes, but a notice was posted on my property, and you'll see I was only two months late. And we wouldn't have been late if we hadn't had to pay four thousand dollars in an unexpected bridge tax this year. No one can keep up. As soon as we pay the tax, another comes. I'm telling you, many are losing their homes and their reputations because the sheriff is taking money that's rightfully yours." Fabrice's fingers tightened on the bars. "I've only been able to keep up because he didn't give me the newest tax. Everyone else in the village had to pay, but we didn't."

The dungeon breathed fresh life into Adam's childhood anxieties of swallowed by the dark, but he turned to face Fabrice and folded his arms over his chest, resolving himself to hear the man out. "And why is that?"

Anger flashed in the old man's eyes, causing Adam to take a step back. "Because Gabe Aston wants my daughter! He'll do anything, including throwing me in jail, to get at her. When the newest fine came about, she went to him without my knowledge and agreed to take him up on his bribe."

"What bribe?"

Fabrice's voice shook with palpable pain. "He said he would drop the tax on our family if she agreed to go away for a weekend with him." Fabrice cringed as he gripped the bars, his eyes squinching tight. "I value her more than anyone else in the world, and that swine of a sheriff treats her like trash and trinkets to be traded. Do you know how that feels?" He sniffed, his wet nose running and red. "The eviction notice was just to scare me. The false charges for arrest are truly dangerous, though. If he takes me away, then my daughter will have no one, and he'll win."

Adam gaped at the old man, wondering how he'd stumbled into such a tangled web that had apparently been going on right under his nose. All he'd seen were the numbers. The annual household income, and the average mortgage price. He hadn't understood why the people in the West Village couldn't pay their rent. On paper, it certainly looked like they had the means. He'd assumed they were lazy, uneducated or frivolous, but apparently it had been something else entirely.

For the second time that day, Adam's doorbell rang. "That'll be the police. Faster than I was anticipating. Stay here, and I'll get it all sorted." He pointed at the old man with a menacing finger. "Never come to my house with this much drama again."

It was the humble, "yes, sir," that made Adam cringe. Had Fabrice been petulantly silent or begged for more time to make his case, Adam would've felt justified in his own gruff behavior. Adam clenched his fists but didn't say anything. In fact, just for the man's sweetness, which had no real place here, Adam shut the door without turning on a single light, taking the candelabra with him, and shrouding the old man in blackness.

Adam stomped up the stone steps. The chill in his house was far more unforgiving in the basement, making the drafty main floor feel like a heated sunroom by comparison. He stalked over to the front door and flung it open. "Sheriff," he greeted the dark-haired officer, but didn't invite him inside.

From a single look, Adam had a hard time finding holes in Fabrice's story. He'd never seen a cop wearing fine leather shoes before. Gabe's black, coifed hair was perfectly done, and his face was shaved so closely, it looked like he'd just come from the barber. He wore four gold rings, each of them shiny, jeweled, and begging to be gawked at.

It wasn't the opulence that put Adam off – he himself had plenty of baubles in the safe upstairs – it was the bawdy impracticality, and the obvious display of wealth that didn't seem befitting with the "servant" aspect of "public servant."

"Do you have the suspect inside?" Gabe adjusted his gold name badge and flashed a perfectly white-toothed grin at Adam. His uniform shirt was two sizes too small, which allowed him to show off his musculature with the simplest flex.

"Depends. I do a lot of entertaining. You'll have to be more specific. Who are you looking for, and what's he being charged with?"

Gabe's smile fell. "You were the one who called in the tip. Surely Fabrice is here. His old beater is still in your driveway." He jerked his thumb in the direction of the car.

Adam grimaced at the hideous vehicle, and silently marveled that it had made it all the way to his home from the West Village. "What's he being charged with?"

The squat, portly cop standing on the stoop behind him shoved his hands in his pockets as he spoke up. "Public disturbance." The deputy had part of his shirt untucked, his pants were too big for his shorter frame, and he had a clubbed foot.

Adam glowered at the two. "Well, as you can see, he's not in public, and he's only disturbing me. I'll not press charges for that. Show me the warrant, and then tell me why you posted an eviction notice on his property. I'm the mortgage holder. You can't carry through that process unless I initiate it, and I haven't."

The deputy shifted nervously, and scratched a spot on the back of his head. His brown hair was messy, and didn't look like it had been trimmed in months. "You saw that, did you?" the deputy mumbled.

Gabe didn't waver, but Adam could see the lie blooming in his haughty eyes as it curled his upper lip. "Must've been a paperwork mix-up, then. I'll remove the notice. I know he's late on his payments, though."

"And how would you know that?" Adam folded his arms across his broad chest, not holding back his stature that towered a couple inches over the strapping Gabe.

Gabe shrank marginally. "Word around town spreads."

Adam's puffy upper lip coiled in a sneer. "You posted an eviction notice on hearsay?"

Gabe backpedaled. "I was over their house. I'm dating Fabrice's daughter, you know." He adjusted his belt, as if to brag to Adam about the prize he'd nabbed. "Anyway, I saw the late notice in the mail on the table. Thought I'd do you a favor."

Adam scoffed, understanding enough of the story to

realize Fabrice had been telling him the truth. "How about this: if Prince Henry looks into your dealings with Fabrice and his daughter and finds anything shady, I'll have you thrown in your own jail. How does that sound?" He snarled as he clenched the doorknob. "I don't need a crooked cop doing me any favors, and I certainly don't need him breaking the law and blaming it on my company."

Gabe's jaw twitched as he took a step back, bumping into his partner, who fell backwards off the cracked concrete dais. "I can have the charges dropped, if that's what you need."

"I need you to do your job. If you're not capable of doing that, Prince Henry will replace you."

Gabe raised his hands, his sneer juxtaposing with his humble words. "Consider the charges dropped. And I'll remove the eviction notice first thing."

Adam was about to slam the door in his face, but the cough of an old red sedan caught his attention as it pulled into his driveway and parked. He frowned, wishing the outside world would just leave him alone, but paused his impending tirade when the squeaky car door opened, and its owner stepped out.

Adam hadn't seen any woman aside from Rory in so very long. She had long legs, which she put to use stomping toward Gabe with a steadiness that belied the tremble in her slender fingers. With a look of brazen determination on her heart-shaped features, she beelined for the porch with an angry story on her face. "Gabe, how could you? Where is he?"

Gabe hopped down the steps and offered her a cocky smile he produced out of nowhere. It had a sideways tilt, and his voice carried a note of bravado that Adam found off-putting. "Here I am, tasty cakes."

Adam's face soured at the term of endearment. He didn't need to know the woman to understand that the nickname didn't suit her – or anyone, for that matter.

A ripple of disgust marred her beauty. "Where is my father?"

Her hair was the color of pure maple syrup. Despite the bun it had been fashioned into, several bits had fallen out, and blew back with the bite of the wind. The snow was deep enough that her jeans were wet at the ankles, which for some reason bothered Adam. Her gloves were just as tattered as her father's, but the holes in her winter-wear made him irate instead of indifferent, as he had been with Fabrice.

"Belle, calm down. You're always so tense. Let me drive you home. Your face is positively red with the cold." Gabe leaned toward her with a smarmy grin that made Adam recoil. "Or perhaps that's a little blush I see."

Adam felt as if it could be seen from space how much she loathed the man who was clearly making a pass at her – and badly, at that.

Belle didn't address Gabe, but made her way past him up the porch. When she took in Adam standing in the doorway, her big brown eyes grew impossibly wider. She seemed to forget her mission at the sight of his beastly features, but finally her shrunken voice found the words. "Sorry to bother you, sir. Have you seen a man around here who answers to Fabrice?"

Adam hadn't been addressed by a beautiful woman in ages. Sure, the kingdom was enamored of Rory's delicate features, but he'd known her since they were children, and didn't appreciate her beauty the way the public did. He straightened his posture and wished he'd changed into proper clothes that morning. Or showered. "You're welcome to come in and wait for him here."

Gabe spoke for her the moment she opened her mouth to respond. "I'm sure she would rather wait in my squad car. Come on, Belle. We'll make Rufus ride in back." He let out a haughty laugh that Rufus joined along with halfheartedly.

Adam held open the door for her and jerked his head to indicate the choice was hers.

Despite her obvious reluctance to be near the deformed man in pajamas whom everyone knew was a gruff shut-in with mental health issues, Belle braved the unknown rather than stay another second in Gabe's presence. Apparently, she would take a chance on the monster who used to be a man, rather than stand another second next to the man who was truly a monster. "Thank you, sir."

The moment she stepped inside, Gabe moved to follow her. Adam stood in the doorway, his barreled chest blocking the path and proving to the arrogant sheriff that he would not be intimidated. While Gabe was powerful in his village, Adam had deep pockets and even deeper connections. "You don't step inside without a warrant, Officer. You can call to confirm that the eviction notice has been removed, and then I never want to hear from you again." He slammed the door and locked it, wondering how his day had gone so very off the rails.

STRIKING A DEAL

When Adam turned to face Belle, it was with an odd lump of anxiety in his throat. She was shivering, and her jeans were wet up to her calves. But despite the cold, she looked most worried about his presence. There was a hesitance in her eyes that he'd seen around town the few times he'd been out and about. He'd shut himself away from such stares, but hers had wandered into his home without warning. She seemed at a loss for words, so the two just stared at each other for a few beats, taking in the anomaly that was a woman standing in the long-forgotten castle.

Adam cleared his throat before he finally spoke to her. "I'm Adam," he offered, but his voice was so froggy that he wondered if she understood him at all. Then it dawned on him that of course she knew who he was. Everyone knew *of* him, but few actually knew him.

The woman's chin remained level with the ground, no signs of cowering in Adam's presence. "I'm Belle. It's nice to meet you, though I wish it wasn't like this. I'm sorry about all that. It's not your problem, and we brought it literally to your doorstep."

"Yes, well," Adam didn't argue, which made the awkwardness compound until the few feet between them felt like an ocean of difference. "Your father is downstairs."

Light flooded Belle's eyes, highlighting emotion Adam hadn't permitted himself to indulge in for so very long. She had such an expressive face, which made her a captivating woman to watch. "Oh, thank you! He's been through so much. He always forgets to take his meds, and this morning was just..." She held up her hands. "Not your problem." She cast around for the stairs, but the house was so massive, she knew she'd be lost if she wandered off in search of the stairwell.

"The poor darling's freezing. Be a gentleman, Adam! Offer to take her coat for her." Audra had moved from the office upstairs to the top of the steps, and looked down on him with disapproval.

Adam shot the nosey teapot a glower that told his mother figure to back off.

Belle glanced around in confusion. "Oh, I'm alright. You don't need to go to any trouble."

Adam quirked an eyebrow at Belle, wondering if she often spoke out of nowhere. It was only he who could hear the objects in his home speak. "I won't. Your father's just that way."

Audra huffed with indignation. "Oh, you are insufferable. Would it kill you to pretend like you were raised with manners? You can expect your tea to be lukewarm if you don't at least offer her something warm to drink. Poor thing's frozen through!"

Adam ignored Audra, but Belle craned her neck up the steps in confusion, calling up in the direction of the voice. "You really don't have to worry about me. I'll just be collecting my father, and I'll be out of your hair."

"Who are you talking to?" Adam inquired, glancing up the steps in Audra's direction. Sure, it was odd to have a teapot perched at the top of the stairs, but it was his home, and he wouldn't be judged for his eccentricities.

"I'm not sure. Whoever's upstairs."

Adam frowned. "There's no one up there."

Belle opened her mouth to argue, but shut it when a shiver rolled through her from the lingering cold. "Can you show me where my papa is, please? This place is enormous."

"This way." Adam led the path to the dungeon. With every step, he began to regret throwing the old man down in the dank, unlit space. He'd been called a monster many times before, but when the candelabra clutched in his fist revealed Fabrice huddled in the corner rubbing his hands together, he truly felt like one.

Belle gasped and pushed past Adam, crying out in

horror when she saw the state of her father. "No! Did you shut him in here? My father is not a criminal!" She rattled the bars with a passion she expected could open the irons, but the cell remained firmly locked.

"You might need these. Here." Adam jangled the keys. He couldn't venture a look at her disapproval, but he refused to shrink under her outrage.

"You imprisoned my father in a dungeon?" she seethed. "Get him out now!"

Fabrice moved like an old robot toward his daughter, his limbs stiff from old age, coupled with the cold. "It's okay, Belle. He was just following orders. Sheriff Aston put out a warrant for my arrest."

Belle closed her eyes, steadying herself from coming undone right then and there. "I can't stand this anymore! First the eviction notice, and now he's trying to get you locked up?"

Fabrice was shaken, but his kindly demeanor was never compromised. After Adam shoved the key in the lock, Belle flung herself into her father's arms, though he looked to Adam more like he could be her grandfather. "There, there. It's alright, Belle. See? Nothing's wrong at all. We can't let things like this bog us down."

"Things like you being thrown in a dungeon? Things like losing our home for no reason?"

Adam watched the two embrace with fascination. He couldn't recall the last hug his father had given him, or his mother, for that matter. While they had been kind enough, they had never been all that openly affectionate.

When footsteps echoed down the stairwell, Adam rolled his eyes. "I should've known you couldn't leave."

Prince Henry's indignant expression matched his tone. "You should know I know you well enough not to let you unleash your temper on an old man. On my drive back to the freeway, I saw cop cars coming to your place, so I turned around. What's going on?"

Adam pulled Henry aside and explained everything as best he could, so as not to intrude on the father-daughter moment.

Henry's face went stony. "I'll look into the Sheriff's books first thing. All because he wants to get with this one?" He motioned to Belle, who was still holding onto her father.

"I guess so." After spending barely five minutes with Belle, Adam could see clearly the madness that would lead a man to risk his career for this woman. It was more than her captivating eyes that could drive a man to bend the law to be near her. Belle had a firmness to her soft demeanor that intrigued him. Most people were one or the other – strong or soft – but she seemed to have a handle on both aspects. His eyes kept finding their way back to her, studying her expressions carefully while she talked with her father and warmed his fingers. There was a strangeness to the stirring in him that made his eyebrows knit together in consternation.

Belle turned to Adam, her slender nose scrunched with temper. "How could you put my papa in a dungeon? I didn't even know these existed anymore!"

Adam stiffened, drawing up his posture so as to make good use of all six-and-a-half feet nature had blessed him with. "I can do what I like with suspected criminals in my own home. I let him go once I figured everything out. You're welcome."

Belle drew in a long drag of annoyance. "If I thought the police force had an ounce of integrity to it, I'd tell them to lock you up!"

Henry's eyes widened when he saw Adam's hands raise in surrender. Usually Adam loved a good fight. It didn't matter if he was right or wrong. When anyone else lost their temper with him, it was usually his green light to unleash all of his acerbic wrath. "You're right; I shouldn't have taken him down here. It was a misunderstanding, Fabrice."

Henry's jaw dropped at the sudden stroke of humility exhibited by his oldest friend.

Fabrice waved off the apology. "How could you have known? You were only doing as the law ordered. Though, the next time the sheriff wants to lock me up, I wouldn't say no to a nightlight and a pillow."

Adam's mouth tightened, but he didn't bite back. "Let me get your coat," he said before he left the three.

HENRY SAW HOW CAREFULLY ADAM WATCHED BELLE, AND the unprecedented respect he doled out for her father. "Take your time, Adam." Henry put his hand on the old man's elbow to steady him as they walked slowly down the stone corridor toward the steps. "Tell me about yourselves. You live in the West Village. You make music boxes." Then he turned his attention to Belle. "How about you?"

"He's an inventor, too," Belle chimed in. "He's a genius."

Henry inclined his head to Belle. "I was actually asking about you. I already had a pleasant chat with your father earlier."

Belle brushed the cobwebs off her father's back. "Oh. I'm a caretaker. I do in-home nursing."

Fabrice coughed three raspy times before puffing his chest out with pride. "My Belle is the best nurse in all the villages in all of Avondale, even though she's vastly underpaid. She treats sick folk with no health insurance on the weekends, but she's too modest to tell you that."

Belle rolled her eyes with a small smile. "Oh, Dad."

Henry's gaze was thoughtful. "I'm sorry to hear you've fallen on tough times."

Belle held tight to her father's hand. "They wouldn't be so tough if the sheriff didn't tax us to pieces. People can't afford in-home care as much, so my hours aren't enough to get us through anymore."

A smile danced in Henry's blue eyes, as it always did

when he was scheming up mischief for the greater good. "Are you available to take on a new patient?"

Belle paused, her chestnut eyebrow arching. "I am. What do you need?"

"It's not me. It's your father's prison warden." Henry glanced up the stone steps to make sure he wasn't overheard. "Adam is my oldest friend, but he's got some quirks."

Belle narrowed her eyes at Henry. "That's a nice way to put it. In the village, we call it being an entitled jackass."

Henry snorted, taking in her sass with a measured dose of humor. "Yes, well, it's a bit more complicated than that. You know of his curse?"

"Sure. Everyone knows what Malaura did to him."

"Adam's isolated himself here. Won't let anyone in to clean. And he hears voices. Thinks his household staff were changed into teapots and coatracks and such."

Belle's eyebrows rose. "And were they?"

Henry blinked at her, his arms folded over his chest. "No, miss. Of course not. Adam is unwell. He needs someone to take care of him. He has medication he refuses to take. He has only me in his life now, and my patience isn't what it used to be, nor is my available time enough to look after him as he needs."

"You want me to work for Adam?"

"Actually, I *beg* of you to work for Adam, and I'll pay you a ridiculous sum of money to put up with him." He motioned around the castle. "This place is unsanitary, so it wouldn't be just for nursing, but for housekeeping duties, as well. I know that isn't in your normal job description, but he won't let a cleaning service in the front door. Believe me, I've tried."

"Well, I used to clean houses when I was working my way through school." Belle dropped her father's hand, a lump forming in her throat. "How much money?"

"If you'll promise to stay even when he's difficult? Name your price, then double it. That's what I'd pay to get my best friend the help he needs." He glanced between Fabrice and Belle, noticing how they were constantly taking turns guarding each other. "Wouldn't you do the same for your father?"

Without skipping a beat, Belle replied, "I would do anything for my family." Then, taking a breath, she nodded. "Even take on a more challenging patient like Mr. Fontaine."

Fabrice shook his head. "No, Belle. We'll find a way. We always do. He's rough, and there's anger there that's set in deep. You shouldn't have to be around someone like that."

Her hand slipped into her father's and squeezed, but she didn't drop eye contact with Henry. "I want a contract, and I need the first payment up front. There's no point in working to pay the bills if our home is taken away from us before the first paycheck comes in."

"Fair point. He needs round-the-clock care. I can't be here all the time, and I'll sleep easier if I know someone is here to watch him."

Belle kept raising and lowering her chin – her constant battle between bravery and decorum. "If you're asking me to give up my other clients and move in, you'll have to replace my wages."

"Try me," Henry challenged playfully, a smile teasing his sculpted lips.

Belle's voice came out quiet but unwavering, with a hint of both shame and pride. "I make twenty-seven grand a year right now."

Henry rubbed the nape of his neck. "I shouldn't have told you to double it."

Belle swallowed hard and touched a lock of her hair that the wind had knocked loose from the sloppy bun. "It's alright. We've gotten by so far just fine with the job I have now."

Henry shifted his weight from one foot to the other. "I meant I should've told you to triple it. You can't get by on that. How does a hundred thousand grab you?"

Belle stood stock-still – a deer caught in headlights. "You can't be serious. What are you expecting me to do for him for a hundred grand? I only do in-home care. Cleaning and cooking is fine, but I'm not a geisha on the side."

Henry chuckled at the firmness of her frown. "I never assumed otherwise. It's for in-home care plus house-keeping duties. It might seem like a lot of money now, but after a week dealing with Adam, I'm sure you'll demand a raise." His eyes grew serious. "Ask me for a raise before you up and quit on him. I mean it. He's gone through fourteen housekeepers in less than ten years, and I'm not sure how many in-home nurses. He's... difficult. But I've got a feeling about you. I think you might be just what this house needs." Henry extended his hand to Belle, willing her to release her father's grip to take him up on his offer.

Belle stared at the prince's hand for a few moments, weighing the sizeable pros and cons. The thing that tipped it was when her father coughed into his sleeve. He needed medicine they couldn't afford.

Belle rolled her shoulders back and gripped Henry's hand. "You've got yourself a deal."

5

A UNIQUE WARDROBE

It didn't take long to move Belle into Adam's home. Henry hired movers to expedite the entire process. They unpacked the last of her boxes in her new bedroom within forty-eight hours, which gave her just enough time to cash her first advanced check from Henry, and bring their mortgage up to date. Other nurses were more than thrilled to pick up her dropped patients, so they could have more hours and pay their many bills. Belle had poured over Adam's charts from his previous nurses while her meager belongings were moved to her new address.

Adam had been diagnosed as having major depressive disorder with psychosis, and was prescribed pills that he refused to take. He was agoraphobic, and didn't leave the house unless under extreme coercion. Belle's brow furrowed at the injuries he'd been treated for. Some had been self-inflicted years ago, but now it seemed he was mostly treated for wolf bites.

She shivered and hoped his property wasn't lousy with the likes of the Lupine. They could be a murderous bunch when provoked.

Adam locked himself in one of his many offices on the second floor and didn't greet her on the morning she arrived. He was gruff, calling through the door when she knocked. "I don't care what Henry says. I don't need a nurse. I don't need a housekeeper. I don't need anyone taking up space in my home."

Belle blinked at the closed door. "Do you want me to take my things and go?" She closed her eyes and prayed that wasn't the case. They desperately needed the money, and she'd already spent the first check on bills.

A second voice surprised her, coming from inside the office. "Sir, you can't send her away. Henry loves you. At least humor him. Give her a month."

"Yes, give me a month. Please, Mr. Fontaine. If you don't need me, then I'll leave after thirty days."

The long pause didn't do anything to quell Belle's nerves. When Adam finally answered, it was with a growl of aggression she couldn't imagine she deserved this early on. "Fine! If it takes a month to pacify Henry, then you can stay for one month. You'll see that I'm fine how I am. I like my space, so stick to the east wing. The west wing is mine, and I don't want to see you in it."

Belle debated between arguing and backing down,

playing with a lock of her hair as she decided which version of herself she wanted to be. "Yes, sir."

One month. Belle began mentally repacking her things and moving them back into the West Village. How she wanted this to work, but if he wouldn't even let her examine him, there wasn't much hope.

Belle moved through too many hallways to her bedroom on the first floor, her chin low at the dressing-down she didn't feel she deserved. It wasn't the first time a patient was rude to her, but each time, the cruelty cut her.

Upon entering her room, Belle decided that if she had thirty days, she would make the most of them. "I'll do such a fantastic job, he won't be able to fire me."

Belle made quick work of locating a duster, some polish and a few rags. Her new bedroom was massive – almost as large as her entire house back in the West Village. There was a fireplace, with a section above the mantle that was ornately carved bronze, cut into swirls that would have been whimsical, were they not tarnished and covered in soot. The fixtures were ornate, curly and made everything look like a dignified dream, but she couldn't fully appreciate it with the thick coating of dust and neglect that covered every surface. It looked like the room hadn't been touched in a decade, so she took her time, starting in the corner and pacing herself.

"It's a castle. It's going to take time to get all the rooms looking as they should. You've got this, Belle," she said to herself.

"Oo! That tickles!" said a female voice.

Belle paused, the feather duster poised above the mantle. She looked over her shoulder, but saw no one. "Who said that?"

"I wish you could hear me. I would thank you for putting me to good use!"

Belle glanced toward the source of the voice, which was coming from... the duster? Belle's mouth dropped open when she saw the dove-shaped handle twist in her grip. "Did you just..." Belle looked over her shoulder to make sure the door was locked.

When she glanced down again, there was no mistaking the movement of the dove's white beak that opened and closed as it spoke to her. "My, she's pretty," the duster commented.

Belle gasped and jumped back, dropping the duster on the floor. "That didn't just happen! You didn't talk, and I didn't hear you."

She echoed Belle's gasp, and found with delight that she could turn her neck. Normally she could only move on her own if no one but Adam was around, but finally, finally she could speak for herself to someone who wasn't so surly. "Mademoiselle, my name is Vivienne. Don't be frightened!" she fretted as Belle backed up and plastered her back against the cobwebby wall.

"Vivienne?"

At this, the duster sprang up, the handle floating, so that the feathers barely brushed against the hardwood floor. "Yes! Oh, mercy, mercy in Heaven! You can hear me! I've been silenced for so long."

Then it wasn't just the duster, but the wardrobe who came to life. The old blue-painted wooden wardrobe that was pressed to the wall near her bed opened with a creak, the drawers sliding as if to peek out and see if it was really true. "You can hear us?"

Belle's wide eyes darted to the wardrobe, and she let out a bleat of distress. "But I'm not supposed to hear you! I'm not crazy!"

"Crazy? No, no. Enchanted – that's what you are. Only Adam can hear us usually. I'm Simone."

"Simone?" Belle whimpered. "Will someone please tell me what's happening?"

Vivienne floated nearer, lifting up so she was in Belle's eyeline. Her words tumbled out so quickly, Belle had to really focus to make sense of it all. "We were cursed! Most people think it was just Adam, but it was all of us. We used to be servants in the castle, but now we're objects. No one can hear us except for Adam, and we can't move or speak freely when other people are around. That's why the rumors spread that he'd gone mad. He tried for months to convince his friends that we were real, but only he could see us move and hear our voices. That you can hear us now?" Her voice caught with a shaky quality as she broke into tearless sobs. "It's a miracle!"

Belle shook her head. "No. No, this isn't real. Someone must've Pulsed me with hallucinations or something. It's not possible!" It wasn't until the wardrobe started walking toward her with heavy sideways steps that shook the floor that Belle finally lost it. She screamed for help, afraid that she might be crushed by her own delusions.

Though the castle was large, the walls were mostly bare, and there was no carpeting to muffle the sound of her cry. Belle's cry echoed up the steps and down hallways, and before he knew it, Adam was on his feet.

"Calm down, honey. We won't hurt you. Is it too much? Is it because I'm so big?" Simone's voice was loud and had a bawdy charm to it. "Vivienne didn't seem to scare you too badly, but it looks like I'm pushing you over the edge. I'll take a step back." The massive wardrobe was as long as an office desk, and at least seven feet tall. The blue beauty had gold etchings on the top, curling and swirling to match the rest of the room's opulence. Simone's movements were abrupt and shook the door with how heavy she was. "Is that better?" she asked, her middle drawer opening and closing to act as her mouth when she spoke. There were two drawers at Belle's eye level, and the handles that should have been immovable bronze folded in on themselves, and then flattened back out, looking to Belle as if they were two eyes blinking at her.

"What's his Pulse? His charts said it was a variant of boldness and persuasion, but were they wrong?" Belle demanded as she inched for the door. "Did he do this to me?"

"Adam's Pulse is stripping away a person's inhibitions.

He can make you speak your mind, but he can't force hallucinations. We're real, buttercup," Simone said matter-of-factly.

When Adam charged into her room, Belle had never been so grateful to see his face – gruff or not. She lifted her hand and pointed to the floating duster. "Do you see that, or is it just me?"

Adam swore, his eyes going wide. "Viv, how are you doing that? You've never been able to move around anyone but me. How..."

Vivienne chirped with glee. "She can hear us!"

Belle kept tight to the wall, as if it was the only thing holding her to the planet. "You were tried for murdering your household after you were cursed, but they couldn't find any evidence – only that the entire staff had disappeared. This is what happened to them?"

Adam was flabbergasted, his mouth opening and closing without sound as he took in the giant leap he'd hoped would one day be possible – that someone might understand his plight, crazy as it seemed. "Yes. I tried to explain it, but no one believed me. Only I could hear them and see them move. Not even Henry or Rory could. You can really... Is it true?"

He moved further into the room, taking in her anxiety with curiosity. Usually it was him people were afraid of, but Belle didn't recoil as he stepped toward her. Instead, she threw herself into his arms, as if he could offer her some kind of protection from the unknown.

But *he* was the unknown. He'd gone to great lengths to make it so. Still, in this moment of uncertainty, it seemed she was determined to make him her safe place.

His fur-covered hand moved to her hair, hesitating before taking a chance and touching the tresses to calm her. "It's alright." His low voice had a bass note to it that vibrated the constant knot in his chest. "They're nothing to be frightened of."

"I know the laws of magic. This isn't possible."

He chuckled at her fight to hold onto logic. "I'll let you think that, if you need to."

Belle's voice came back insecure and small. "I think I might."

His fingers sifted through her bun, enjoying the feel of something so silky. "It's alright, Belle," he said again, lending comfort that hadn't been offered to him when he'd discovered the odd twist of the curse years ago.

Adam hadn't held a woman in ages. Rory always tried to enforce gentle touches, but he rarely reciprocated after his change. This was different. Finally, he wasn't alone in his plight. There was someone who didn't write him off as mentally unstable, and give pacifying nods while calling for a script to lessen his "hallucinations". His arms were stiff around Belle, but neither of them pulled away. He let Belle hold onto him, which was the most contact he'd had since Rory forced a hug upon him over a year ago.

Belle shivered in his arms, and clung tighter when Simone piped up from the corner. "Oh, isn't that splendid?

They're already bonding." There was sheer joy in her voice.

Vivienne floated higher so she could get a birds-eye view of the two, who were still locked in a tight embrace. "Her head is on his shoulder!"

Belle knew she should pull away. This wasn't exactly appropriate patient-nurse decorum. But each time Vivienne caught her eye or Simone spoke, Belle clung tighter to Adam's swollen biceps. "Tell me I'm not seeing things. Tell me you see the floating duster, too," she whispered into his broad chest.

"You're seeing what I see. That's Vivienne and Simone. There are others who live here. Would you like to meet them?"

Belle hesitated, but then nodded quickly. When she pulled back, it was with a sharp intake of breath. "You have to go off your meds! If I'm seeing this, then you're not suffering from psychosis. You're not having hallucinations. Those pills can cause serious damage if they're taken when they're not needed."

Adam took in her bossy streak with a small smirk. "I know, which is why I never took them. I believe I'm labeled as 'obstinate' somewhere in my files."

Into the room scampered a barking footstool that was covered with a light blue and rose swirl-designed fabric. It seemed to match the rest of the castle's décor, but for the fact that it was jumping up to paw at Belle's jeans with its wooden legs.

Belle all but climbed up Adam's body to get away from the enchanted objects. Adam merely chuckled at her fear, his hand finding its way to the small of her back. He kept it there until she calmed enough to release her stranglehold on him. His hand felt right, like it belonged in that most sacred of spots. "This is Sultan. He's a cocker spaniel. He belonged to my father, but was always more affectionate toward my mother. He won't bite. Here." Adam turned his head to the side and sneezed three times, and then took Belle's hand and extended it toward the footstool. The dog was so excited he could move about freely and interact with a new person, that he began chasing his own tassels, running in a frantic circle as he yipped. "Are you afraid of dogs?"

"No, I'm afraid of possessed footstools who run around like dogs!" Belle replied incredulously. "I feel like freaking out is a normal reaction to this kind of thing."

Adam chuckled, and was immediately perplexed by the sound. He couldn't recall the last time he'd laughed. "I'm sorry," he said, covering his mouth at her scolding look. "It's just that you're so amusing. It's been only me who could see them all moving about. I feel as if I'm the one hallucinating now."

"Well, I'm very much real, and I'll burn your dinner tonight if you laugh at me again. I'm on the verge, here."

"Sit, Sultan." Adam moved her hand slowly, but eventually Belle made contact with the dog, who wagged his hind tassel amiably. "Good boy."

Belle finally felt confident of her surroundings just enough to drop to her knees to indulge the pup in a good belly scratch. "Is this real? Am I dreaming?"

Adam studied her, perplexed that finally someone could witness what he'd seen all this time. "I was just about to ask you the same thing."

6

THE MASTER DOESN'T LIKE
CHANGE

Belle's first day in the castle was spent being introduced to the household staff, who were overjoyed to meet her. They'd only had Adam to interact with for so very long, and he often spent his days shut inside his office. She'd been overwhelmed at first, and despite his appearance, which usually drove people away, Belle clung to Adam's hairy arm, using it as her touchstone when the nuances to her new abode grew to be too much.

"Lucien is the candlestick. Bosworth is the antique clock. The stove is Chef Bouche. Thomas is the coatrack." She rubbed her temples. "Does the floor have a personality? Am I walking on someone's face?"

Adam shook his head, wondering if he would be permitted to put his free hand atop hers, which was looped through the crook of his elbow. It had been ages since he'd given anyone a tour of his home. His previous nurses had been given a gruff, "Stay out of the West Wing," and that was that, if they'd been let in the door at all.

He coughed a few times before speaking to her. "You've met nearly everyone. I daresay it's the most they've all talked in quite some time. They grew tired of my company long ago."

"No kidding? Maybe it's got something to do with your sunny disposition," Belle teased. "Are you hungry? I was going to make some dinner. Get better acquainted with Chef Bouche."

At this, Adam stiffened and dropped her arm. "I eat alone. You can pick up whatever you like. Call up Harris' Grocer in town and charge whatever you like to my account. Don't shop for me, though. I feed myself."

Belle touched his arm, but he instantly recoiled. She recalled her professional manners and folded her hands, letting them hang before her. "I don't mind cooking for the both of us. It's part of my job: nurse and housekeeper. I wouldn't be living up to the hype if I let you starve."

"I don't need you to cook for me. I haven't needed mothering since I was a child. Clean the house if you like. Cook for yourself if you like. Leave me alone to do my job during the day." He sped up his pace. "I've indulged you enough. There's no need for us to spend any more time together."

Belle's mouth fell open, dumbstruck at having stepped on some landmine in his tightly-woven psyche she couldn't have seen coming. She made a mental note to ask Chef Bouche about Adam's eating habits. She was his nurse, after all.

Belle tucked away her sadness over being snapped at and raised her chin, reasoning that there was work to be done. The castle was a filthy mess. Whether her patient was cordial or not, she had a job to do.

"Don't mind the master," Audra said sympathetically when Belle turned the corner. The white China teapot had been listening in – her golden swirls turning to a nose, mouth, eyes with expressive eyebrows when she spoke. "He's sensitive about food."

"I can see that. I was going to make dinner. Any suggestions?"

Audra pfft'd irritably. "You'll find nothing but cobwebs in the cupboards. Make sure to buy all you need to feed yourself. The master doesn't eat regular food anymore. It's all I can do to force a cup of tea into him every now and again."

Belle rubbed her temples. "What does he eat?"

Audra looked up, making sure to meet Belle's big eyes before she answered. "His curse will turn him into a member of the Lupine when he turns thirty later this year. He started eating dog food last year. It's his way of punishing himself, preparing for the inevitable."

Belle's lips tightened. "But that's..." She wanted to put to words all the obvious reasons why this was not the way to handle one's life, but instead focused on what she could rationalize as part of her job, leaning away from just plain meddling. "I'm his nurse. Show me where the dog food is."

Audra's eyebrows lifted – the gold swirls moving like waves on the delicate china. "What are you going to do?"

"I'm throwing it out. He'll eat as a person, or he'll starve. Self-pity has a time and place. I'd say nine years of it is enough. Wouldn't you?"

Audra smiled deviously. "Oh, he won't like that."

"Yeah? Well, he'll just have to get over it. Dog food doesn't have enough nutritional value to sustain a person. No wonder he's so irritable."

"Rare steak, then," Audra suggested, hopping on her tray with giddiness that someone was finally going to help the boy she'd raised. "Barely cook it at all. He used to love my potatoes. I can teach you how to make them. Chef Bouche tries to make everything fancy, but I know my boy. He likes them mashed, with a mushroom sauce of my own invention," she informed Belle with a gleam of pride as she drove her teacart down the hall next to the woman.

Belle pulled out her old cell phone and ordered enough food for two for the week, and then turned to the magical objects. They flocked to her, watching her with anticipation of being noticed. She smiled down at them all with an indulgent love in her heart for the long-forgotten people who'd had lives and loves of their own, once upon a better time. "I think I should probably start cleaning this place. Would you all like to help me?"

The objects looked around at each other hesitantly,

with covert guilty glances that they'd let the castle fall into disrepair. The candelabra hopped up to her, and Belle scooped him up, so he could look at her on eye level. "Mademoiselle, the master doesn't like change. If you clean things around here, believe me, he'll have something to say about it."

The corner of Belle's mouth lifted. "Would that thing be, 'Belle, the house looks amazing. I'm so inspired that I think I'll buy Lucien some new tapers just for the heck of it.'" Belle and Lucien shared a chuckle.

Bosworth chimed in from the floor, his brass arms on his shapely laquered hips. "Now, now. The master won't like us messing with the state of the home. We tried that years ago, remember? We moved the stand in the foyer a foot to the left, and he was spitting mad for days."

Belle studied the enchanted trinkets with a new bloom of compassion. It wasn't exactly easy for a teapot to operate a broom. "Look, I'm not entertaining any sort of delusion that everything will be up to snuff within the thirty days Adam's given me. Still, I have to try. It's unsanitary for anyone to live in such conditions. His coughing is no doubt from the dust. I'm his nurse."

Lucien leaned forward and squeezed her face with the two pedestals that held the unlit melted white tapers. He brushed his brass nose across hers affectionately. "Then whatever you need, we are here to assist you." His voice turned sharp after Belle kissed his cheek and set him back on the floor. "Alright, everyone! You heard the lady of the house. Bosworth, find the mop and bucket. Audra, let's start in the kitchen. That's one of the rooms that still gets used on occasion. I'll not have the lady of the house dining in filth." He turned over his shoulder and gave Belle a wink and a conspiratorial nod of his head.

Belle felt energized with the zing of fresh optimism as she located the pile of unused dust rags. Though Adam was stuck in his mess, Belle realized that she didn't have to carry on as if she was also stuck.

7

SOMEONE WORTH GETTING UP IN THE MORNING FOR

The foyer, Belle's bedroom and bathroom, the kitchen, the dining room and the hallway that connected the two took all day to clean, but when they were finished, the staff lounged with Belle on the settee in one of the nearby living rooms, uttering several gusts of well-deserved satisfaction. The castle was enormous, but finally there was marked progress. They were all filthy, but happy.

"I need to go get washed up. Then I'm going to start dinner. Do you guys... Do you eat?"

Lucien shook his head. "No, but we can appreciate smells. If you cook? Oh, the fragrances that will fill the castle! Tell me you cook with plenty of garlic. I haven't smelled that in far too long."

Belle's hand fell on the footstool, who was lapping at her shoe with his tassel and yipping happily. She scratched his fabric and then sat back to bring Lucien onto her lap. The staff were starved for touch, so every time she sat down, they inched closer with hopeful faces, wishing to be stroked or picked up.

Bosworth was the only exception. He kept a respectable distance, his posture unbending and his tone always a little haughty. "Garlic is a smell that fills the house like a loud noise. Thyme. That's what I long to smell. It's a slight bit more sophisticated than being whacked over the head with an odor."

Lucien rolled his eyes. "Don't pay attention to him. He loves garlic, too. He just wants to impress you with the extensively snobbish palate he used to have, back when we were human."

Belle sniggered at their dynamic, and then excused herself. Lucien and Audra followed her down the hall, with the pup nipping at Belle every so often. Before she shut them out of her bedroom so she could change, she asked for a pen and paper to write a note that she read quietly to Lucien and Audra, taking care not to wake the sleeping Simone. "Dear Adam, Dinner is at 6:30 sharp. I'll see you in the dining room then." She placed the note on the teacart and smiled at Audra. "Can you deliver that to him? I don't know where his bedroom is, and he doesn't want me sniffing around in the West Wing."

Audra exchanged a hesitant look with Lucien. "Are you sure, dear? He doesn't like to eat in front of people. The master doesn't take kindly to being ordered to do something he's said he doesn't want to do."

Belle held up her dirt and soot-stained fingers as proof. "Him calling the shots resulted in this. I'm the nurse, so I get to decide what's best for him. I don't think I'm pushing the boundaries too much by telling him when dinner will be ready."

Audra still looked uncertain, but gave Belle a nod and zipped off to deliver the note. Lucien stayed behind, tucking in the edge of Belle's freshly-washed sheet. He clapped his hands, and the wardrobe came to life with an operatic burst of welcome. "You've come back to me! Come, come. Let me look at you." Her drawers arced in a slight grimace at Belle's disheveled demeanor.

Lucien took charge, reclaiming his role as butler with pride. "The lady of the house needs something nice to wear to dinner. This is no attire for a fine woman to be wearing around the house. Can you whip up something more delicate?"

"Of course!" Simone replied. Everything she said sounded to Belle like the aria of a throaty soloist who had no need for a microphone. "I was working on a few outfits this afternoon. I'll have something for you right away. Go, go. Wash up."

Lucien tottered into the adjoined bathroom and got out a fresh towel, shampoo, and fancier soaps than Belle had ever used before. "I think this will do nicely, but let me know if there's anything else you need. Anything at all."

Belle glanced around the bathroom with new appreciation for all the gleaming fixtures. Everything had been so dingy mere hours ago, but now the sconces and moldings sparkled with new life. The white jacuzzi tub was huge and beckoned to her aching limbs, but Belle opted for the shower, so as not to get the tub filthy all over again. She envisioned herself reading in the bathtub, the way she'd seen people do on TV. She had just the book in mind. It was tucked away in her belongings, and though she'd read it dozens of times already, the luxury of the bathtub seemed like it might make the old story come alive with new light.

Lucien turned his back so Belle could disrobe and step under the heated spray, but he didn't leave her. Instead he gathered up her dirty clothes and sent them down to be washed. "Lucien, do you think Adam would submit to a physical exam? I know now that his diagnosis of major depressive disorder with psychosis is wrong, but I worry his doctor learned that Adam hears voices and stopped the medical exam there. His patient file didn't really give me a broad enough scope. Plus, it's years old."

"The master doesn't like doctors, for obvious reasons. When you're written off as crazy, there's not much motivation to convince people otherwise. Though he did try for a time; I'll give him that. But if you asked? I admit, I do not know if you can convince him. Just yesterday I wouldn't have thought that anyone could come in here and transform so much in such a short time."

Belle took her time lathering up, enjoying the hot water on her sore back. "It was only some cleaning products and elbow grease."

"To you, maybe. But to us? To us, it's hope. We haven't had a reason to be at our best in years. Now we have purpose. We have someone to please whose smile lights up the room."

Belle dimpled as she rinsed off. "That's a high compliment, coming from someone who literally lights up every room he wanders into."

"Just be patient with the master. He's not used to someone like you."

"Someone like me? A nurse?"

Lucien shook his head with a note of melancholy to his smile. "Someone worth getting up in the morning for."

Belle turned off the water and took the towel he offered her, cinching it around her curves before stepping out. "Oh, you charmer."

Lucien moved to the doorway, looking back at Belle with a contented sigh that was laced with a little worry. She was a breath of fresh air, but Adam was the type to bolt the windows against anything that might be good for him. "I think I'll go help speed the master along. See you at 6:30, milady."

Belle was nervous when she tiptoed down the steps half an hour later. She hadn't worn a dress since she'd been a child. The wardrobe had been so proud of her creation, and to be fair, the dress was lovely. It was a bright mossy green and had a long, belled skirt. The bodice hugged Belle's slender frame as if it was made for her, which Belle learned that it had been. The slight dip showed off a hint of her cleavage, which Belle had never exposed to the public. Now that the wardrobe had her measurements, she promised Belle that she could make a whole assortment of couture for the new girl to try on. Belle's footwear consisted of only sneakers and a pair of nude ballet flats, so she opted for the flats to move through the castle, hoping she didn't look quite as strange as she felt in the fancy outfit.

The dress moved easily with Belle's quick walk. The draft that licked at her bare, freshly lotioned legs felt like a glorious scandal she reveled in that she'd never experienced in her usual jeans. Her long brown hair had been pulled back with a light green silk ribbon, making her feel feminine and delicate after a day spent scrubbing on her hands and knees.

She wandered into the kitchen and scolded Chef Bouche with a lighthearted tease for starting without her.

"But it's been so long since I've been able to cook anything! You can't put steaks in the fridge and expect me not to put them to use." His backsplash splintered off on both sides, forming arms he used to gesture with, stir pots and tend to his meals. "Tell me of the most magnificent steak you've ever had, and I'll top it."

Belle giggled as she started boiling potatoes, following the instructions from Audra, who was perched on the counter. "The best one I had could easily be topped, I'm sure. I don't really remember what Papa did to season it, but I remember the day. I'd just come home from a long day of cleaning homes, which is what I did when I finished high school. I'd been down that week, because I'd gotten into the nursing school I applied to, but the tuition was too expensive. Papa made us steak that night, which was a real treat. I remember thinking how utterly wasted the luxury was on me, depressed as I was. When I sat down to eat with him, on my chair was a letter from the Johnstone Foundation. They'd granted me a full scholarship." Belle plopped a few potato pieces into the boiling water. "Best steaks of my life, that day. Of course, it probably could've been hot dogs, and I would've said the same. That's the thing about a beautiful blessing. It paints the whole day with glitter."

When Belle looked up, she saw much of the staff in the doorway, wearing wistful expressions and hanging on her every word. They'd been starved for happy stories of glitter. Too much of their world had been dust and doom.

"You're lovely, Mademoiselle," Lucien said with a look of rapture about him.

"I think you look good enough for a dance," commented the wheeled coatrack. Thomas Chapeau's wooden arms animated for Belle as he rolled into the kitchen and bowed.

Belle laughed at the sweetness they lavished on her. "Why thank you, kind sir." She fanned out her skirt and curtsied, pretending like she was a fine lady worth the fuss. When she righted, Thomas swept her away from the stove in a waltz that enchanted them both with its melodious levity. She didn't care that she struggled to keep the rhythm; she was dancing, and found that she was adept enough to keep up with the likes of a coatrack. Audra sang an upbeat dirge while the staff banged and clapped as best they could to give the two some makeshift music to hold onto.

Belle's smile was contagious, giving them all something beautiful. They illuminated the room with sheer delight, which gave birth to stories of their own memories of their best steaks ever.

Lucien danced around Bosworth, who stood stock-still with a disapproving frown painted on the face of the antique clock. "Mine was in the artisanal town just north of Hinlay, but it wasn't the steak and it wasn't Hinlay that brought me to my knees. It was Vivienne. Ah, she's always been a sight. And what of yours, Bosworth?"

Vivienne swept Lucien's face with her feathers, giggling at the compliment.

Bosworth scoffed and turned up his nose, which had the clock's hands sprouted from the center. "A steak is a steak. A woman is a woman. A city is a city."

Lucien shimmied, shaking his imaginary breasts in Bosworth's face. "I don't think you understand the world if you can say Hinlay is just a city." He motioned above to where duster was floating above them, twirling in time with Belle's skirt as the woman continued dancing with Thomas. "And if you think Vivienne is just a woman, then you're blind, my friend. She is perfection."

Vivienne pretended she hadn't heard the second compliment, but the proud smirk that lifted the righthand corner of her mouth gave her away. She shook her feathers with a more deliberate sensuality, beckoning him to look, and to never stop staring.

Thomas twirled Belle with ease that awoke parts of him that he'd long written off as being of lesser importance. There was no one to twirl, so he'd stopped trying to make the world into a dance. He didn't mind her clumsy footwork; he was dancing. Belle's throaty laughter filled the kitchen while the potatoes boiled, sending light-hearted melodies into the castle that had forfeited its will to play long ago.

So lost in the moment was she that when Thomas spun her out, she gasped when she smacked into Adam's chest. He'd been watching in the doorway for who knows how long, but was startled at the laughter that painted Belle's lips. His arms fell around her hips to steady her sway, and for the briefest of moments, his body was tempted to fall into the easy rhythm of the waltz. It had been so long since a woman had looked at him and smiled. The levity didn't die on her lips, even this close up. All of his scars and hairy spots that should be smooth were on display, but still, her eyes crinkled in amusement. "You came down for dinner! Thank you." She moved a stray lock of hair back, beaming up at him. "You're early, too. I was worried I'd have to fight you about coming down for every meal."

Adam's brows pulled together in dismay. "Yes, well, I came down to tell you that I won't be joining you for dinner. Though it looks as though you've found enough company. I won't be missed." When he realized that his arms were still around her, he stepped back. "Excuse me."

"You came down to tell me you won't be coming down?"

Adam cleared his throat, his palms stinging to be placed back on the curve of her hips. "I would have sent you a note, but someone refused to deliver it," he growled at Audra, who turned up her spout unapologetically. "So don't go to all this trouble. I prefer to dine alone." He motioned around the kitchen, his nose crinkling. "Did you clean?" He said the word "clean" with the same disdain one might reserve for the word "fart".

Belle refused to be deterred by his mood, which always seemed to be some shade of irritable. "Well, I already did go to the trouble. I can't exactly eat two steaks. Tomorrow, I'll remember that you eat alone. Tonight, let's test out the dining room. If you think the kitchen is clean, wait until you see the table out there. You can actually eat off it. You'll be amazed."

Adam frowned. "I don't want you messing up my home."

"I unmessed it, actually." Belle's lightness slowly began to descend, her heels weighting to the floor. "Henry hired me to be your nurse and your housekeeper. Since you don't have major depressive disorder with psychosis, you clearly don't need a nurse as badly as he thought. So I threw myself into being your housekeeper. I'm not going to take a paycheck for doing nothing. That's not me."

He motioned to her dress. "And you look different. I assume I have Simone to thank for that? She always tends to go a bit overboard."

It was the first dress Belle had worn since her kindergarten graduation. When she'd gotten dressed, she had hoped she looked beautiful in the green gown, but Adam's comment came out flat, revealing her insecure underbelly. "Simone made it for me. I thought it looked nice, but maybe it's too much." When Adam didn't correct her, she shrank, feeling foolish that she'd just accepted that she belonged in a nice frock, in a huge castle, eating steak like a rich person. Belle turned and switched off the stove so the potatoes didn't boil over. "You're right. I look ridiculous. I don't know what I was thinking. I'll go change."

Belle flitted out of the kitchen, her chin lowered.

Lucien and Audra glowered at Adam, who shrugged as if he didn't understand what all the fuss was about. "What? You've all never thought that Simone gets a little carried away every now and then?"

They didn't answer, but continued their irate glares. Chef Bouche responded by tossing Adam's steak onto the floor, while Lucien stepped on it, never breaking eye contact.

Adam rolled his eyes at their dramatics. "She's the one who said she looked ridiculous. I didn't say it."

Audra shook her head at him, disappointed. "It's like you want her to hate you. She's done nothing but her job, and you can't say one nice thing. Saying nothing at all would've been better than that."

Adam clenched his fists at his sides. "I don't think you all understand who the master of this house is. I don't need your lectures. Where's my normal food? I'm not eating that," he said of the steak on the floor.

The staff turned up their noses at him and exited without a word. When Adam moved further into the kitchen, Chef Bouche lit his stovetop flames up high so that they almost scorched the ceiling. "You didn't clean the kitchen. You didn't cook the food. You don't even eat anything I make. This isn't your space anymore. You've made that clear. We'll do what we like with it, and you'll say nothing about it. Belle has free reign of the kitchen. If she cooks for you, you'll eat it, so help me. You've turned up your nose at my hard work, but I won't see that sweet girl insulted like that."

Adam backed away from the flames that made the chef's face in the backsplash seem to glow with an underworldly vehemence. "Fine! I didn't do anything wrong, by the way. I didn't ask her to clean or cook."

"You'll eat what she cooks, or you'll starve to death!" Chef Bouche threatened at a shout. When the flames finally died down, his tone returned to normal. "I forget. Did you prefer white wine or red?"

Adam held up his hands. "Whatever you choose is fine." He inched out of the kitchen, unsure when it was that he'd lost hold of his staff. They were talking back now, and telling him what to do. They'd given up on his behavior long ago, but now suddenly it seemed his redemption was worth fighting for.

For the first time in too long, Adam thought about his deportment. Mirrors had long since been forbidden in the castle, but looking down, he finally started to notice how unkempt he'd let himself become. He turned around, finding Lucien in his path. "I'm wearing my pajamas."

Lucien folded his brass arms and cocked his hip to the side. "You are. Belle was wearing a dress, but now you've ruined that."

Adam's hand moved over his chest and stomach in confusion. "It's the middle of the day, and I'm wearing pajamas."

Lucien softened his frustration, seeing the new light dawning on Adam in slow motion. "You are. Dinner doesn't start for another half an hour. Perhaps you would like to freshen up?"

Adam looked down at his fingernails, and for the first

time was repulsed at how overgrown they were. They had mutated into claws upon his transformation, but they were gnarled now, and curved slightly at the pointed tips. "That might be a good idea. Lucien, would you mind…"

Lucien was never one to hold a grudge. Compassion lit his features as the flame atop his head danced with a bit more spirit. "I would be glad to assist you, Master."

8

WALTZING PARTNER

When Belle came back down to the kitchen to bring out the food to the dining room, the staff shooed her out. "Sit down, sweetheart. You've been working hard all day." Audra took in Belle's change of wardrobe back into her simple blue nursing scrubs with a compassionate tilt of her head.

When Belle sat at the dining room table, she'd had no delusions that Adam would join her. She sighed, knowing it would be an uphill battle to get him off of dog food. She'd had many difficult patients before, but none she'd had to convince that dog food wasn't a proper dietary option. Belle had brought a book down from her bedroom, anticipating the possibility of dining alone.

Opening up the familiar worn cover brought about a measured beat to her breath that was almost trance-like. Though she'd read the tale of Michel Fourniret too many times to count, there was something about the elegance of the Poe-like language that soothed her. Even though the tale was dark and dreary, she knew the story so well that she felt like she could hide in the maple cupboards of the backdrop when the silver-tongued killer skulked by.

When Audra brought out her dinner on the teacart, Belle forked the delicate greens, moved at how elegant the setup was. The fine china was eggshell colored with gold on the rims that broke off into swirls every few inches. There were dainty bluebirds painted on the lip of the plate that looked so cheerful, she half expected them to start chirping merry tunes at her. Audra poured Belle a cup of tea while the coatrack unfolded her napkin for her and laid it across her lap. Despite her shapeless scrubs, she felt like a refined lady at their pampering.

"Thank you, Thomas."

"Anything for my favorite waltzing partner."

"I thought *I* was your favorite waltzing partner, Thomas," Adam said from the doorway.

Belle straightened at the sound of Adam's voice, and met his eyes with confusion. His pajamas were gone. He looked freshly showered, dressed in khaki pants and a pressed lavender business attire shirt that had vertical blue pinstripes. The more animal aspects of him were still there, but he appeared less unkempt, and more like an upright man than a beast.

Adam cleared his throat, suddenly aware that everyone was gawking at him. "6:30, right?" His gaze sharpened into a glare at Audra. "I hate to think I came down here just to be stared at."

"I'll get you some dinner, Master." Audra hopped onto the teacart and zoomed into the kitchen to fetch him a salad.

Belle felt vastly underdressed now, but refused to apologize for her scrubs. She was at work, after all, and this was her work uniform. Besides, it was because of his scrutiny that she'd changed out of the green gown in the first place.

"I threw out your dog food," she admitted, testing his temper to see if that would make him fly off the handle.

"Chef Bouche mentioned something to that effect." Adam sat down when Thomas moved over to him and tentatively pulled out his chair. "You should really ask me before you go throwing out my belongings."

Belle put her book down and leaned back in her seat, her eyes narrowed. "Are you a dog?"

Adam didn't answer, his mouth pulling in a tight line. He'd chased away the softness in her when he'd criticized her gown, and now he was left to deal with the strength he could see burning in her eyes.

"If you're not a dog, then I didn't throw out your things. I threw out your dog's things. And wouldn't you know? Sultan didn't seem to mind."

"You've got quite a mouth on you."

Belle flipped open her book and started reading again, refusing to be baited into a fight.

After a few beats of silence, Adam spoke up. "What are you reading?"

"A book," she replied succinctly. "It's about a big man with a bigger mouth and an even bigger ego who gets stabbed to death in the end by the help because he's insufferable." She covered her mouth in faux apology. "Oops! I just ruined the ending." Then she waved her hand to excuse the slip-up. "Don't worry. She makes him suffer for being a condescending butthead."

Adam scoffed. "Did you truly just call me a butthead?"

Belle smirked at his affront as Audra came back out with his salad. "I think I did. I mean, if your head is acting like a butt, spewing crap out at random people who were otherwise having a nice day, that's something worth noting to your doctor. Not your nurse, obviously, since you won't let me examine you. Perhaps you'll have better luck with your proctologist."

Adam gaped at Belle, and then barked out a laugh that startled even him. Audra jumped back, confused at the sound coming from the man. Lucien stood in the doorway, utterly perplexed and amused. Adam's smile showed off his teeth, two of which had grown into fangs as he neared his permanent transition to a member of the Lupine. He rarely smiled, and couldn't recall the last time he'd laughed so loudly. "That was brilliant. Truly. I'll try to remember to bring my A-game to dinner tomorrow."

Belle quirked her eyebrow at his compliance. "I was planning on serving breakfast at eight o'clock tomorrow.

Do you think the stick up your butt might be dislodged by then, and you'd like to join me? Perhaps your proctologist makes house calls."

Adam chuckled further at her sass. "Eight o'clock is fine." He swallowed hard, the levity dying on his lips as he eyed the salad and the fork. He hadn't used a fork in a couple of years, and had never been all that enthralled by salads. He kept his eyes on his food and chose his words carefully. "Do you think you'll have food for Sultan for breakfast? I don't think he prefers salads. And he doesn't usually eat at the table."

Belle reined in her tongue, looking across the long, polished table thoughtfully, considering his roundabout admission. "I think Sultan's punished himself enough."

Adam kept his eyes on his food, and for all of his etiquette lessons as a boy, realized he'd completely forgotten how to properly hold a fork. His eyes climbed to Belle, so he could study her movements and mimic them as best he could. His grip on the utensil was more akin to a serial killer fisting his machete, but he managed to guide a few leaves into his mouth. His wrist faced the ceiling as the tomatoes dribbled off the fork and plopped on his lap.

Adam growled in frustration, shooting a glare at Belle, who turned her focus back to her book. Her refusal to acknowledge his frustration gave him the space to work through the mechanics of eating upright. Every now and then, Belle would make a show of holding her fork properly, and bring a small bite to her unpainted, pink lips.

After he mimicked her, she would take another bite, not making eye contact the entire time.

Adam grew frustrated when the third dried cranberry fell onto the floor. "This is pointless! There's no need for me to eat at a table. You and I both know I'm destined to become one of the Lupine. This is all frivolous!"

Belle didn't take the bait, knowing that if she looked at him, that would only give audience to his frustration. "If you're okay with giving up, then give up. And here I thought you got to be the largest mortgage broker in Avondale because you're a hard worker. Maybe it's just because of who your parents were. There's no shame in nepotism."

"You act like this is easy for me!"

"I just said it was hard work. You're the one who isn't up for hard work. That's fine. Should I send Audra to tuck you in? Read you a bedtime story? Bring you a blankie?"

Adam growled at her and stabbed at his salad again, angling his head under the utensil when the food started to drop off. He caught a few leaves in his mouth, but could hardly count that as a victory. "There! Are you happy?"

"I'm always happiest when I'm being yelled at," Belle droned, and then her eyes cut to him in a glare. "You told me I looked ridiculous earlier. If you could also call me fat, I'd be ecstatic."

Adam's upper lip curled, but he didn't back down. Now it was a challenge he couldn't back away from. He'd made his peace with being a monster long ago, but being lazy? That had never crossed his mind. Leaf by leaf, Adam worked his way through the entire salad, stomaching every boring bite that cost far more effort and pride than it was worth. "There! I had dinner with you. Are you satisfied now?"

Belle quirked an eyebrow at him. "You call that dinner? That's what we simple folk refer to as a salad." When Audra came back out with their plates filled with steak, mashed potatoes with mushroom gravy, and baby carrots, Belle picked up her knife with a note of a challenge in her eyes. "I don't care if you make a bigger mess than a toddler slurping down spaghetti. I care if you wuss out."

"Wuss out? Do you think living like this is easy for me?"

Belle made a show of picking up her fork and knife, and daintily sawing off a chunk of meat before popping it in her mouth. Her eyes rolled skyward as she groaned. "I think this steak is worth being uncomfortable for."

Adam gave a few attempts and nearly stabbed his hand with the knife, finally cutting off a chunk that was far too large. "This isn't worth it!"

"Would you like some help?"

"What I'd like is my regular food back!"

"I'll put that on the grocery list, right underneath the shiny new unicorn I was going to buy for myself." She softened at his frustration. "If I cut your meat for you, will you show me how to get Sultan to calm down? He's adorable, but the constant yipping is grating after the fifth straight hour."

"It's because you're too easy on him. He wants to play with you." He sighed and threw his fork on the table. "But sure, I can show you where you can lock him if he becomes bothersome."

"Thank you." Belle moved slowly as she stood, taking in Audra's looks of caution and Lucien's raised hands as a sign that this might not go over all that well. Instead of picking up his knife and fork, she stood behind his chair and wrapped her arms around his sides. She rested her hands atop his, maneuvering them to pick up the utensils, as if he was her puppet.

"This is humiliating," Adam complained as Belle directed his hands.

"Audra? Lucien? Would you give us a moment?" She waited until they exited with wary expressions before she leaned in so she could whisper in his ear. "We're alone now. I'm no one, so there's no humiliation, because no one's watching you."

Adam swallowed hard and allowed her gentleness to wash over him, covering his vulnerable spots with her softness. When she pressed her cheek to his temple, his heart quickened at the intimate touch. "What's your Pulse, Belle?"

"Getting grown men to let me feed them. What can I say? It's a talent." Her attempt at levity worked as they kept on cutting, his movements less resistant to her guidance.

"It's Discernment. If I put my Pulse into people, they have a clearer head when it comes to decision-making."

"And you're a nurse? That seems like a wasted avenue for your gift. You could be working alongside King Hubert himself."

Belle chuckled. "I'm not sure the king is looking in the West Village for people to put on his staff. I was working at a hospital for a while. My Pulse helped the doctors and surgeons better care for their patients."

"Why'd you leave?"

Belle paused, and Adam could tell she was debating between the hard truth and the G-rated answer she doled out for acquaintances. Finally she gave in, letting the quiet of the dining room cover her confession. "They were..."

But Adam never heard her true reason. Thomas came in to check on them, but was promptly pulled back out by Lucien.

"It was just time to move on," Belle amended. "How about you? Tell me about your Pulse." Even though they were alone again, Belle's moment of confession had come to an end, and she was eager to shift the focus. She already knew the answer to her question, but redirected the conversation anyway.

"I can persuade people. Take away their inhibitions so they can act on their whims."

"Sounds like you missed your calling. You should've been a salesman. Or a pimp."

Adam laughed through his nose. "Most women pull away when they hear what I can do."

Belle finished sawing through the last piece of meat and then shifted the utensil in his grip, setting down the knife. "I know myself well enough. If you took away my inhibitions, it would only go badly for you. I called you a butthead with my filter firmly intact. Can you imagine the names you'd have to endure if you took away my manners?"

Adam chuckled at her forthcoming nature. "Worse than butthead? I'd better not use my Pulse on you, then."

He expected her to go sit down in her chair across from him, but when she wrapped him in a light hug from behind, he stiffened, his eyes going wide. She said nothing when she released him and went back to sitting in her seat, her eyes drifting back to her book while she ate.

As Adam worked his way through his meal, he thought to himself that, frustrations aside, it was the most enjoyable dinner he'd had in years.

9

DINING WITH ADAM

Three days passed with Adam eating breakfast, lunch and dinner in the dining room with Belle. Belle spent every day with contentment in her heart, feeling as if she was starting to belong in the castle, cherishing even its most dingy nooks and crannies as she meticulously cleaned them. She ended each evening with a phone call to check up on her father, trading laughter and stories with him about their days.

Lucien invested more time grooming the master of the house, now that Adam allowed it. Though he still looked animalistic in nature, he didn't appear quite as wild and unkempt. Belle and Adam shared lively chit-chat across the table, until one afternoon Adam moved his sandwich and bowl of soup down the long table to the spot next to her. Belle quirked her eyebrow when she came into the dining room, but said nothing of it, so as not to put his burst of bravery on the spot.

Belle usually read over lunch while Adam poured over paperwork, making sure his mortgage company was running smoothly from his remote location. He stood as he spread out his papers, casting her a shadow of a smile when she moved around the table toward her seat next to his. "I saw what you did in the ballroom. I admit, I didn't think it possible to make the walls shine again. It looks even better than it did back when I was a boy."

Belle wore scrubs while cleaning between meals, and changed into jeans for lunch, so she didn't get dust all over the food. Today, Simone had laid out a simple peach-colored flowing skirt that fell to her knees, and a beige blouse that left no mistake that Belle was very much a woman. "Thank you," she smiled demurely at him, her eyes widening when he pulled out her chair for her and slid it back in place as she sat, making her feel like a lady. "It was the staff, really. They're so motivated. We're making good progress."

He sat next to her, grateful she didn't comment on his close proximity. He wanted to be closer to her because her presence soothed him, but he didn't want to admit that to her, or have a whole conversation about it. He sorted through the mail that was bundled in a rubber band, surreptitiously watching her flip to the first few pages of the book she'd finished over dinner last night. "You're reading that Michel Fourniret book again? Is it possible the ending will be different this time?"

"Haven't you ever read the same book twice?" She kept her eyes on the worn page. "I guess in my case, it's more like a couple dozen times. It's a comforting story. I can't explain it."

"You told me it's a horror story that ends in a bloodbath. And that's comforting to you?"

Belle sniggered at the summary of the story she'd explained to him in great detail over lunch the day before. "It's not the gore. Well, maybe it's a little bit the gore that I like. It's that she's avenged. Everything she went through couldn't be erased, but it could be avenged." A shadow flickered across her features, but just as quickly, it was gone.

"Will you read it to me?" he asked, fishing through his mail and discarding several notes of no importance.

"No," Belle said flatly as she ladled out a spoonful of creamy tomato soup.

"No?" Adam balked, surprised she would be obstinate about something so trivial.

"No. This isn't a lunchtime book. If I ever read it to you, it would need to be at nighttime. There's nothing scary about the middle of the day. It would ruin the ambiance. We'd need a fireplace and somewhere creepy."

"You're reading it now, and it's the middle of the day."

"Yes, but you're a scaredy cat, and I want you to get the

full effect. What can I say? It brings me joy to watch grown men cower."

Adam sniggered, but then frowned when he came across a letter that wasn't addressed to him. "This is for you."

Belle closed her book and glanced at the sender's scrawl, her jaw tightening. "Huh. Looks like that letter never made it to this address. Weird." Then she took the envelope and tore the whole thing into two pieces, tossing the remnants onto the table. "Must've gotten lost in the mail."

Adam stared at the torn note, now wondering desperately what might be lurking inside that would rile her so easily. He noted the lack of a return address. "Who's it from?"

"I didn't have my mail forwarded here. He shouldn't know where I am." She stood abruptly, gathered up the remnants of the letter and moved toward the doorway. "I need to make a quick phone call. I'll be right back."

Adam studied her jerky steps, which were usually fluid. Her easy smile abandoned her as if it had never graced her lips. He forced himself not to follow her, but to grant her a few minutes of privacy. He glanced at his expensive watch, knowing he wouldn't make it to five whole minutes. Usually only he was the thing that vexed her, and they'd hit such an amiable stride that he was frustrated with whoever it was that dared bother her.

Though, with her gone, he didn't have to suffer

through the tedium of a spoon. He tipped his bowl to his lips, taking in the steaming soup with uncouth slurps.

It was just ticking to minute four when Belle came back. Adam was reading a memo from his stack, pretending to be absorbed in its contents. Her frustration with the unwelcome letter ebbed when she took in his feigned ease marred by the tomato soup that painted his beard and clung to his mustache. "Sorry about that. We were talking about reading dark and scary tales." She sat back down, still intrigued by his sudden preference for close proximity.

"Is everything alright?" he asked, his eyes glued to his paper, doing everything he could not to appear overbearing and demand to see the letter in question.

"Why wouldn't it be? I was thinking of running errands this afternoon. It's supposed to snow this weekend. Is there anything you need?"

"I usually send an email, and the delivery service drops off whatever I desire. There's no need for you to go out."

"I checked, but the delivery service won't giftwrap the unicorn I had my eye on."

Adam snorted, but didn't smile. "What was in that letter? Who sent it?"

"No one. Absolutely and completely no one. He's no one, and doesn't deserve a name or a place at this table. I mean, isn't this a beautiful table?" She ran her finger along the edge. "I wouldn't want to muddy it up with people who... This sandwich looks amazing."

Adam frowned, but refused to look at her. He knew if he saw the troubled look behind her confident expression, he would badger her about it. Besides, he could always just go fish out the letter from whatever trash bin she'd thrown it in, which was exactly what he planned to do once they'd finished their meal.

He was fixated on the letter, when he should have been watching his elbows. When he brought the memo down to rest on the table, his arm caught on the lip of his soup bowl, and the whole thing tipped over, flinging warm crimson liquid onto Belle, who cried out at the sting.

"Oh! Belle, I didn't mean to. Are you alright? Here, let me... Lucien!"

The candelabra scooted into the room, gasping at the sight of Belle covered in tomato soup.

"It's fine," Belle assured them both as Lucien scurried to the kitchen to fetch some rags to mop up the mess. Her beige blouse was utterly ruined, and her skirt had splatters of soup across her lap.

"It just figures," Adam grumbled, handing over his cloth napkin. "The one time you wear something nice, I wreck it."

Belle gripped the armrests through the worst of the heat, which quickly cooled as it spread. She dabbed at the red on her neck, dipping into her collar as a chunk of tomato slid over her cleavage. "Are those letters important? You might want to move them to the other side of the table."

"Right." Adam shuffled the papers out of the way and snatched up his napkin, bringing it over to her to wipe off the splatters on her arm. "I told you I don't eat this kind of food anymore! I eat on the floor, okay? I don't use silverware because I'm going to be turning Lupine in less than half a year. This is all wasted effort, you know. I didn't want to do this!" he scolded her through his shame.

Belle leaned in, pretending to need his arm to brace herself. "Adam?"

He knelt down at her side, bending to her gentle touch without a second thought. "Yes?"

"That is, without a doubt, the worst apology I've ever heard."

"I didn't apologize," he retorted, stiffening.

"I know." With that, Belle picked up her bowl and flung its contents over his dress shirt. Though she loved seeing him in nice clothes as opposed to pajamas, there was nothing more satisfying than his roar of indignation that she'd pulled one over on him. "I think you've got something on your shirt," she laughed.

"I can't believe you just did that!" Adam's shock only brought out more of her giggles. More than irate, he was flabbergasted that she'd done it on purpose. Everyone cowered to his temper. Even Henry backed off when Adam raised his pitch.

"I can't believe that's the first time I did that. It felt amazing." She moved her finger down his chest, giggling to herself at her daring. She'd had problem patients before, but Adam pushed her to her limits with his irrational temper. "Red is totally your color."

"That was good soup!"

She swabbed up a dab from the end of her finger and offered it to him with merriment dancing in her big, brown eyes. "Then you probably shouldn't have asked me to fling my bowl at you."

"I did nothing of the..." He caught her tease and narrowed his eyes at her, letting out a short-tempered growl that did nothing to perturb her. "You're ridiculous."

"You're impossible."

Neither of them expected Adam to lean forward and pop her finger into his mouth, but when he did, the mood shifted to something that shut down his irritation and her laughter. He held her wrist firmly, but she didn't make any attempt to pull away as his tongue laved over her digit. Adam locked eyes with Belle, the serious moment sneaking up on him as much as it did her. Her wide doe eyes didn't look afraid of him, which did wonders for the male prowess he'd long since cast aside. She bit down on her lower lip, as if holding back a torrent of questions and admissions that threatened to spill out if she opened her mouth.

Neither of them spoke. Even as he slid her finger from his lips, they stared at each other with something other than frustration. It wasn't anything as enormous as love, but it was pure, unfettered curiosity that bloomed between them.

It wasn't until the corner of Belle's mouth lifted that Adam realized he was staring at her pink lips with perhaps too much fascination. He cleared his throat and straightened, trying to regain control of the situation that had spiraled out of the tight grip he usually maintained over his household. "I, um... I should probably go wash up."

"Why?" Belle asked, looking innocent as ever. "Our outfits match perfectly."

Adam's face coiled into a smile, indulging himself with the suppleness of her skin as he thumbed her wrist before returning it to her. His lightness fell back to the way of the storm clouds when he glanced at the doorway and found much of the staff crowding the space, gaping at him in astonishment.

His fists tightened at his sides, and his shoulders remembered their position of tension. "The dining room needs mopping," he growled at them, and turned to glance over his shoulder to glare at Belle for forcing levity upon him.

Belle's smile tightened, but it didn't fall to disrepair. She knew that every laugh exchanged was a gamble, and wasn't afraid of the occasional loss if it meant she had more moments where Adam was playful, and just a little bit vulnerable.

10

THE WEST WING

The days passed with small but marked progress in drawing Adam out of his room. The two laughed over meals, and worked and read in a quiet, pleasant rhythm together.

Though Adam had warned her not to invade his personal space in the West wing, she reasoned that perhaps he needed his boundaries pushed a bit, especially when she saw several letters marked "urgent" that had been left on the kitchen table. After she cleaned up the lunch, she scooped the letters up, holding them to her blue scrubs shirt. As she started to climb the steps, Lucien met her at the top of the stairs, which branched off in two directions. "Good afternoon, Mademoiselle," he said with a bow.

"Good afternoon, Lucien. I need to give these to

Adam," she explained before trotting up the forbidden stairwell to the left.

"Actually, I can take those, if you like."

"I got it." She didn't look back, but knew Lucien was worried for her. She'd survived four days with Adam. She was his nurse, and hadn't even been able to give him a physical. Her nursing degree had been largely discarded for this job thus far, and while she didn't mind playing the role of his housekeeper, she felt irresponsible not checking his living conditions. If his room was anything like the rest of the untouched house, he would never stop coughing, and would be at a higher risk of influenza and any number of respiratory hang-ups. The snow was falling fast outside, which meant the drafty house was just a bit nippier.

When she moved down the cobwebbed, unlit hallway, she was struck by the sadness of it all. There were tapestried walls, but they were so caked with dust that the soft blue hue was barely visible through the brownish-gray layer of neglect. One door was cracked open, so she ventured a guess that this might be his bedroom. She lightly rapped on the door, and then pushed it open. "Adam? I've got your mail."

The light switch didn't work, so Belle made her way over to the windows and slid open one of the heavy crimson curtains that stretched from the floor all the way to the ceiling. She sneezed over and over as the cloud of dust flew out at her, making her wonder when the last time was that these curtains had been opened. She glanced around, seeing an undressed bed in the corner, but no sign of Adam. There were broken trinkets everywhere, making Belle grateful she'd worn her shoes. A shattered glass lay near a desk in the center of the room, and something that smelled like scotch and regret stung her nose when she drew near.

Atop the desk was a glass dome that encased a red rose. It was suspended by some kind of magic. Belle possessed the basic magic everyone in her world developed by the time they hit first grade. She could make a few things levitate, change the color of fabric, and use her Pulse to touch people and grant them a burst of her particular gift, which was discernment. But she couldn't make a rose float for prolonged periods of time, and certainly not out of her sight. Everyone knew you had to be looking at the thing you were levitating, but glancing around, Adam was nowhere in sight.

Belle's breath drew in sharply when she realized this must be the rose that would bloom for ten years – until he turned thirty. Then he would go the way of the Lupine. Everyone knew the story of Malaura's curse on Adam, but no pictures had ever surfaced of the rose that served as the ticking timeclock on his destiny. Belle held her breath, lest one false move cause a petal to fall and shorten the time he had left to entertain her with his endless shortcomings when it came to eating soup and pretending at politeness.

Beside the rose was a series of sealed envelopes that

were all addressed from him, ready to be mailed. They were only missing stamps. Belle quickly traded the addressed envelopes for the stack of letters she'd brought up from the lunch table, making a mental note to send them out for him and take one thing off his to-do list. They were all addressed to Rory Johnstone, the Chancellor's daughter. It was widely known that the beautiful woman had been betrothed to Prince Henry, but had bucked the arrangement and married a man of her choosing – a Lethal, which set the wheels of controversy spinning. Belle assumed it must be official political business he was writing to her about, since she was the only daughter of the most notable politician in the land, aside from King Hubert himself.

On her way back out, her eyes caught on a four-foot-tall slanted frame. The gold had long since lost its luster, but the oil painting was in far worse disrepair. Belle gasped, her fingers touching her lips as she saw Adam as he had once been, before the curse. This man wasn't scarred, angry and hairy. Though she'd seen pictures of him before his change in the paper, this was different. This was a full-color oil depiction of the man she'd just flung soup all over. The haughty expression hadn't changed over the years, nor had his stately deportment that came from having an expensive education. It his was green eyes that captivated her, though. In person, Adam's eyes were always angry about something, and didn't encourage careful study of his features. But here she could stare as long as she wished, soaking in the chartreuse that seemed to cover over his many thoughts about the world with an acerbic sharpness.

Heat rose in her cheeks, unbidden, confusing Belle with the swirling, unnamed emotions that threatened her casual demeanor. The deep green enchanted her, bringing out things she didn't understand in herself.

Without meaning to, her fingers reached out, as if something inside of her wanted to touch his face. Confused, she retracted her hand, wondering what had come over her that she was so drawn to a painting of a handsome face that had once been the object of many women's affections. She stepped back and clutched the letters to Rory against her breast, running out of the room and darting down the hall, embarrassed that she'd stared for so very long.

Belle busied herself picking up where she'd left off, cleaning the ballroom with the staff after she sent out his mail.

11

ADAM THE PHILANTHROPIST

"**I** told you not to peek!" she chided him, and then leaned up on tiptoes to cover his eyes.

Adam sighed, but complied. "Surprises are childish. I already know what I'm going to see. You do this every time you finish cleaning a room. There's the grand unveiling, then my look of feigned surprise, a congratulations to you and the staff, then I'm allowed to continue about my day."

"This time, there's an elephant."

"An elephant?" He frowned, but kept his eyes closed behind her dainty hand. He was standing in the hallway, waiting for Belle to build up the suspense enough to suit her whimsical nature.

"It was hard to sneak past you, but I think it really pulls the whole room together. I was thinking we could open a petting zoo. Wouldn't that be fun? I know how much you love having people in and out of your home."

Despite his best attempts to remain stoic, Adam laughed through his nose. "A petting zoo with an elephant? My, that is inventive. And inside my castle, too? We'll have to charge top dollar for admission."

She led him forward, smiling that he was getting better at trusting her, moving where she pleased with his eyes closed. "Oh, we won't charge for tickets. I've decided you're going to become a philanthropist."

Adam scoffed, turning his chin in her direction. "Oh, you've decided, have you?"

"Yes." The cloud of melancholy he used to live in visited him far less frequently since she'd moved in, but it settled on his shoulders and weighted his levity on occasion. "Soon enough, I'll be one of the attractions. Children can come in and throw scraps of bread at me. Adam the Lupine."

Belle stiffened and brought her hand down from his eyes to cup his cheek, making sure he saw only her. "Hey. You're not a beast," she assured him. "I'm looking at you right now, and I can see that you're a man."

It was becoming more frequent that Adam found he didn't mind Belle's little touches. No one made the effort to touch him before she moved in. Even Rory and Henry had kept their distance to respect his penchant for a thick bubble of personal space. But Belle ignored Adam's hang-ups, prancing closer and closer until they'd gotten to the point where he craved her delicate fingertips brushing over his cheek when moments of misery gripped him.

This time, he met her effort halfway, and pressed his forehead to hers, his eyes shut tight. "Tell me again," he begged.

"You're a man," Belle assured him, taking in a drag of the cologne he'd started wearing. It was faint, yet utterly intoxicating. She was so taken with the fragrance that she had to remind her own personal space bubble not to vanish completely each time it infiltrated her senses. Whenever it seduced her, she fought hard with the desire to lean in for another inhale, and still another. She cleared her throat. "You're a man who appreciates the elephant I got him."

"I hope you searched around for a bargain."

"Why bother? I just charged him to your account. You said to buy whatever we needed for the household."

"And we needed an elephant?" he teased, enticed by the sweetness in her game. His lashes lifted, filling his vision with the wonder that was Belle up close. Perhaps in his younger years he might not have pursued a beauty like her. She had an elusive allure about her, whereas he'd preferred women who put their curves on display. He'd been drawn to the bawdy laughter and the scantily-clad legs. But with Belle, there was a subtlety that hooked something deeper inside of him, drawing him in when usually he'd pull away.

Belle blinked up at him, equally transfixed until she dropped her hand and all but jumped away from his side. Color haunted her cheeks, and though she tried to remain unaffected, the green of his eyes played on her unexplored desires.

It was Adam's turn to tease her, once he recognized her pink hue for the compliment it was. "Are you blushing?"

"No!" she protested, feigning being appalled at the notion. When he sniggered, she scrubbed the sweetness from her cheeks. "Oh, shut up, or I really will buy an elephant and charge it to your account."

Adam's chest puffed out with pride that hadn't filled his masculine nature in almost a decade. He'd given up on desire, or being found desirable by anyone, but once upon a better time, he'd been one of the most sought-after bachelors in the land. He knew that blush, and reveled in the color of it on Belle. "I think this is the part where you show me the surprise."

Belle kept her chin down to conceal her chagrin, and motioned to the third living room that had been checked off the list. "Ta-da."

Though Adam had known this would be the surprise, he rolled out a dramatic gasp for her sake. "Wow! You really did a number on this room. I admit, I didn't even remember that we had teal antiques." His eyes fell on the ornate furniture with rounded edges that had been restored to actual usefulness. "My mother picked out that vase. She always had pink roses in it. One time, Lucien put orange lilies in it, and within the hour, they were switched out and given to the mailman." His eyes clouded over with the memory, picturing his mother fretting over the flowers with her usual eye for detail. "She was particular like that."

Belle was quiet for a few beats. "Do you think she'd like the setup of the furniture? Where would she have wanted the couch?"

Adam motioned to the far wall. "Well, it used to be over there, near the window. She would read while I did my lessons when I was a boy."

Belle crossed the room and put her hands on one of the ends. "Help me move this?"

It had taken only two weeks for Belle's sweetness to wear down his acerbic demeanor. He didn't even question his feet that moved where she beckoned, gripping the other end of the couch to help her shift it over to the window. "I can do this. It's too heavy for you. You'll hurt yourself."

Belle smirked at him. "I've got news for you, pal. I lift patients for a living. I got the elephant in here easily enough."

Adam chuckled as they scooted the couch into place, bringing the whole room into a more familiar focus for him. "Speaking of which, where is my brand new elephant? He seems to have wandered off."

"Weird. I gave him a piggyback ride into the house. You know, he probably has to go to the bathroom. I told him to use your bed as his toilet. I hope that's okay."

Adam lost count of how many times he laughed in her presence, but appreciated each moment of lightness he'd assumed it was fine to live without. The laugh led to a deep, barking cough he'd never been able to shake.

When he collected himself, he glanced around the freshly cleaned room, taking in the lemony scent of the floor polish that really made the dark hue of the hardwood shine. The main rooms had marble floors, but the smaller ones had the coziness of wood, which looked even more inviting when cleaned. It was strange how right Belle looked, standing by the couch with him. Though the room was decked in antiques and fine furniture, and she was clad in scrubs, she was the most captivating thing in the space.

"Let's test out the couch, shall we?" He slid onto the cushion, recalling the stiff backing he'd squirmed against many times in his youth. It brought back memories of studying Latin next to his mother while she looked over legal documents for the family business.

Adam patted the space next to him, and suddenly a flood of vulnerability swept through his insides. Just as quickly as it rose up in him, the anxiety faded when Belle sat down at his side.

The urge to drape his arm around her shoulders caused his forearm to tense up, wondering if that would be far too forward. He was constantly aware that he might spook her, or perhaps spook himself if indeed she was comfortable enough with him to allow such things. He'd never been so self-conscious before, but now he questioned every move, to the point of freezing completely next to her like a scared schoolboy.

When she yawned, he began to see a slight tiredness etching itself around her eyes. "Did you sleep alright?"

"Something like that." She cracked her neck and leaned into the cushion, taking a deep breath. "The Lupine were especially vocal last night. Kept me up for a bit with their howling."

In truth, the incessant and angry howling frightened her. She'd clutched the comforter tighter around her, and asked Simone to sing her a song to drown out the nightmares she was sure were coming.

Adam's mouth tightened in a firm line. "They do that sometimes to remind me my time is coming."

"It's fine. I'm being a baby about it." Belle smiled at her handiwork, a restfulness relaxing her sore shoulders. The staff had given them a bit of privacy for the unveiling, noting that each time Belle showed Adam a new part of his house that was able to be used again, the two drew an inch closer. "Do you like it?"

"It looks wonderful. I can't believe how quickly it's all coming together. It seems like every day, I add new available rooms to my free zoo for children."

It was subtle – an accident, even – but Adam felt Belle's smallest finger brush against his. She didn't pull away at the closeness, but left her hand there, connecting herself to him as if she had a right to try something so brazen. He didn't pull away, but savored the smallness of the connection, wondering if the simplicity of the touch was what made it feel spectacular.

"You got another unmarked letter today. Lucien left it for you on the counter in the kitchen," he said quietly, broaching the subject she always shut down. "He burned the last one before I could sneak it out of the trash bin and read it."

Belle stiffened, but didn't pull away. With her other hand, she adjusted her shirt, arranging it around her as if checking her armor to be ready for possibly attacks. "Thanks. I'll throw it away later."

He let the silence build until he could endure it no more. "Who are they from? It's your fourth one since you moved in."

Belle opened her mouth to speak, but Adam's phone vibrated in his pocket. He'd forsaken his pajamas during the day, and wore business casual around the house. He noticed that his pressed dress shirts always managed to draw Belle's gaze, so he made sure Lucien had a full selection of nice clothes ironed and ready for him.

"Yeah?" he said on the phone, his usual gruff demeanor just a few degrees lighter, until he heard the voice on the other end.

"Hey, Adam. Are you busy?"

Adam stiffened and stood, but didn't leave the room. His heart picked up with nerves that came from guilt he'd never been able to reconcile. He'd wronged Rory when last they'd spoken. They both knew it, but she'd never called him out on his selfishness before. Now there was a rift between them, and he'd refused to apologize for it. Oh, he'd written her countless letters berating himself for not coming to her aid sooner.

"Sleeping Beauty" is what the papers had called her. His childhood friend had fallen into the coma that had been predicted since her birth. Before she'd fallen, she begged him to try to wake her with "true love's kiss", as the counter-curse advised, but they had both known it wouldn't work. Adam wasn't in love with Rory, nor did she feel that way about him. Still, as the deadline neared, she pleaded with him to try.

Four months. He'd waited four months before braving the outside world to go and see her. It was a crime she'd never forgiven him for, and he refused to apologize for leaving her in her slumbering state without trying to wake her for that long.

That she was calling him now? Something had to be wrong. "What is it? Is Remus alright?"

Rory's quiet voice was gentler than it had been the last time they'd spoken, when she'd yelled at him to stay out of her life. "Uncle Remus sends his love."

Adam scoffed. "Remus hates me. Always has."

"Remus is smart like that," Rory teased him.

"What do you want?" he asked without preamble, phone clutched in his hand.

"I wanted to say thank you. No, more than thank you. I

had no idea you thought about our fight at all. I figured you were glad to be rid of me."

Adam's brows furrowed. He nodded to Belle when she excused herself from the room to grant him a little privacy. "What are you talking about? Thank you for what?"

"For apologizing. I admit, I wasn't sure you were capable anymore. I was so angry with you for letting me sit in that hospital for so long without trying to wake me. That you see how messed up what you did was?" She paused, and Adam steeled himself against the emotion in her voice. "I forgive you, Adam."

Adam frowned, affronted and confused. "You *forgive* me? It was never going to work, and I told you as much from the start. I couldn't break your curse, so I came down when I could. I have a company to run, if you didn't remember. Several, in fact. And I did come for you, and I did try to wake you, but all I got from you was heaping piles of guilt for not coming fast enough when you snapped your fingers." He began to pace, his anger rising again as he balled his fist at his side. For two weeks, the knot in his sternum had loosened so much, but it was back now, tightening as his conscience warred inside of his chest.

Rory's softness melted away. "So your letters were all a lie? Why apologize to me so beautifully if you didn't mean any of it?"

"What letters?" Adam stilled, recalling the countless notes he wrote out to his childhood friend, confessing his culpability in the mess. He'd poured his heart out in those pages, knowing he would never send them. It was a ritual he did whenever he felt the need to say things he knew he never could. He would write them in a letter, then address and seal it, and then burn all the letters every so often, expunging himself of having to publicly own up to the humiliation of being wrong. "I never sent you any letters."

"Why are you doing this? I know your handwriting. They were sent from you, and they made everything better! Why are you trying to break us all over again? I swear, Adam, I know you better than anyone, but I'll never understand you!"

He could hear her tears over the phone, and clenched his jaw. She'd always been the more emotional of the three of them. Henry knew how to handle Rory when she got worked up, but Adam had never acquired the patience for comforting women. It was only fair; he never permitted them to comfort him, either.

He heard Rory's husband, Cordray, in the background. He arrested the phone from her to speak to Adam directly. "This is the last time you'll ever make my wife cry. Never call her again."

Then then line went dead, leaving a pit of perplexity bobbing in Adam's chest. He slid his phone back into his shirt pocket and made a beeline for his second bedroom, throwing open the door to find a stack of mail, but his letters to Rory nowhere in sight.

"Lucien!" he roared through the hallways, bringing the candelabra ambling up the steps as fast as he could come.

"Yes, Master? How can I help you?"

"Have you been in my second bedroom?"

Lucien held up his hands. "No, sir. I know no one's allowed in there."

"Well, someone's been snooping in here, and they mailed out letters that weren't supposed to be sent!"

Lucien backed away, seeing the familiar flare of temper that had abated in the last two weeks. "I don't know what to tell you. Perhaps you mailed them by mistake?"

Adam hadn't set foot in his second bedroom in a week and a half. It was the room he reserved to torment himself. The enormous oil painting of his former countenance served as the therapeutic slice through his wrists and kept him in his dismal state. He hadn't felt the draw to that room quite so often since Belle had livened things up.

Adam's nostrils flared. "Has Belle been in the West wing?"

Lucien's guilty expression said it all. "I'm not sure."

12

NO LONGER WELCOME

He hadn't yelled in too many days. The unleashing of his volume felt like a release, admitting to himself that he was already the monster he would one day permanently become. "Belle!" Adam ignored Lucien's pleas to calm down as he stomped through the hallway toward the staircase. "Belle!"

She scampered to the expansive foyer, running up the steps in her thin blue scrubs. Concern tugged at her features as she reached him at the top of the wide staircase. "Are you alright? Did you hurt yourself?" She looked him over, but it did nothing to soften him.

On the contrary. He chose to see her concern as meddling, which he had a low tolerance for after years of journalists trying to weasel their way into the private life of the most notorious shut-in. "Did you go into the West wing?"

Belle tilted her head at him, confused that this was the source of his upset. "Today? No. What's wrong?"

"Have you been snooping in the West wing?"

Belle shrugged, trying not to shrink under his visible anger. He was tall, but somehow he seemed impossibly more gigantic as his temper reached new heights she hadn't seen in person. "Of course not. I mean, you left a bunch of documents and mail on the table in the dining room last week, so I brought them up to you. I saw some letters on the table, so I mailed them out for you, but that's all. I didn't touch anything important."

"Nothing important? Do you realize what you've done?" he shouted in her face.

Belle took a step back, shocked at how quickly they had gone from hints of closeness to out-and-out yelling. Belle refused to get louder, knowing that never worked to fuel effective communication. "Adam, I'm sorry. I didn't mean to make you mad. I thought I was taking something off your plate to make your workday easier."

"No one asked you to do that! In fact, the only thing I've asked you to do was to stay out of the West wing!" He glanced down at himself angrily and unfastened the top button of his dress shirt, feeling foolish at how much he'd allowed her to disrupt his home since she'd come to him. "You changed my food, changed my clothes, changed my house, and now you've wrecked one of my oldest friendships. Are you happy?"

Belle didn't tear up, but the pressure building behind

her eyes couldn't be ignored. She'd been yelled at before on the job by irrational patients, but Adam's fury hit her harder than her usual layer of thick skin could fend off with a light joke. She backed away, refusing to let him see her break down. "I'm sorry. How can I fix it?"

"You can leave. Do you think this is what you were hired to do? Meddle in my things and mess up my life? You're no longer welcome here."

"Master, no!" Lucien begged from the top of the steps, watching with horror as the scene unfolded.

Belle's mouth fell open, and the world seemed to go still around her. "I thought I had thirty days. Prince Henry said you would give me thirty days."

"Henry only hired you because you've got a nice ass."

Belle gaped at him, horrified that such venom could come from his lips. "Why are you doing this? Don't talk about my body. Prince Henry hired me because I'm qualified!"

"You can't even follow simple instructions, like 'stay out of my space.' Get out!" Adam roared at her. He took a menacing step forward to spook her into action, but when he saw genuine fear twisting the light and trusting eyes he'd grown to adore, guilt slashed across his chest, tightening the knot in his sternum further. She'd never been afraid of him before, but now he could see it plain as day.

Belle didn't argue, nor did she make a move to pacify his temper. When his hand swept out to motion to the exit while he yelled again, she flinched at the gesture, worried that he meant to hit her. She fled down the stairs, ran to her bedroom and shoved as many of her things in her suitcase as she could find, leaving the many dresses and nice clothes Simone had made for her, and packing up only what she'd brought into the home. Simone tried to get the whole story out of Belle, but the tears were already starting to slide down her cheeks. She didn't want to cry in this beautiful castle. She wouldn't let this be a place where tears fell freely. She loved the home she'd been meticulously cleaning, and the staff that filled it with so much life.

When she whirled around, it was Audra in the doorway, sitting on her teacart with an expression of woe tugging at her porcelain features. "Please don't go," she begged. "The master doesn't know what he's saying. We can help set him straight for you."

"I can't stay here another minute. I'm sorry."

"Please, Belle!"

"He fired me!" she cried, hurt that anyone would assume her incompetent, or talk down to her for something so small. "I've never been let go from any job ever. I graduated at the top of my class – the only nurse to come out of the West Village in seven years."

"You can't go out in this weather, child. The snow's really piling up out there."

"I don't care. I have a nursing degree, you know," she said as she zipped up her suitcase. "I was cleaning because I love this castle, and because I cared that he was coughing and sneezing so much from the dust. But I don't have to put up with his crap."

Belle ignored Audra and ran down the hallway, barely sliding on her threadbare coat before she threw open the front door, wincing as the icy blast bit at her cheeks. She hadn't been outside in over a week, and had severely underestimated the cold. There was no turning back now, so she thrust her body into the wind, holding her hand up to shield her face from the snow that was coming down in heavy sheets. Her beaten-up old car was in the garage, which was a fair hike from the house. Her scrubs were thin. Within the first few steps, they were soaked through from the wetness of the snow that seemed mixed with a light smattering of sleet. Her coat was old, thin and had a couple holes in the sleeves.

In the distance, she heard the haunting call of the Lupine. They usually stayed away from people, but the sound of their cries sent a shiver of fear through her that rivaled the shiver of cold she was already quaking from. Still, she soldiered on, determined to run far away from the castle she loved.

13

FLEEING IN A SNOWSTORM

Belle couldn't feel her fingers when she finally reached her old red sedan. The heat always took at least fifteen minutes to kick in, and she knew she couldn't wait that long. She wanted to get off Adam's property, and away from the painful image that was his face twisted with rage.

She dropped the keys four times before she managed to shove the proper one in the ignition. The car coughed to life, groaning to Belle that she hadn't taken it in yet to get the catalytic converter fixed. It was on her list of bills to pay and things to take care of when more paychecks started rolling in, but those plans were now over. The tears finally broke free and rolled down her cheeks, marring the fun she'd cooked up for herself in the amazing castle.

The roads were icy, and her bald tires skidded off the road twice, but she managed to make it back onto the unsalted asphalt. Her grip on the steering wheel tightened as she turned each corner. What felt like hours covered only a few miles of road as she puttered along, praying she didn't swerve again.

She chided herself for believing she was making a difference. The fact that she was the only other person in the world who could hear the staff in the castle tugged at her. She knew that as much as she would miss them all, they would miss the opportunity to be heard even more.

A pickup truck with too much bravado barreled past her, swirling up the wind and temporarily blinding her when it kicked up too much snow for her windshield wipers to combat. Belle slowed, but the road was too slippery. She swerved again, only this time, her car didn't stop until it took a nosedive past the shoulder and dipped over the edge, gaining unwanted speed before it veered off into the snow-covered ditch. Belle screamed when she crashed into a tree, finally able see just enough out the front windshield to make sense of the madness of the misadventure. Her head banged against the steering wheel, knocking her until she saw stars.

It was several minutes before Belle found the wherewithal to straighten her neck, fearing the horrible cracking sound it made. Her lower lip trembled, and she fumbled for her purse. She cursed her low battery and dialed roadside assistance, and then her father, who wasn't picking up.

Her engine died, giving up its grand fight to the death

through thick snow and thin budget. She shivered, not even having much of a chance to relish the warmth from the rickety heat vent.

When her phone rang, and she scrambled to answer it with clumsy fingers. "Papa?" she sobbed. "Papa, I spun off the road and crashed into a tree, and the car isn't starting. Roadside assistance said it would be hours before they could get to me because I'm all the way out by Adam's place, and there are so many accidents because of the snow. I'm cold and I can't feel my fingers. Can you come get me?"

When no response came, she broke down in audible tears. "Papa? Please, hurry! I hit my head on the steering wheel, and it's just... I'm having a bad day!" She wept for a few seconds before she croaked out a desperate, "Tell me it gets better than this."

"It gets far better." It wasn't her father's voice that responded, but Adam's. She hadn't checked the caller ID, but assumed it was her father returning her frantic call. The usual note of aggression was replaced by worry. "Belle? Where are you? I'll come get you."

"Adam? Sorry, I thought it was my papa calling me back. Never mind. I'll try him again."

"Can you see any cross streets?"

Belle blinked, but the snow was quickly covering her car. "I have no idea. I slid off the road a few miles from your house on the main road that leads to the freeway. It's fine, Adam. Roadside assistance is on their way."

"You just said they were backed up, and wouldn't be able to get to you for hours!"

"That's when I thought you were my papa. But you're you, so I don't need any help. We don't know each other anymore. Your issues aren't mine to deal with, and my problems have never been yours to handle."

"Stay in the car. I'm on my way."

"You don't leave your home," she countered stubbornly. "Do you even have a valid driver's license?"

"Probably. Keep the heat on."

"My car won't start!" she fretted, knowing how quickly one could lose digits to frostbite in weather like this. She groaned when her vision started to swim. "My head hurts."

"Are you okay? Is anything broken?"

"My car is broken." She touched her forehead to keep the world from spinning. "I hit my head on the thing."

"I'm coming, alright? Stay on the line and tell me something. Anything. Tell me how mad you are at me. Just don't fall asleep."

"I don't have a concussion," she argued.

"How would you even know that?"

"Because I'm a nurse. I know all the things." She let out a high-pitched whine of distress when she realized she couldn't bend her fingers anymore.

"You veered off the road on the right, correct? I'm looking for you on my right?"

Belle heard the roar of his engine, scolding herself for

the relief that flooded through her unbidden. "Sure." She gazed out the window, only able to make out a few feet on either side of her car.

"Belle, I'm on my way. Five minutes. You can…"

Belle gasped, hoping she was seeing things. It wasn't Roadside Assistance or Adam, but a wolf who found her in the snow. Only this was no ordinary wolf. Staring at her with glowing yellow eyes standing out in the sheets of white was a member of the Lupine. He howled, alerting the others of his find, and Belle's heart dropped. "Adam, listen to me. You have to call the police. You can't come out here. It's them. It's the Lupine."

But Adam didn't respond. Belle pulled her phone from her ear, panic welling in her throat when she saw that her phone was dead.

14

HUNTED

*M*ere minutes ago, Belle had been cursing her rickety old car, but now she clung to the insides as if they were her steel fortress. The Lupine she'd seen through the snow was drawing closer, stalking with a certainty that sent chills down her spine.

Then the one wolf was joined by a second, and a third. Then even more came through the snow, eyes fixed on their prey. Like the rest of the magical community, Belle had been taught to fear the Lupine from a young age. They were made up of a mix of cursed men and women. Belle shuddered, knowing that Adam was destined to become one of the violent wolfy castouts in less than half a year's time.

Belle clung to her useless phone, and then began to rapidly flick through different options in her mind if it should come to hand-to-paw combat. She didn't think her

Pulse would do much good in this situation, since pulsing discernment into the wolves would involve getting near enough for them to bite her.

A flash of hope raced through her mind when she remembered that she'd bought a can of pepper spray that she kept in her purse. She'd purchased it after Sheriff Aston had taken her away for the weekend. She never considered she'd have to use it on oversized wolves. Her fingers were stiff as she fumbled in her suitcase for her purse, praying the can wasn't frozen.

Belle pursed her lips to hold in a scream when the first wolf launched his body into the window. Another climbed atop the dented hood and began butting his head against her windshield. Belle groaned at the long fissure, courtesy of the car's crash into the tree. It bespoke of forthcoming doom, and Belle prayed the windshield would hold. Her fingers scrambled against the crack, frantically adding resistance.

More Lupine the size of mid-grown bears joined in their quest to either bust out her window by force, or tip the car over. Belle bit back a scream each time the glass rattled, clutching the pepper spray in her fist and searching the car for anything else that could be used as a weapon. The snow scraper wasn't as handy as a baseball bat, but Belle refused to go down begging for her life. She would fight for each last breath, and they would get damaged enough in the fray to regret their choice to single her out.

Belle's eyebrows pulled together as she clung to the wheel to keep her steady as the car rocked. Why were they targeting her? She was no one important in the magical community. Sure, she was one of the few with a degree in the West Village, which was largely illiterate, but that was no reason to illicit an attack.

"Why?" she demanded without a hint of despair. She refused to beg for her life, but she would ask for answers.

No matter what they wanted to say, she wouldn't be able to understand them anyway.

That's okay, she thought. *I just want them to think it through. Think before killing. If it doesn't save me, then maybe it'll get their conscience going, and the next person they go after will be spared.*

Belle gripped the snow scraper with trembling and numbing fingers, adrenaline pumping in her veins as the wolves on her hood bashed their thick bodies into the glass. Her head spun as she tried to hold onto lucidity, fighting through her head injury and the cold in her bones to stay in the moment. She prayed her father knew how much she loved him, and that he would remember to take care of himself after she was gone. Her chin trembled when she thought of how quickly he might deteriorate without her.

Each slamming body against her car rocked the metal frame, which oddly erased her fear that much more. It was inevitable now, and she wouldn't meet her end in tears.

She wiped off her icy cheeks and steeled herself against any further woe-is-me sentiments.

The next thud spread the crack on her windshield to the very edge, and she knew she was almost out of time. She made eye contact with the creature on the hood, her mouth in a tight line to let him know that she wasn't about to cower.

The wolf on her hood was gray with patches of black throughout his snowy fur. He had several scars marring his maw, no doubt from throwing himself into unnecessary fights like this one. He snarled at her, crouched down with his hindquarters raised, and geared up for the final push. Belle knew she should shield her eyes from the possibility of shattered glass, but she couldn't look away. They could take her life, but she wouldn't forfeit her grit to the beasts.

The wolf slammed his body into her windshield one final time, and finally crashed through, his neck bleeding as his jaws snapped. His back legs were still on the hood as his body thrashed and fought to make the hole bigger.

Belle couldn't help the scream that erupted from her as she cracked the wolf across the face over and over again with her snow scraper, and then used the sharp end to jab at the monster's eyes. Soon the wolf's cries were joining hers, floating out into the air in hopes the snow would carry the sound away.

Suddenly a loud bang shot through the snow,

drowning her cry of distress. The wolf yelped in agony, and then seconds later, went limp.

"Belle, hold tight! I'm coming!" Adam called to her through the blizzard.

She couldn't see him, only the wolf that was now dead, slumped halfway through her windshield. "Adam, run!" she warned, worried when the wolves on the sides of her car were no longer focused on rocking her vehicle.

Another shot blasted through the snow, and another. Belle was frantic, worried that he would get hurt coming to rescue her. She knew she couldn't have that on her conscience. Despite the fact that she was wearing thin scrubs under her worn jacket and didn't have proper snow boots on, she flung herself out of the car the moment she was able to kick herself free from the jarred steely frame that had bent from the crash. Belle ambled through the two-foot deep snow, calling out to Adam so he didn't shoot her in all the confusion.

The wolves were moving toward his tall figure, and though she couldn't make out the details of his features, she could see the gun in his grip that aimed and took fire again and again, dropping the Lupine that had haunted his nights for months.

Adam kept firing until the bullets ran out. Then the wolves took their opportunity and charged him, not bothering to strike for a kill, but sinking their sharp teeth into his skin just to hear him howl. Adam's roar thrust Belle forward through the snow until she was able to crack one of the four remaining wolves over the head with her snow scraper. It was plastic and not all that heavy, but the sharp end used for breaking off ice from a windshield cut one of the wolves on the back of the skull, drawing blood that brought Belle a small burst of satisfaction.

"Run, Belle!" Adam growled.

But Belle knew there was no way he could make it to safety like this. His thigh was badly bleeding, and the wolves were taking as many bites from his arms as they could. It was clear they didn't want to kill him, but punish him and remind him that they owned his future, and he certainly wouldn't be anywhere near the ranks of the alpha in their tribe.

That was when she heard him. Though she had only the basic knowledge of wolves and Lupine culture, it was rumored that when you heard the howl of the alpha, you knew it. The baritone bark was elongated, so it sounded more like a foghorn than a call from an actual animal.

The wolves all turned their heads in the direction of the call, some of them lowering their haunches to submit to the voice, though Belle still couldn't see the head wolf through the thick curtains of snow.

The low-toned call of the alpha shook Belle's trembling bones with a power she didn't understand, and instinctively feared. The wolves looked at each other, as if deciding via pack-speak whether they should continue their assault on Adam, or go to the alpha. When a few turned back to Adam, Belle knew it was all about to go south.

Belle took her window of opportunity and stumbled forward, unleashing her pepper spray on the wolves, aiming downward so she didn't blast Adam in the face. Their growls quickly turned to whimpers of agony as they fell away – all but one, who rammed into her, knocking the can from her hand as she fell backwards in the snow.

The last determined wolf who wasn't writhing in the snow from the pain of the mace kept his maw firmly latched onto Adam's forearm. Belle scrambled to her feet, picked up the nearest weapon and whapped him hard on the back of the head with the snow scraper, but he still didn't let go. It wasn't until Adam's growls of fury mutated to pain that Belle let loose her stored-up scream that was laced with fear and frustration.

The scraper wasn't enough to break Adam free of the last wolf's determined attack, so Belle cast her snow scraper aside, knowing there was a chance the wolf might be powerful enough to send them both into an early grave. Trumping all logic and self-preservation, Belle pummeled the wolf, finally breaking the hold he had on Adam's arm.

The wolf was too turned around to shift his attack onto her, which gave Belle just enough of an advantage to scramble in the snow to retrieve her second weapon. She gritted her teeth and turned her chin as she blasted him directly in the eyeballs with a spray from her icy can of mace.

The wolf yelped and scrambled away, licking his wounds with the others as they scampered and limped off into the woods, leaving their dead behind for the snow to bury.

Belle indulged in little more than a breath of victory before she turned to Adam, who was bleeding too much to tough it out.

"Belle," he rasped, and her name sounded like a prayer on his lips. His chest was moving up and down in heavy pants, but he was upright...

Until he wasn't.

Adam collapsed with a gust into the snow, taking Belle's screams as the last sound he heard before unconsciousness claimed him.

15

WOMAN IN RED

*B*elle knew this wasn't the time for tears, but they sprang to her eyes anyway. She cursed each one of them for marring her vision that kept her from being the best nurse for the job. She felt for Adam's heartbeat, but her fingers drew in no sensation from anything, icy as they were. Belle glanced around and saw what she guessed would have to be his car parked up on the shoulder. It was sleek, expensive and probably had a working heater, she reasoned.

She summoned all her gusto to heft him up, but it wasn't enough. The car was so far away, and Belle's limbs were starting to freeze over. She didn't mean to drop him in the snow, but when she fell backward, so did he. Her fear of the wolves was replaced with the very immediate worry of hypothermia, which didn't take all that long to set in. She knew she had to get him to safety, but her body was starting to give out on her.

"Belle? Get to the car," Adam instructed her when he roused.

"Can you stand?" she asked, scrambling clumsily and crawling through the snow so he could see her face.

Adam made an attempt, but his left leg was useless. He let out a growl of frustration through clenched teeth. "Go, Belle! Get warm. The wolves might turn around and come back for us. Run!"

A gust of harsh wind whistled through the trees toward them, giving her two entire seconds to throw her body over his, shielding him as best she could from the icy blast. She shuddered as the wind sliced through her thin coat. A bleat of pain escaped her lips at the ache that felt etched deep down in her bones. "I'm not leaving you!" she promised, her brown hair whipping around them to give Adam something to focus on other than the blur of white. "We'll try again. Use me as a crutch."

She was too clumsy from the cold as she tried to sit him up. Her body wasn't stable enough for herself, let alone to support a second person. Still, Belle remained stalwart in her decision to get Adam up the incline to the car.

"I can help," came a feminine voice behind her.

Belle turned, and in the motion, realized that she was losing mobility in her joints, since her neck was barely able to rotate to take in the stranger. A blur of red caught

Belle's eye, and before she could respond, the woman had hold of Adam's other arm.

The young woman who couldn't have been much more than twenty years old wore a long red cape over thick winter gear. Her face was barely visible, surrounded by the brown and gray fur of her black coat's lining. When she helped Belle heft Adam from the snow, she paid no mind to his howl of agony. The stranger took most of his weight on herself, so Belle could have a better shot at staying upright.

After a few steps, Belle knew she'd been out in the snow five minutes too long. Her legs refused to move, and she toppled forward, her body locked in one elongated shiver.

"Rafe, grab the girl!" the young woman called over her shoulder, continuing the trek to get Adam back to his car.

Belle couldn't move much, but she found that her heart was still beating when it started to race at the sight of an enormous white wolf approaching her.

Without being told, Belle knew she was coming face-to-face with the alpha. She screamed, eliciting a shout from Adam beckoning her to run to him, but when the wolf made contact, it was a gentle tug on her coat's collar, rather than a sharp bite through her skin.

Too muddled to ponder the meaning of it all, Belle's body went limp, trusting the wolf to take her someplace warm. There were a few bumps as the wolf dragged her up the incline, but eventually she found herself next to the open door of Adam's silver vehicle. The red cape swept out again in her vision as the young woman lifted her up and set her in the driver's seat.

The car was turned on, and the heat was on full blast, with Adam gritting his teeth through the pain in the passenger's seat. Despite his cold, he turned the vents onto Belle, bathing her in heat that felt like chocolate melting over her body.

Belle wanted to thank the woman for rescuing them, and give the wolf his due praise as well, but her jaw was locked tight from chattering.

The woman leaned over Belle's body and grasped Adam's hand. "Stay strong," she said by way of a goodbye. "A curse is not the end."

Adam protested her departure, but the woman merely smiled at him, as if the cold didn't bother her one bit. In a move Belle didn't expect, the woman bent down and pressed a kiss to Belle's temple. "Once you've thawed, get home. The roads are terrible, and it's not likely to let up for weeks, if not longer. Get indoors, and stay there."

"Thank you," Belle worked out just before the driver's side door closed, and the woman disappeared with her wolf into the snowstorm.

For several seconds that stretched into whole minutes, Belle and Adam stared at each other, breathless. Their eyes talked about things that their mouths wouldn't admit to – that they were scared, and grateful the other one didn't leave them to die in the snow.

The heat worked its magic while their breathing steadied to a companionable rhythm. Adam finally reached forward and turned up the radio, letting classical music fill the interior with a sad violin that made the snowy death outside seem like a mere playground.

"Adam," Belle whispered, unsure what she wanted to say. Somehow just uttering his name made her feel slightly better.

"Shh," he replied quietly. "We're safe." Then he reached across the console and coiled his fingers around hers.

The gesture of comfort and camaraderie warmed Belle, but alerted her to the greater danger. "I can't feel you," she admitted, her fear growing at the prospect that perhaps the snow had steeped them in damage unfixable.

Adam's green eyes zeroed in on hers with a determination that everything would somehow be alright. "Then I'll just have to keep holding you."

Belle's lashes swept shut at the sweetness, and she willed her worries not to overwhelm her. She managed a tight nod, and went back to the quietness of the violin, hoping it would soothe all that was wrong in the world.

In those minutes of silence, Adam said things to her with his eyes that he couldn't admit to aloud. He wanted to hold her, which wasn't a longing he had entertained all too often during his life. He blamed it on the near-death experience, but still, the desire called to him.

"You should have left me," he chided her stiff fingers.

"But you didn't leave me," she countered. When she spoke again, she allowed her vulnerability to shine through as her eyes opened to focus in on him. "You hurt me when you yelled like that back at home."

Any softness in Adam's features clouded over with defiance that hardened the regret that clawed at his insides. "You shouldn't have been in the West wing."

Belle winced as if his words had cut her. "When the storm clears up, I'll leave. But the woman with the red cape was right; we shouldn't try to go anywhere tonight. The nearest hospital is at least twenty miles away."

Adam pursed his lips. He didn't want her to go, but asking her to stay would involve apologizing, which he had never done before. "Just give me a second to tie off my wound, and I can drive us home," he promised after a few minutes of silence. The car was a sauna, but the two were only just starting to get a little feeling back in their extremities.

"No, no. I've got it. I can feel my fingers well enough now." She slid her hand out of his grip. Though Adam wasn't ready for her to let go, she turned toward the steering wheel and did her best to acquaint herself with the expensive vehicle. "This thing is like a spaceship. Why do you need so many buttons?"

"They do things like provide heat, so I wouldn't complain. It's a reliable little spaceship. Have you ever driven a stick before?"

Belle shook her head, chagrinned. "Talk me through it."

Adam was surprisingly patient as he explained the basics of shifting in the sleek car. When she put it into gear, there were a few false starts, but eventually she got them turned back around in the direction of the castle. She stalled twice when she shifted incorrectly, so Adam placed his hand atop hers, gently guiding her hand so they could shift together.

Neither of them spoke, but allowed the music to say the things they couldn't. The violin with all of its might did its best to smooth over the rift between them.

16

BEDSIDE MANNER

Belle was a little steadier on her feet, and acted as Adam's crutch as they made their way inside. The staff were overjoyed to see her, and horrified at the injuries Adam had sustained.

"Master, I'll fetch the first aid kit. Do sit down."

"Take off your shoes! Oh, and your shirts and pants. You're both soaked!"

"I'll heat up some soup for you both, and some tea."

"What happened to you, Master? Come, Thomas. Give him something to lean on. The lady of the house looks as if she might fall over."

Sultan's yip was a mixture between excitement and worry as he circled Belle and sniffed Adam.

Belle didn't protest the coat hanger coming over and offering one of his wooden arms for Adam to lean on, but she didn't let go of him. She flicked through her brain to the nearest room with a fireplace. "My bedroom, Thomas. Lucien, can you light the f-f-fire in my room for him? Adam's soaked through. Audra, can you grab Adam some clean pajamas? He can't make it up the stairs."

"I can make it up the steps," Adam grumbled.

Belle's lips drew together in a tight line before she spoke. "You'll shut up and let us help you, or else I really will just leave you down here to fend for yourself."

Adam sighed. "Fine."

Belle and Thomas slowly got Adam down the hall and into Belle's bedroom. Her fingers were stiff, but they were starting to work alright. It was her balance that was giving her trouble at the moment. Living with a fifty percent hearing loss in her right ear didn't slow her down most days, but the chill was messing with her inner ear. She stumbled a few times, trying to remind her body where up was, and that it needed to stay clear in its focus not to fall.

After she greeted Simone, she sat him in the chair by the desk and knelt down to untie his boots. The room gave a disturbing tilt, but she gripped the floor to steady herself, and then continued on her task.

"I can do that," he groused.

"You're welcome," she countered with a tart frown angled up at him. She lightly pinched his fur-covered big toe after pulling off his sock. "Can you feel that?"

"Mostly. Only because your hands are so icy."

Belle didn't want to lean on him for many reasons, but it suddenly became necessary when her inner ear proved problematic again. Her hand gripped his kneecap through three labored breaths before she felt stable enough to kneel on her own.

Adam's brows were knit together with worry. "Lucien, can you build the fire bigger?"

"Of course, sir. It's coming, it's coming." Lucien had already kindled the beginnings of a fire in the hearth, but he added more wood and blew on the cinders. Then he took Adam's shoes and socks when Adam slid them off with Belle's help. They were wet with blood and snow, but Lucien still carried the garments as if they were fit to be worn by a king.

Adam shifted away slightly when Belle tried to undo his shirt. "I don't need my shirt off."

Instead of fighting with him, Belle stood and leaned over to get right in his face, bracing herself on the armrest. "Look, I know I was your housekeeper here, but I'm actually a very competent nurse. The hospital is too far to make it to safely, so I'm your only option if you don't want some of these cuts to get infected. I know you don't like people to see your body, but I need to sew some of these gashes up."

A shadow of insecurity flickered over Adam's face. "I'm sure I'll heal."

"I'm sure you will too, because I'm going to take care of

you." It was more of a warning than a statement, ordering him to fall in line and let her make the decisions.

Belle moved slowly, her fingers slipping on the buttons of his shirt as she trailed down the row, maintaining eye contact until the last button popped open. She took in his grimace as she slid the fabric off his shoulders, and watched his body shift as he tried to find a comfortable spot through his pain.

Had she not received years of training, she might have gasped at Adam's chest. It was far hairier than anyone she'd ever seen, and there were scars that looked like they had no rhyme or reason to them. The hair was thick, brown and straight, and looked more like a wolf's fur than a man's.

"I don't need your pity," Adam snarled.

"Good. Then I can actually do my job instead of having to hold your hand through all your whiny, superficial hang-ups."

Adam's mouth fell open in shock at her sass, and then a low chuckle vibrated his chest. "Your bedside manner leaves something to be desired."

"Yeah? Well so do your actual manners, so I think we'll make it through this alright." She prepped her supplies from the first aid kit Lucien had brought down for her. She took a breath and shot Adam a look of warning before she touched his side. "This is going to hurt, so, you know, I don't want to hear about it."

Adam tried to remain stoic, but Belle smirked when

she caught his grimace a few times as she knelt at his side, cleaning and stitching his arm. Her fingers were feeble and trembling, but she was well-practiced in the art of suturing up a patient.

"Mademoiselle, you should change into something warmer. Perhaps something dry, no? You're soaked through!"

Belle shook her head, praying she didn't lose her balance and topple over in the middle of a stitch. "Not until he's alright. Then I'll thaw out."

Adam glanced down at the tear on his forearm, and then on his side that had been quickly cleaned and neatly sutured. She hadn't once complained about his fur getting in the way, or acted like touching him was a chore. He met her eyes with a calmness that started to settle in his soul whenever he was around her for more than a few minutes. "I'll be alright. Take a few minutes and get changed. You're shivering."

Belle paused, considering his words as she measured how detrimental the trembling in her fingers was becoming. "Alright. I'll just be a few minutes." She banged into both sides of the doorjamb as she made her way into the bathroom, her balance taking a serious hit and making her nauseous the longer she tried to fight with her inner ear.

Thomas sidled over to the bed and picked up the pile of clothes Simone had selected for her. He walked her over to the adjoining bathroom, disappearing inside with her.

"Thomas, you'll stay out here. Belle can get undressed without your assistance," Adam ordered with a growl.

Thomas came back out with his wooden arms raised to proclaim his innocence. "Master, of course I would never try anything."

Belle froze in the bathroom at the strangeness of the conversation. "It's fine, guys. Thanks anyway, Thomas. Adam, he's a coatrack. I hardly think that's the tawdry peepshow you're imagining." She leaned over the sink, willing herself not to vomit.

"Thomas is a man, Belle. Never forget that."

Belle gulped as she shut the bathroom door and peeled off her thin, icy scrubs. She shivered violently as she stepped in the shower to thaw her frozen extremities. It took more time than she was anticipating, but eventually her limbs found movement. She leaned her throbbing head against the shower wall, breathing out the ice as she inhaled the steam. She found scratches on her body, and a bite on her arm and her calf that she hadn't noticed before.

The nightgown Simone had made her was far fancier than anything she'd ever owned, and a fair bit sexier, too. The green silk did nothing to warm her but looked elegant as the hem brushed over her knees. The low-cut lace kept her cleavage on display, held up by thin straps that made her feel like a woman, despite the ache that felt deeply set in her bones. Belle blushed furiously when she emerged, unable too look at Adam, or anyone else in the room. "Simone? Do you have a sweater or something? I'm so cold, and this nightgown is... a little flashier than I'm used to."

Simone's drawers arched downward, looking like a frown. "I think you look lovely. I don't make many sweaters." She said the word as if it had offended her.

Adam's throat had gone dry, but he snapped to life when he saw Belle shiver, and wrap her arms around herself. "Lucien, fetch two bathrobes from my bedroom. One for me, and one that might fit my nurse."

Lucien bowed, casting Adam a relieved look that he was making an effort to think of others. "Very good, Master." He blew on the fire, coaxing the flames higher, and then scurried out to do Adam's bidding.

"I'm sorry," Belle said, still unable to look at him. "All my things were in my suitcase, which is in my car, covered in snow by now."

Adam shifted to the left and pulled the comforter off her bed, crooking his finger to her to beckon her forward. "Here. Until the bathrobe comes." He wrapped the thick warmth around her body, rubbing her arms through the downy fabric as she shivered before him.

She glanced at his leg with a frown. "I was working my way down to the cut on your thigh next. Can you take off your pants, or do you need help?"

He stood and unbuttoned his pants, bending, but

stopped short when he winced. "Actually, yes. Would you mind helping me with these? The cut on my leg is starting to itch, and I'm freezing." He narrowed his eyes to his staff. "Out."

The staff obeyed, shooting each other gleeful looks of anticipation.

17

BATHROBES AND BEDTIME

Belle shut the door, leaving them alone with Simone, who closed her doors to give them the appearance of privacy. "Hold still."

Belle set the comforter back onto the bed, shivering as she unzipped his pants. Though she'd helped hundreds of patients undress before, she was acutely aware of just how exposed her breasts were to public view. She was careful as she bent down and peeled off his pants, discarding them in the bathroom where her ruined scrubs rested in the sink. She tried not to think about his navy cotton boxer briefs and raised her chin with the air of professionalism.

When she turned to come back into the room, her vision blurred, and she grabbed onto the doorjamb to steady herself, closing her eyes.

"Are you alright?" Adam asked, not holding back his worry.

Belle held up her hand to stop him from getting up. "I'm fine. Just hit my head, is all. I have an inner ear issue that sometimes acts up and messes with my balance."

Adam had the comforter wrapped around his hairy shoulders. "Come here and warm up."

"Your leg is cut. I have to fix it."

"My leg can wait until you don't look so dizzy. Sit with me, Belle." He opened the blanket, taking in her hesitance as she stepped closer, glancing toward the door to make sure it was shut.

Both of them sighed with contentment that ran deep when Belle sat next to him on the mattress, allowing him to drape the blanket over her shoulders, leaving his arm to coil around her hips.

The perpetual knot in his sternum began to dissipate when she moved to rest her head on his shoulder. He kept her wrapped in the warmth of the comforter, hemming her in so that he felt her breasts against his skin. Though he'd been positively icy minutes ago, finally he began to thaw, his knees weakening when her unsteady hand reached up to stroke the fur on his broad pectoral. Moments like these had long since been considered extinct by him after he'd been cursed, and yet, here she was, pressing her body to his and trusting him enough to allow him to warm her.

"You're an ice block," he commented in a quiet voice.

His hand rose to rub circles into her lower back, pressing her more tightly to him. He coveted the small of her back and didn't bother chastising his hand when it found its way there.

Belle's body was pliable with weakness, but her voice was firm – exhibiting that strong softness that did him in every time. "I wouldn't have been this cold if you hadn't sent me out into the worst snowstorm this country's seen in years."

Adam stiffened. "Those letters weren't for you to touch. And now Rory's read them all."

Though Belle was intent they would duke this out, she couldn't bring herself to pull away from him. The hair on his chest was soft and thick, giving her something to hold onto while she shivered against him. "You left your mail on the dining room table, so I was bringing it up to you. I wasn't trying to hurt you by helping."

"You shouldn't have been in the West wing!" he argued, irate that she was sneaking in valid points.

"Well, you should learn to control your temper!" she spat back, her cheek lifting from his shoulder so she could glare up at him.

Adam took in her frustration and measured it against his own. He tilted his head to the side, unsure what to do with a roommate who stood up to him and didn't cower to his temper. "Yes, well, I may have heard that a time or two before."

Belle dropped her anger a few notches and chuckled. "You don't say."

When Lucien came into the room dragging a sack with the two bathrobes, the etchings over his eyes raised at catching the two in an intimate embrace. "Here you are, Master. I'm so glad you'll be staying here, Belle. For the few hours you were gone, the sun didn't shine at all."

Belle glanced down at Lucien with a sadness she tried to temper so she didn't seem like a pouting child. "I'll be here until the roads clear up, Lucien, but then I'm going back to the West Village."

Adam stiffened. "Will you stay out of the West wing?"

"Only if I miss the sound of you yelling at me."

He released her from the shelter of the blanket and reached down to grab the sack. He pulled out an emerald bathrobe that was thick, fuzzy and softer than a freshly shorn lamb. Instead of covering himself first, he wrapped her in the robe, silently chiding the cold for making it a necessity to cover her up. He threaded her arms through and cinched the belt around her slender waist, smirking at the sight of her in his nightwear. He threw his sapphire robe over his shivering form and then brought her to his side again, missing the feel of her so close. "I want you to stay," he whispered, his large hand again migrating to rest on the small of her back.

"You yelled at me, and then you fired me. I've never been fired from anything before." She pulled away and motioned to the chair. "Sit down, so I can look at your thigh."

Adam obliged, and Belle took in the wince he gave when he lowered himself slowly onto the chair. It wasn't just the bites that had injured him. She knelt down between his knees and started cleaning the wound, rolling up the too-long sleeves on her bathrobe while she worked. Whenever a swoon hit her, she leaned against his undamaged inner thigh to steady herself until the world came back into focus.

She didn't look up at him, so Adam pushed out a confession. "Rory and Henry are my oldest friends. She's the Chancellor's daughter, Aurora Johnstone."

Belle nodded, but kept to her task. "I know of her. The cursed Sleeping Beauty and all that."

"Then you know the only thing that could wake her was true love's kiss. We all knew Cordray would be the one who could wake her, but she was scared as the deadline drew nearer. She came to me and Henry and begged us both to try."

Belle's eyebrows quirked. "You're in love with her?"

"No. I love her, but not like that. Not in a curse-breaking way. I told her as much, but she still wanted us to try. Henry went to her hospital room the day she fell into her coma, but he couldn't wake her. Cordray had been kidnapped, so he couldn't even try to wake her."

"I remember the headlines when he was found. Good

strategy on Malaura's part – going after the cure instead of the cursed."

Adam kept his eyes away from Belle, for the first time admitting aloud his fault in the fight. "I waited four months before going to see her."

Belle paused her stitching to glance up at him with a tightness to her mouth.

"Don't look at me like that."

"Like what? Like you're a tool for standing up your best friend when she told you she needed you? For making her rot in that hospital bed for four months while you did friggin' nothing about it? Why would she be mad at you for that?"

Adam glared at her. "You act like it's easy for me to go out in public. I don't look like Henry, or whatever boyfriends you've got pictures of in your yearbook. Rory knows who I am; she shouldn't have expected me to be any different. I told her it wouldn't work, and it didn't. I was right."

"You were wrong," Belle countered, giving her words a few beats to sizzle. "What you did was wrong, and you know it. That's why you're being such a baby about it now."

"Do you want me to throw you out in the snow again?"

"What was in the letters I mailed out?"

Adam's expression grew sour. "Nothing important, which is why I didn't want them mailed."

Belle tied off the suture and moved unsteadily over to

the desk in the corner, pulling out a pen and paper and scribbling out a few sentences. "Here. Call Rory up. Read this to her, and then sit quietly and let her yell at you."

Adam scanned the page and glowered up at Belle from his seat. "You must be joking."

"I'm not. I'm the nurse, and I say this is what you need. It's my unofficial prescription." Belle postured, trying to look commanding in the oversized bathrobe. "Call her, or I leave right now dressed in this."

"No, you won't. You barely escaped frostbite the first time."

Belle leaned over to the nightstand where Lucien had deposited his cell phone. "How many people are you going to hurt with your pride? You already took Rory down. Who's next?" She touched his wrist, pressing a Pulse of Discernment through him.

Adam's nostrils flared at her challenge. "You don't understand. She won't forgive me."

"Good. She shouldn't. I don't care if she forgives you; I care if you're a good man. I care if you fight for the important things in life, rather than just plain fighting."

Belle held his gaze long enough that Adam began to see that she meant business. His eyes narrowed at her as he dialed the number he hadn't called in far too long. "Get out," he warned Belle, who didn't heed his instructions.

Instead she leaned in and pressed a kiss to his temple while the phone rang, sending softness rippling through him. Then she seemed to catch herself in the act, and drew back too fast, her balance suffering as the room shifted at a dizzying speed.

"Easy, now," Adam cautioned, reaching for her as she stumbled. Before he knew what he was doing, he pulled Belle to sit on his uninjured thigh, coiling his arm around her hips. "Rory?" he said, his voice husky. There were so many things he wanted to say to the friend he'd left high and dry, but his pride shut his mouth.

"Adam? What's wrong? Henry told me you couldn't find Belle. Did you find her? Do you want me to drive down the freeway and look for cars on the side of the road?"

Adam closed his eyes, and though he knew Belle was Pulsing Discernment through him as she draped her arm around his shoulders, he didn't need her Pulse to clearly see the error of his ways. "I found her. She's a little banged up, but we're back home and warming up. But I didn't call about that." Adam's mouth went dry, so he read from the script that Belle had written out for him. "I'm sorry, Rory. You've always been good to me, and I was terrible when you needed me most. I shouldn't have waited four months to try and wake you."

The silence that stung the phone gave him pause until Rory finally answered. "Adam? Are you alright? Does someone have a gun to your head?"

Adam chuckled, and the sound felt like a breath of fresh air to him. "No. But Belle might murder me if I don't apologize to you. For leaving you in that hospital bed for four months. For yelling at you this morning. All of it."

He had meant to stabilize Belle by bringing her close, but it seemed he was the one who needed steadying now. He squeezed her tighter, only drawing a full breath when her body curved into his.

Without hesitation, Rory rushed out a breathy, "Adam, I forgive you. I always have."

18

DON'T BE COLD

hef Bouche sent over stew, and Audra brewed them enough hot tea to warm their insides to the point of sleepiness. The two didn't leave Belle's bedroom, but brought over the desk to the middle of the room and dined there, relishing the fireplace that made everything feel cozy. The sun was just beginning to set, and after the craziness of the day, the two were ready to turn in early.

"I should probably get some sleep," Adam said, wincing as he stood.

"I'm not sure where you think you're going with your bum leg, but it's certainly not up any stairs."

Adam quirked his eyebrow at her. "That's where my bed is."

"Unless Lucien can carry you, you're not going up any stairs tonight." She pointed to her bed. "You can sleep here. I'll take one of your other many bedrooms."

"None of them have been cleaned yet. And have you forgotten your own injuries?"

Belle's mouth drew to the side in a frown. "I'll sleep on the couch in one of the living rooms."

He shot her a baleful look. "Hilarious that you think I'd allow you to sleep on a couch."

Belle's eyes widened that he cared about such things. "What do you need from your room? I know you're too finicky to let me up to the West wing, but Lucien can get you whatever you want."

"I'm already in my pajamas," he observed, looking down at the soft pants and long-sleeved thermal poking out from his robe. He hobbled to the door and called for Lucien. "Can you bring me a book from the study? Something from Poe."

Lucien scurried off and Adam made his way to the bed, taking Belle's help in stride when she braced him so he could move without hurting his leg further.

"Feel like a good murder mystery tonight?" she asked of his book choice.

"No, but you do. I don't care one way or the other, but your favorite book is out in your car. Thought you might want to read something at least in the same genre before you went to sleep."

Belle blinked at him, pausing after she helped lift his legs so he could sit in the bed with his back against the headboard. She tucked the covers over his lap, unsure what to say of the considerate gesture. "Thank you. The thought of my book out there in the cold just kills me."

Adam tugged on the sleeve of her robe, bringing her face closer to his. He took a chance, coming off the high of his vulnerable moment with Rory on the phone, and spoke from his heart. "The thought of *you* out in the cold killed me. I shouldn't have yelled at you." He stared hard into her eyes, summoning up courage he didn't normally care if he possessed. "I'm sorry."

Belle met his eyes with a hardness that wasn't ready to let him off that easily. "You said Prince Henry only hired me because he liked my ass. Is that true?"

Adam shrank, his chin lowering. "No. I was angry. I shouldn't have said that."

Belle swallowed, fighting through the urges inside of her to punish him further for being so terrible to her. There were several weighted seconds that passed between them before she decided that being livid required more energy than she could muster that evening. "Okay, then. I forgive you."

"Good. Then get into bed. I'll not kick you out of your own room. We can be civil for the night. Besides, no bedroom will be as warm as this one. The fire's been going for a while."

Belle was hesitant, her heart fluttering as she moved into the bed next to Adam, settling against him as he leaned on the headboard. She didn't know why she was so nervous, but she realized when his arm wound around her back to pull her closer, she didn't want to be anywhere else. The fur on his arms was warm and drew her in like the most cuddly kind of teddy bear. It had been a long time since she'd indulged in comfort like that.

When Lucien opened the door to deliver the book, Belle shot out of the bed with a guilty look on her features. "Nothing happened!"

Lucien looked shocked to have found the two of them in bed together, and grinned at Belle with a bow. "Of course not, milady. Back under the covers with you. I'll not have the lady of the house freeze under my watch."

"No, no. I'll go sleep in one of the other rooms."

Adam's expression soured. "Of course. You don't want anyone to hear you've bedded the beast."

Belle ran her hand down her face. "Give me a break. That has nothing to do with it." Her eyes climbed to the ceiling in frustration. "It's that I don't want anyone to think I got my job back by sleeping with my boss."

Adam froze as his unwarranted snarl evaporated from his face. His eyebrows lifted in surprise as the corner of his mouth quirked upward. "That's what you're worried about?"

"Obviously."

"Who's going to tell?" He motioned to Lucien, who mimed zipping his lips. Then Adam gave a shiver and grinned up at her with a hint of innuendo. "Perhaps this is the wrong time to ask for a head-to-toe physical."

Belle kept her eyes glued upward as she pinned her lips together to fend off her embarrassment.

"Are you... Are you blushing?"

Belle touched her heated cheeks with chagrin. "Oh, shut up."

Adam's laugh turned into a cough that rattled the bed. The sound was deep and had a bark to it that drew Belle toward him. She felt his forehead with a frown. "You're feverish. That's not good. Maybe we were out in the snow a little too long."

Adam flipped back the comforter on her side of the bed once his coughing subsided. "See that more tea is brought in while we read, Lucien."

"Yes, Master," Lucien said, and then excused himself.

Without a word, Adam extended his hand, gently guiding her to lay next to him. Her movements were skittish as her eyes darted around the room, but eventually she sank down onto the mattress.

Adam's eyes widened with faux surprise. "Why, Nurse Belle, are you sure this is the normal routine treatment for the sniffles? Do all your patients have to lie in bed with you?" He moved her hand to his taut pectoral and gasped. "Nurse! Where are you planning on putting that thermometer?"

Belle let out a tinkling laugh that relaxed them both. It didn't take more than a bat of her hand at his wicked grin to dismiss her reservations. She pulled the comforter up to her chin, her head resting atop his outstretched arm. For several moments, their eyes danced with playfulness, sparking something precious and tender between them.

He brushed a stray lock of hair that had fallen slack from her bun, tucking it behind her ear. "Are you still dizzy?"

Belle had been feeling slightly steadier as the warmth chased away the cold. Her voice was quiet as she drank in the wonder of his emerald eyes up close. "I think I'm feeling better now."

He held her gaze for a few beats, and then drew her closer, loving the feel of her body molding to his in their cozy haven. "How about now?"

Belle rested her temple to his cheek, letting the crackle of the fire lull her into a wealth of relaxation. "Mm... Perfection."

When the oversized bathrobe fell off her shoulder, he was quick to slide it back into place. "As long as I'm here, you'll never be cold again," he promised quietly. "The thought of you wearing those thin scrubs in the snow sent me into the early stages of a panic attack."

"Don't be cold," she whispered. "The snow, I can handle. When you turn frosty on me, it's the worst kind of slow death."

He nodded once, as if sorting his thoughts into a proper working order, pushing out selfishness to make room for her wellbeing. His chest swelled with the pride in accepting a commission that resonated deep within his soul. "I can keep you warm, Belle."

As Adam flipped open the leather-bound book and began to read to her, he vowed he would never again be caustic with the woman who was brave enough to snuggle up to the beast.

19

THE NATURE OF GABE ASTON

Belle woke to sweat that, upon closer inspection, she realized wasn't hers. "Adam?" She had fallen asleep in his arms, and found herself curled up in his embrace while he spooned her. She twisted in the sheets and felt his forehead, swearing at the heat that was far too much. "Okay, we've got to get this robe off you."

Adam groaned, in the throes of a fever so grand that he scarcely comprehended her words. They'd fallen asleep to the sound of him reading Edgar Allen Poe, contentedly wrapped in each other after the far too eventful day they'd barely survived. Belle chided herself for not noting that Adam's docile and gentle behavior while he read to her in bed should have been an indicator that he was being taken down by a virus.

She went through her nurse's list of taking care of a

patient, not skimping on even the basics. Lucien brought her a washcloth, which was kept cool by dipping it into the ice bucket on Audra's tea tray. Since Adam wasn't aware enough to be caustic, Belle was able to perform a cursory medical examination, assessing his breathing, musculature, ears, nose and throat from a clinical angle. She'd never worked on animals, but longed to have a docile wolf to study to see if the abnormalities she was noting were simply because he was getting closer to his transition.

It was a terrible thing to bear, this curse that slowly stripped his humanity away from him. Belle touched his cheek, admiring the shorter chestnut beard that was more fur than facial hair. It was soft, begging her to stroke it again and again. Belle found herself studying his lips longer than any medical professional would deem necessary.

She only drifted from Adam's bedside for twenty-minute stints – gathering his mail, slowly making her way through cleaning the room next to hers, so she could hear him if he roused.

It wasn't until two days after their catastrophic fight that Adam felt well enough to demand he be able to get back to work.

"Well, since you asked so nicely... No," Belle spouted back as she polished the fixture while perched atop the ladder in the receiving room. "Can I ask you a question?"

"I highly doubt saying 'no' would stop you."

"This is the third living room I've cleaned. Why do you have so many?"

Adam motioned around to the make-believe masses. "To welcome all my many adoring fans, of course."

Belle let out a one-noted laugh. "Hilarious. If I had a house like this, no way would I let it go to waste. You should have a ball."

"A ball?" Adam repeated with distaste. "You must be joking."

"It would be nice to see people appreciating all these gorgeous rooms. Did you know you have a vase from the Artrarian Era in the second living room?"

"You don't say. Then we should invite droves of people over, so they can knock it over and shatter my mother's collection of vases."

Belle rolled her eyes at his grumping. "I'm not sure why you're dressed for work," she said of his khaki pants and lavender dress shirt. "I'm not giving you back your laptop, phone, or the key to your office. That's going to stay nice and hidden until I say you're better."

Adam's upper lip curled, trying to appear menacing. Both of them were too companionable to really believe his attempt to intimidate her. He dropped the act when she merely sniggered and went back to polishing the brass fixture on the wall.

"You're a bit overdressed for housework."

"If that's a compliment, you should put a little more sugar on it next time. 'Belle, you're so beautiful. Everything you do is art.'" Since her suitcase with her clothes was lost in her snow-ridden car, Simone had let herself run free with Belle's new wardrobe. She adjusted the green strap of her dress. It showed off her trim waist and belled out at her hips, making her look truly feminine and far fancier than a housekeeper normally dressed while on the job. She wore a beige apron over the gown so as not to get it dusty. "You can thank Simone for my new outfits. Not quite me, but since I have nothing else, I've decided not to complain." She waggled her eyebrows at him. "Do you want me to put on a musical for you? I'm certainly dressed for it."

"I'll pass. Where's my laptop?"

Belle's eyes rose to the ceiling, as if wondering where she'd stashed it. "I think you'll have to beg me."

Adam clenched his fists, his shoulders tensing as he uttered a begrudging, "Please."

Belle pressed her hand to her heart and tried to hold back her laughter. "That looked painful."

"It was. And you're my nurse; you're not supposed to be the one inflicting pain. Give me my laptop."

"I prefer my begging in song."

Belle finished with the fixture and slowly lowered herself down the rung, not expecting Adam to actually comply with her whims. When a low voice drifted toward her to the tune of Sonata in A, Belle froze midway down the ladder, eyes wide.

"Will you please give me my laptop? I need it so I can

help you. After your father told me what Sheriff Sheriff Aston did, trying to evict you unlawfully, I alerted a few contacts at the Department of Criminal Investigation and the Department of Taxable Wages. I need to keep up with them, so we can put the criminal where he belongs. Far, far away from you."

Belle's mouth was dropped open, flabbergasted that he'd actually sang, and that his reasons for wanting to work more were unselfish. "Are you serious?"

Adam's face was red, but he postured, as if daring her to laugh at his singing. "Did you really think I'd sit back and let the sheriff kick people out of their homes without a valid eviction notice? No wonder so many in the West Village haven't been paying on their mortgage; he's kicking them out prematurely so they can't even try to catch up on the payments. He's cheating me out of my revenue when he raises levies like that, too. That money's going straight into his pockets, and the Department of Taxable Wages is closing in on him. No doubt he's so buried in audits that he hasn't had time to terrorize your father at all."

Belle's feet touched on the floor, and she leaned her head on the side of the ladder, closing her eyes in worry. "You... I... Be careful, Adam."

Adam's posture remained straight and gentlemanly. "Gabe's the one who should've been careful. I don't fear common crooks."

Belle spoke with deliberate measure. "Gabe's the kind

of guy who takes what he wants. People who don't comply end up…" She stopped herself, clutching the fabric over her breasts as if it was too thin to be considered a covering.

Adam took a step forward and lightly tugged her away from the ladder. He drew so close, his nose almost touched hers. He stroked his thumb across her jaw, Pulsing a little of his ability to take away one's inhibitions into her. "What did he do to you?"

Belle searched for the words, but the pain that slashed across her face told him enough. She couldn't work out a response, instead folding her arms across her breasts as if to cover them. Her chin bent downward, and her shoulders drew in to protect herself from the bitter chill of life.

Adam curved his arm around her hips, bringing her in for a hug meant to shield her until the pain of her memories passed. "Those letters you get that you throw away. They're from him, aren't they."

Belle draped her arms around his waist, permitting her anxiety to rest in his embrace as her cheek pressed to his chest. How she could have used someone sturdy like him to shield her from all the bad things in life when they threatened to bury her. "Mm-hm. When Gabe wants something he can't have, he steals it. He stole me two years ago. Stole what wasn't his." She shuddered against Adam, the story itself making her feel icy inside.

Adam cupped the back of her head, raking his fingers across her scalp to soothe her. "Tell me what he did."

Belle couldn't say the words aloud. Though the

receiving room didn't have any listening ears nearby, Belle whispered to Adam all the ways Sheriff Aston had pursued her, stalking her, impounding her car whenever he found out she had a date with someone else, and how he'd given her the option of going away for a weekend with him in order to forgive the newest fine that year that would have bankrupted her and her father. Gabe had taken her by force when he grew too frustrated by her cold shoulder.

"Can you prove any of it?" Adam asked softly, his cheek pressed to hers. His hand found its way to the small of her back, as if he had the power to protect her from shadows.

"I shouldn't have to. I was the victim."

"Not prove it to me. If I bring in someone more official, could you testify against him?"

"I tried when it happened, but you can't exactly report the sheriff to the sheriff." She thought for a moment, sifting through her mind for proof of all he'd done to her. "Gabe's got a scar on the upper part of his right inner thigh," Belle replied dryly. "No one would know it was there unless they've seen him naked."

Adam stiffened, fighting back all the rage that was on the brink of taking over. But he knew Belle didn't need that right now. Holding her was the high point of his year, and he would gladly endure frostbite, frustration and his worst fears if it would give him a few minutes of her trusting him enough not to brace herself as she leaned her body's weight onto him. "Right inner thigh?"

"Yeah. Matches my hunting knife."

Adam chuckled, his chest vibrating against hers. "That's my girl. I'll need my phone back so I can make a few calls."

"You don't have to. What's done is done."

"That may be true, but at least what was done to you won't happen to anyone else if we get him locked up."

Belle let loose a breath into his neck that she'd been holding onto for two years. Her exhale tickled his skin, unleashing a shiver of intrigue that rolled through him. "After that story, I think it's time for you to lie down, and for me to be the one who brings you tea."

Belle shook her head. "I'm really fine. It is what it is. Plus, I want to finish up this room this afternoon."

Adam laced his fingers through hers, touching her knuckles to his cheek just to feel the softness in her that life hadn't managed to stamp out. "Humor me."

He led her out of the living room and didn't let go of her hand until he'd tucked her into the bed. He sat on the side of the mattress, sandwiching her hand between his. "I'm sorry the world was cold to you. How can I warm you up?"

Belle's eyes misted over. "Don't say another nice thing to me. I can't take it right now."

Adam frowned. "I promised you that you'd never be cold in my presence again. This very much applies."

"Damnit, Adam!" Belle wasn't prone to emotional outbursts, but he stayed with her when her tears started to fall. He contented himself brushing her hair back from her face and dabbing at her cheeks with his handkerchief. He promised her all the ways he would make things right. Adam knew enough about himself to accept that he would do whatever it took to see those vows come to fruition.

Adam had never put much stock in comforting women, but for the first time found that he couldn't leave her side when she was in the slightest bit of pain. So he held her hand after she cried herself to sleep, making sure someone was there to watch over her and keep her warm, so she could finally rest.

20

A SECOND DANCE

Belle returned Adam's laptop to him the next day. Each new morning presented her with a myriad of options for scrubbing down the place, so she cleaned another two rooms before she helped Chef Bouche prep for dinner.

"What's that smell?" Adam asked, popping his head into the kitchen.

Audra was on the counter next to the stove, instructing Belle how to make the alfredo sauce. "It's garlic." When she picked up her head from her project, she was so surprised, she dropped the spatula into the pan. "Oh, wow."

Adam had shaved, and though the shorter beard that was only half an inch long would be its standard two inches by morning, the effort made him look younger, and more like a man. He looked down at his clothes curiously, wondering if he'd accidentally put his trousers on backwards or something. "That 'wow' better have been a compliment."

Belle swallowed thickly. "It was."

Adam's chest puffed, but he said nothing more about it. "I can smell dinner all the way down the hallway, and it's making me starving. How long until we eat?"

Belle tore her eyes from his features, her cheeks rosy when she realized she'd been thinking how handsome he looked with his face more exposed. There were still the animalistic nuances, but this way he was about fifty-fifty between man and beast. "About twenty minutes. If you're hungry, there's some celery in the fridge."

Adam fished around in the refrigerator and pulled out a stalk, munching on it as he sidled up next to her and peered into the pan she was stirring. His free hand found its way to the small of her back, his insides warming when she leaned into him. "Mm. Satisfying," he lied as he crunched the celery.

Belle sniggered and bumped her hip to his. "It'll tide you over. I've never made alfredo with parmesan and goat cheeses, but I've learned Audra's never wrong."

"That's right," Audra spouted proudly.

Adam knocked his hip to hers, and the two began to fight for space in front of the stove, their bodies battling like flirty teenagers. "Would you move it? I'm going to make a mess if you don't knock it off."

Adam grinned at her, not holding back the more

wolfish aspects of his smile. Usually he smiled with his mouth closed, but he didn't mind letting the veil down around Belle. She never balked at his fangs. "You can't stir a pot while someone's bumping you? And I thought I hired an experienced housekeeper."

"You're going to make me burn myself on the pan!" she giggled, putting the wooden spoon down so she could shove him with both hands.

"Audra, Bouche – rally! This monster's attacking your master!"

Audra chortled at their playful nature, wondering to herself when the last time was that she'd seen Adam truly happy before Belle came into their lives.

Before Belle could turn off the stove, Adam whisked her away from the pan, holding one arm out to the side while the other kept a firm command over his favorite spot – the small of her back. He didn't hold back, but pressed her body to his.

Belle had never been to a royal ball, and didn't fall into the waltz easily. Her feet stumbled when their lack of natural rhythm battled with her desire to play. Still, she beamed up at him, feeling like a true lady. "I don't know what I'm doing," she admitted.

"You're dancing with me, and quite well, might I add. It's no surprise; I'm terrific at leading."

Belle rolled her eyes at his self-flattery. After a few more beats of stepping on his toes, she pulled away and moved to turn off the stove. She hid her pink cheeks from view, lest he find out how special the simple dance was to her. "I'm a terrible dancer," she admitted, motioning to the side of her head. "I'm partially deaf in my right ear, so I've never been all that great at catching rhythms." Her eyes flicked to his, clearly embarrassed. "But thank you. Most men value their toes too much to dance with me."

"Dinner can wait. Let's go test out that ballroom. I've got at least seven toes that are still functional. I haven't danced with a woman in ages."

Though she wanted nothing more, Belle held up her finger to stop him. "First off, dinner. Secondly, I'm a terrible dancer, as we've already established."

His mouth fell open. "You truly won't dance with me?"

Belle took in his longing, wishing she was more adept at such things. "As your nurse, I think I should try to keep your toes from possibly breaking."

His eyes grew serious. "What will it take to get a dance with you in the ballroom?"

"You're truly the only man who's ever asked me for a second dance. Are you sure you know what you're getting yourself into?"

"I know exactly what I'm doing," he said with a slight smirk. "Please, Belle. Let me teach you."

Belle blew out a breath as she thought. "I worked real hard cleaning that ballroom. It should be filled with people, not just us."

Adam's shoulders fell, and the smile died from his lips. "You don't know what you're asking. People don't want to come here and be reminded of all Malaura did to ruin me. They want to go about their lives and leave me to my transition. No one wants to get near the wolves."

Belle moved over to him and placed her hand on his chest. "You're not a wolf, Adam. You're a man. If you're going to give all of this up for your transition, don't you want to have enjoyed it while you could? You don't have to throw a huge party, but you should let people in who aren't on payroll."

"So if I invite someone over, you'll have a dance with me in the ballroom?"

A bashful smile found Belle's lips. "Best offer I've ever had. A girl would be crazy to say no."

Adam covered her hand on his chest with his own larger, hairier one, but she didn't pull away from his touch. The desire to Pulse her with his ability to strip away her inhibitions was a glowing temptation he fought to ignore. Gabe had taken her against her will. He would not do the same. He resolved himself to be unselfish with Belle, even if it killed him. Slowly, he brought her hand up to his lips and blessed her fingers with a kiss. Satisfaction like he'd never known bloomed in his heart when he took in the rosy hue that colored her countenance. "Beautiful," he whispered as he thumbed the apple of her cheeks. "Let me make some calls."

Adam had never been much for putting time into romancing a woman, but suddenly the most important thing on his mind was getting time with Belle in his long-forsaken ballroom.

21

A PRESENT FOR BELLE

Adam tried not to let his disquiet show when he entered the dining room Belle had set up for them. The gift he'd gotten her still remained tucked away, waiting for either the perfect moment, or for him to gather up the courage to give it to her. He'd tried twice already that day, but each time, he'd been reminded by the mere sight of her stark beauty that he was no one to be giving someone of her caliber presents.

The table was always nicely set, but tonight there were two flickering candles in the center of the long table. The lights were dimmed, making the whole room practically glow with hushed secrets. He smirked at the setup, wondering if he should comment on the romantic nuance, or if that would embarrass her. For all her confidence in bossing him around and taking charge of the household, she grew nervous and skittish at romantic advances. He had a feeling it wasn't just because he was cursed that she put on more conservative airs, deciding this wasn't the time for him to give her the gift he'd been stressing over.

He set his book down at the table, loving their routine of reading quietly over dinner. It seemed ages ago that he'd reduced himself to eating dog food off the floor. Now that things were starting to get back to normal after their bout with the snowstorm, he was looking forward to their quiet companionable dinners, in which he was a man dining with a woman. She gave him a reason to sit up straight and put to use the etiquette lessons he'd endured in his youth.

Belle and Audra came in with the teacart and set out the salads. "I hope you're not hungry," Belle said as her skirt swooshed while she moved to his place setting. "Because the sauce is so good, I might just eat it all."

"It smells amazing." Adam followed her to her chair, moving her seat out for her. When she froze, quirking her eyebrow up in question at the gentlemanly gesture, he tried not to grow frustrated with how out of practice he was with all of it. "Just sit."

He'd seen his father do this for his mother every night at dinner, and though he'd never performed the ritual of courtship on a woman before, Adam found himself acting on impulses he only entertained around Belle. He slid the seat underneath her, and touched her hand before returning to his seat and opening up his book.

After a few bites, Adam noticed Belle staring at him.

"Everything alright?" he asked, hoping he sounded like a nice guy, and not aggressive.

"Yeah. I just miss reading. My book is out in the snow still, totally ruined and breaking my heart. It was my favorite, and now it's gone." She closed her eyes and let out a pitiful groan. "I hope the wolves didn't pee on it."

"I ordered you another copy, but I can't imagine the mailman will make it out in the blizzard. Do you want to read one of my books in the meantime?"

Belle blinked at him from across the table. "You ordered me my book? You didn't have to do that."

Adam shrugged. "It's your favorite book. You read it every night. I figured buying you a new copy would be easier than trying to break you of your addiction."

"Thank you." Belle picked up her fork and poked at a tomato. "My papa gave that book to my mom before she died. It's got a love note to her from him in the front cover. Now the ink's probably all wet and smudgy. I wonder if he'll write a new note inside the copy you got me."

"I'm sure he would." Something inside of him pushed him forward, shoving his hesitation over giving her the present he'd obsessed over to the back burner. "Let's pick you out something from my collection while we wait out the weather. Shall we?" Adam stood and extended his arm to her, putting on the mannerisms of his father and doing his best to behave like a man. For too long he'd seen himself as only a beast. He tucked her hand under the crook of his elbow as they walked together, noting the daintiness of her wrist.

It was strange how easily Belle fell into step with him, even going so far as to lean into his side while they walked. They turned corner after corner, bringing them to a whole new series of doors.

Belle frowned at the low-hanging cobwebs. "Oh, I haven't gotten this far in my cleaning yet."

"Vivienne and Lucien keep the library clean for me. It's one of the few rooms I use regularly."

"You have a library here? You mean, like, a bookshelf?"

"Slightly grander than a bookshelf. I think you'll like it." Adam's palms started to sweat as he rethought over his gift to her. Perhaps it was too simple, too practical. He'd had the surprise set up since yesterday, but hadn't found the right time until that evening. Belle was the kind of girl who deserved to be romanced with flowers and chocolates, but his gut had led him here instead. He paused before opening the doors. "If you don't like it, you don't have to pretend you do."

"What's not to like about a library?"

With a steadying inhale, Adam threw open the double doors with a flourish that made Belle gasp. There was nothing coherent in Belle's mind when she took in the enormity of the library. It appeared to be four stories tall and stocked with every book imaginable. The shelves were rich cherry wood, giving everything a polished look of wealth to it. There were ladders attached to the shelves that rolled from side to side, so you could reach anything without too much effort. In the corner was a fireplace with two brown leather chairs set before it. One looked big and regal with a high back, and the other slightly less imposing, adorned with a big red bow atop it.

"Do you like it?" Adam asked, the knot in his chest tightening.

Belle wished her eyes weren't misting over, clouding the most beautiful sight she'd ever witnessed. "It's... This must be what it's like in the movies when someone's so overcome with emotion that they faint."

Adam chuckled at her gaping mouth, and held her wrist tighter to his ribs. "Then I guess I'll just have to hold you closer."

Belle was still drinking it all in, unable to steady herself under the weight of such unfathomable beauty. "The library in the West Village only has three shelves of books. I've read them all at least twice. This... I can't... Adam, I..."

Adam exhaled contentedly at the sound of his name on her lips. "Pick whatever you like to read during dinner. Then if you want, we can have a nightcap in here by the fireplace. That's your present, if you couldn't tell by the red bow. I've decided that every time I yell at you, I should get you a gift. I think that sounds fair."

"You got me a chair?"

Adam stiffened. "If you don't like it, I'll get you something else."

Her eyes combed over the buttery leather beneath the red bow. "No! I love it. Let me get this straight: you lost your temper, so I get a gorgeous chair by the fireplace? A chair that's just for me? Are you serious?"

Adam's shoulders lost fifty percent of their tension at her joy. The simple sound of her happiness brought a contentment into him that loosened the knot of consternation that was always tightening behind his sternum. "Of course. I'm thinking each time I lose my temper, the present should be bigger, so I'll have double the reason not to be cross with you."

"I like this plan. Jeez, what happens the next time you yell at me? New car? Elephant? Skyscraper?"

"Well, you do need a new car."

Belle held up her finger. "Don't you dare buy me a new car. I was kidding." She walked over to the new chair, but didn't let go of Adam's arm. She clung to it, as if she needed him to steady herself under the weight of the shock. She glanced up and noticed a series of oil paintings in between the third and fourth story shelves. "Is that you when you were a boy?"

"It is. And my mother and father. Then my father's parents, and my great-grandparents. It's quite the spectacle, but it made my mother happy to look at them, so I supposed I can't complain."

"One day, you should get a new one of you as an adult," she suggested.

Adam's jaw stiffened. "One that will scare small children? I'll pass. Perhaps you can put up one of me in my wolf form. That should draw the eye. Mother would be so proud."

Belle moved to stand in front of him and pressed her palms to his cheeks. "Do you want me to feel sorry for you?"

His upper lip curled in disgust. "No."

"When your transition happens, it happens. Until then, you're a man. You're the man of this house, and you run the Fontaine Mortgage business, along with the Fontaine Security Firm. You deserve to have your portrait up there, next to your father's. He would be proud to see all you've accomplished. There's too much you've built to throw it all away because you might not win a rigged beauty pageant."

Adam's nostrils flared as he debated whether or not he wanted to fight her on this, but finally his shoulders deflated. "Our profits are up eighteen percent since I took over the business."

"I honestly don't know how you do it. I mean, I know there's an office in town where you have a team of people who work for you, but there's so much on your shoulders. Then you go and do this for me?"

"It's the beauty of not having a social life. You like it?" he asked of the chair.

"I love it. Thank you." When he made to remove the oversized bow, Belle placed her hand on his. "No! I haven't had a wrapped present in ages. Leave the bow on a little while longer."

"Your father doesn't get you presents?"

"He makes me things in his workshop, but when money's tight you don't spend on things like wrapping paper. A bow is a luxury." She fondled the edge of the ribbon with rapture.

"Come, let's find you a book. I fear if you keep looking at the bow like that, I'll find myself giftwrapping llamas and whole buildings just to get a repeat of that expression on your face." The fact that he had fulfilled such an obscure childish fantasy of hers – giving her a wrapped gift – was a heady incentive to do whatever it took to give her the world. He cleared his throat in an attempt to rein himself in.

"A giftwrapped llama would be a little much."

"Come, now. Someone made pasta that smells so good, I'm about to ditch you and go grab some. Let's get you a book." Adam guided the ladder while she climbed up it, and slowly slid it to the right so she could see the spines up close.

A wistful expression washed over her face. "Forget dinner. Let's just do this all night. I'll hang on the ladder, and you push me."

Adam feathered his fingers across her ankle, giving her a light tickle. "I've got too much wolf in me to go skipping meals." Then he pretended to bite into her calf, drawing out her giggles with a satisfaction he felt deep down in his soul. Then he checked her creamy skin twice to make sure he hadn't cut her with his fangs by mistake. The prospect of causing her physical harm made him sick to his stomach.

Belle selected a book, and Adam helped her off the ladder, his arms holding her hips like a man who knew exactly how to touch a woman's body. Belle didn't move away, but stood in his arms when her feet touched down on the floor.

She pressed the book to her breast as if it was a beloved teddy bear. "Why are you so good to me?" she asked, not wanting to jinx her good fortune, but unable to shake the change that had come over him in so short a time. He'd been distant and surly. Now he was the gentleman holding onto her waist and showing her his vast collection of books. There was nothing sexier to Belle than a man who read. It was a rare commodity in her hometown, and she didn't take for granted the gift he'd given her in the library. Perhaps the grandest gift of all – even more so than the chair – was the doting smile he blessed her with, as if she was precious and important.

Adam didn't answer, but met her eyes with sincerity and humility he would never admit to aloud. He needed her. It was the goodness she exuded that fascinated him, and made him want to learn how to be a decent person.

Belle had never been looked at that way by a someone

like him. The softness of the green in his eyes lured her in, reminding them both that he was a man – however long that would last. She threw caution to the wind and reached up on tiptoes to kiss his furry cheek, running her fingers along his jaw to enchant them both. "Thank you."

22

DINING ALONE

That night after dinner, Adam didn't retire to his bedroom or his office. Instead he brought a narrow table into the library, so he could sit with Belle and work while she read. "You're sure the typing sound doesn't bother you?"

"Why would it? I don't think anything could bother me at all right now." She motioned around the library. "This is my happy place. It used to be the ice cream parlor on fifth street. This is better."

Adam chuckled as he read through his emails from the office manager at the security firm he owned. "Perhaps we should have ice cream brought in from there when my guests come over to join us for a spin around the ballroom."

Belle sat up straighter and rested the book on her skirt. "Guests? You invited someone over?"

He kept his eyes on his screen to avoid meeting her gaze. "Yes. That was my way of telling you."

Belle rubbed her forehead. "I was kind of hoping you would chicken out; I'm such a hopeless dancer. I didn't think you'd actually have people over!"

Adam smirked at her. "I thought as much. Still, a bargain's a bargain. Looking forward to spinning you around the ballroom."

"You seriously are going through with this?"

"Well, you didn't give me much choice in the matter when you said you wouldn't dance with me unless there were more people than just us to fill the space."

Belle deflated slightly. "But if we dance together with tons of people watching, they'll see that I have no idea what I'm doing!" She groaned with dread. "They'll think I only got this job because I'm sleeping with my boss. Maybe my idea to invite people to the ballroom wasn't so great."

Adam smiled at her frown, thinking again to himself how lovely she was when her mouth drew to the side, as it often did when she was contemplating things that bothered her. "I knew you'd land there, so I only invited Henry and a guest, plus Rory and her husband. After she read all my letters you mailed her, I guess it's time for us to reconvene our friendship."

"They won't think I'm..." She cast around for the right words. "A loose woman?"

Adam barked out a laugh, holding his stomach. "Oh,

I'm so glad I got to hear you say that. Yes, I'm sure they'll draw all sorts of tawdry conclusions." He waved away her concern. "I told Rory and Cordray all about you already. And Henry knows you live here. It was his idea. It's fine." Then he caught his mistake, letting his cards show too early that he thought about her when she wasn't around – that he'd told his friends about her. He cleared his throat and straightened in his high-backed leather chair. "They'll come over when the snow lets up."

"I can't believe you actually did it. Is it too late to take it all back? How about I dance with you tonight without witnesses."

"You want to dance with me unchaperoned? Think of the scandal. *Now* I'll call you a loose woman."

Belle laughed through her nose and, without thinking, she leaned over and brushed her fingers over the furry curve of his cheek, loving the way his face lit up when he was truly happy. Her eyes widened at her gall, and her hand froze on his face before she tore it away, chagrinned.

Adam reached over and dragged her chair closer to his, holding Belle's hand before she could crawl back inside herself. He rubbed his thumb over the smooth back of her hand, his eyes drifting to his computer screen as he spoke. "You should know Rory's husband is a Lethal."

"I heard rumors to that effect."

"They're all true, but you don't have to worry about him. He's on the pill, so his abilities won't be a danger to you. His deadly powers are completely muted. Still, if it makes you uncomfortable to be in the same room as him, I can tell Rory to leave Cordray at home."

Belle shook her head, a note of compassion weighting her tone. "Lethals can't help what they are. And it sounds like he's doing all he can to make sure his wife is safe from him accidentally killing her. I would think anyone who goes to such lengths to protect their family is someone we should be friends with."

"'We', eh?" he teased her.

"You know what I mean." Belle lifted her book to hide the rosy hue that colored her cheeks at accidentally referring to the two of them as a unit.

"I do," Adam assured her. Without looking at her, he reached over to run his finger from her elbow to her wrist. He smirked when Belle nearly dropped her book as a slight chill ran through her.

Without a discussion, without eye contact and without reservations, Belle's wrist turned upward as her hand drifted down to her armrest, which was pressed up against his. The two sat in desire-laden silence, both pretending that what they were reading was the most fascinating thing in the universe, while Adam slowly ran his fingernails up and down the tender inside of Belle's forearm. In his periphery, he caught the flutter of Belle's long lashes. It was the first time his claws hadn't seemed like such a curse.

Lucien came in only to restoke the fire, casting barely contained looks of glee at the tantalizing touches that breathed life into the whole castle.

Adam narrowed his eyes at Lucien, silently telling him to scram so the candelabra didn't jinx it.

The next few nights were spent the exact same way. After Belle had exhausted herself cleaning the castle and Adam had put in a full day's work, the two wound down in the library. Adam made sure to finish his work before dinner so that after their meal, he could read to her by the fire. When the armrests between them became too much a separation, he moved a two-person leather couch into the library. Nothing was better than the feel of Belle cuddled into his side.

Adam's favorite part of all was the nighttime. Though he'd been well for nearly a week now, there had been no mention of him moving back up to his bedroom in the West wing. Every night, he slept in Belle's bed, with her curled up next to him. It was the best he'd ever slept.

Though he desperately wanted to kiss her lips that pouted while she slept, he didn't want to scare her with his fangs. When he'd kissed Rory to attempt to wake her from her coma, he'd accidentally cut his friend's lip, making her bleed. He couldn't bear the thought of accidentally nicking Belle, so he tucked his desires away as much as he was able, permitting the indulgence of sleeping next to her, since he reasoned he couldn't hurt her that way.

That night, Belle kissed his cheek before her head rested on his firm shoulder, as if she had no cares at all in the world. As if she hadn't received another letter from Sheriff Aston that afternoon. Usually she would rip it into dozens of pieces and then burn it in the fire. She didn't like to speak about it, and Adam knew better than to ask. Gabe's letters made her irritable, and she took her anger out on the dust bunnies, muttering to herself as she cleaned more than her usual workload.

Adam didn't question her about the letters, even when they started to come every day. One particular evening, however, Belle was quiet and skipped the dinner she'd made, opting for anger to feed her stomach instead. She'd even ditched out on their nightly ritual of reading together by the fire, losing track of the time (and losing a little bit of herself) while she scrubbed the floors. The entire first floor of the castle was almost completely spotless, but still she wanted to tear her way through more.

She didn't stop until Adam's voice reached her from the doorway. "I realize I can't order you to dine with me. But is there a way I can put it in your job description to sit by the fire with me while we read? Is there some kind of medical condition I can say I've developed that can only be cured by that?" He forced two coughs, wishing anything he did could make her laugh.

Belle's shoulders slumped. "I'm sorry. I didn't realize how late it was. I'll go wash up. Did you need anything?"

"You," he admitted. "But it doesn't look like there's much of you here right now. Anything I can help with?"

Belle sat back on her heels and slid an envelope out of her apron's pocket. She wiped her cheek with the back of her dirty hand, smearing soot across her face. "It's never going to end, is it."

Adam extended his hand, holding his palm out to her expectantly. "I can't help you if you don't let me. Let me read the letter."

"What are you going to do with it?"

"I'm going to turn it in to the Department of Criminal Investigation agent who's handling the case I've quietly building against Gabe. He's been gathering proof of the illegal levies and unlawful evictions. To add stalking and harassment to that? It would move things along a lot quicker."

Belle's hesitation kept the note clenched in her grip. She was ready to deny Adam again, but it was the steadiness in his eyes that pushed her to hand over the note that haunted her.

Adam opened the envelope, feeling his blood pressure rise at the uneven scrawl of a man who knew nothing but how to take shortcuts. He tucked the letter into his pocket when he finished, moving toward her and kneeling in her eyeline. When Belle lowered her chin, he tucked his finger under it and raised it to make sure she saw the sincerity on his face. "Listen to me, Belle. No one is going to take your father's home away from him. That Gabe is threatening to evict your father again if you don't move in with him is just the evidence we need."

"All my money goes back to my father to bring the mortgage payments up to date. I don't understand how he can do this! I know we're not behind on the payments anymore."

"You're current on your father's loan," Adam confirmed. "I checked on the status last week. I'll call him tonight and reassure him that I won't let anything like that happen again."

"You will?" Her phone had been lost in the snow, and she'd been borrowing Adam's to check on her father every night.

"Of course. Sheriff Aston has no grounds for any of this. I'm the one who has to initiate the eviction process, and I've never had to do that on your father's property."

Belle was on all fours, and at his assurance, her shoulders slumped, her hair falling forward from the messy ponytail. "Thank you for checking. I've been driving myself crazy trying to think of how the money could've been misplaced." She blinked rapidly to keep any moisture from falling from her eyes. "Gabe will never leave me alone, will he. No matter how much I take care of things, he'll never let me go!"

At this, Adam chuckled, surprising Belle with his levity. "You live here now. There's nowhere safer. He can try all he wants; he'll never put his hands on you again."

Belle leaned forward, warming to the promise that

seemed too beautiful to hope for. "What about when I go back home to visit my dad?"

Adam drew her into his arms, not caring that his khakis and green polo were getting grimy from the hug. He was content when she looped her arms around his neck, his eyes closing when her cheek touched his neck. She was trusting him with something big, so he swore to himself he would learn to be gentle with a situation that was so very fragile. His whisper tickled her ear when he turned his head so his lips could brush across the shell. "I'll go with you, then. If you want to see your father, I'll take you there. Let the sheriff try his intimidation tactics on me."

Belle inhaled sharply, and then brought her hand to rest on the breast of his polo, tracing the muscle there as she tried to collect herself. "You'd really do that? You'd come to the West Village for me?"

"That you think there's anything I wouldn't do for you just goes to show how little you know me."

Belle smiled through her sadness and squeezed him tighter around the neck. His shoulders were hairier than they'd been the night before, and she buried her nose into the fur as if she meant to hide her sorrows there. "If that's true, then don't let go. Hold me just a little while longer. I was so worried, thinking something happened to the money I sent in. I'm still coming down from it all."

"You are so demanding," Adam pretended to grumble.

"Hold a beautiful woman? Let her arms stay around me? Let her feel safe when I tell her I'll come to her aid? I don't know, Belle." He waited for her soft giggle, and counted her breaths as they grew more measured. "You made me dine alone tonight."

"I wasn't hungry."

"How about this: instead of cleaning all night, I draw you a hot bath. While you're unwinding, I'll get you something to eat."

Belle pulled her face back from his, her mouth popping open. "But you don't cook."

"For you, I just might." Then he rolled his eyes. "Chef Bouche will most likely do the actual cooking. But I'll bring you food, okay?"

They paused when the sound of wolves outside broke the sweetness of their connection. The howls were a warning, letting Adam know his time was nigh.

Adam's jaw clenched, and he gripped Belle a little tighter until the howling at the moon finally stopped. Now it was him who needed to be held, so Belle squeezed him tighter around the neck.

"I only have a short time left that I'll be able to eat upright. Don't make me dine alone again," he begged quietly.

"Never," Belle promised. "And when you turn, don't leave. Stay here with me." She fought with her daring, but chickened out. "Audra loves you."

The corner of Adam's mouth drew up. "She does, does she? Well, I love her, as well."

In a move so fluid, Belle could scarcely understand how it happened, she found herself swept up in his arms as he stood, unimpeded by the weight of her as he walked through the hallways to her bedroom.

23

HOWLING IN THE NIGHT

elle fell asleep that night with her hand atop Adam's broad chest, her fingers tangled in the fur. He could've gone back to his bedroom days and days ago, but they both preferred he remain with her. When he would wake in the night, afraid and filled with anxiety over his impending change, Belle would soothe him, her eyes lidded and lips puffy from sleep. After each time she comforted him back to slumber, their bodies wound more tightly around each other.

It wasn't until three in the morning that Belle roused fully to the piercing sound of a wolf's howl. She startled, untangling her limbs from his as she sat up, perplexed as to why the wolf sounded so near, like he was in the bedroom.

The second bark sounded from just outside their window. Belle's head whipped toward the sound, every bone in her body on high alert. "Adam?" she whispered, but he was still fast asleep.

When his lips parted but his eyes didn't open, she expected him to mutter something in his sleep. She jumped when a loud howl erupted from his mouth and filled the room. He wasn't even awake, yet he was answering the wolf outside. Wolf-speak was a language that was unknown to the two-legged folk, yet it seemed Adam's mind was making room for the new method of communication.

Belle eyed his fangs, which had never bothered her before. Now they seemed sharper, longer and if possible, hungrier. She knew she should probably get out so she didn't run the risk of getting bitten, but she found that she couldn't leave his side. He began to twitch and twist in the sheets, as if in the throes of a nightmare as he answered the wolf out in the snow.

Belle got out of bed and fetched a washcloth, running it under cold water to lay across his forehead, hoping it might soothe the angst that was slashed across his face even in slumber.

When the sun rose, Belle was exhausted, and Adam had no idea that he'd progressed in his transition during his sleep. He made animated chit-chat over breakfast about the mini-ball they would have that night, since Henry and Rory agreed that the snow had let up enough to bring their dates over for an evening.

"You look tired," he observed across the dining room table over his oatmeal. "Did I snore?"

"Something like that." When Belle explained what she'd witnessed, Adam's spoon lowered until his appetite was gone.

"So it's getting closer, then," he observed quietly. "I'll sleep upstairs tonight and bolt the door."

"No! No, Adam. It didn't bother me to get woken up. Please don't pull away."

Adam hung his head, ashamed that there were complicated sides to him that were better left untouched. "It's only going to get worse, Belle. Eventually I'll be more wolf than man, and I'll belong to the pack. Who knows what I'll do in my sleep. What if I'd bitten you last night? What then?"

"Jeez, if only I was a nurse who knew how to sew up a minor flesh wound," she cast out flippantly with a toss of her hair over her shoulder. "You act like I didn't know what I was getting myself into. I know all about your curse, Adam, and I'm not afraid of you."

"Well, *I'm* afraid of me! I'm afraid I'll wake up to find I can't tell you how much I..." He leaned his elbows on the table and ground his knuckles into his forehead. "I'm afraid of what's going to happen when it all slips out of my fingers."

"We'll figure it out when it comes," she assured him, standing up to move to his side. She lightly scratched his back, placing a kiss to the top of his head. "When we were down for the count out in the snow, do you remember who saved us?"

"The woman with the red cloak."

"The woman with the red cloak and her wolf. He still had his mind about him. He worked *with* the woman in red. He had enough of himself not to turn completely feral. That could be you." She leaned her cheek atop his head. "That could be *us*."

Adam inhaled a lengthy, cleansing breath through his nose as he straightened in his chair. He held onto her wrist, bringing it to his lips to press a chaste kiss to the inside of the tender flesh. "Do you really think so? I'd never seen a human communicate with the Lupine like that before. But you're right, it did seem like they were able to work in tandem."

"See? Then those are worries for another day. Today you're having your friends over. You're a regular guy who does normal things. Let's go with that for now."

"You truly want to stay with me after I transition? You'd live in the castle with me and keep things as they are? You'd look after the staff and not abandon them to ruin?"

"Of course. I like it here."

This seemed to seal something for Adam. He nodded once to himself, and then slid his chair back from the table. "Very well. Then I have some things to see to." He stood, leaving his bowl of oatmeal half-eaten.

UNEXPECTED ARRANGEMENTS

Belle frowned when he left, unsure what he was up to. She hoped he wasn't slipping back into his melancholy. Belle finished her breakfast with Bosworth chatting her ear off about the grand plans he had for the quaint ball that evening. He followed her around the castle as she cleaned, taking notes on everything she wanted done, and assigning duties to the staff, who grumbled and asked under their breath how exactly *he* was planning to help. Bosworth huffed with a haughty air, arms akimbo as his hour hand and second hand screwed up on his face, as they usually did when he was working up a good indignant rant. "I'm tending to the Lady of the House, if you don't mind. If she needs something, I'm first to know."

Belle sniggered while she swept the rooms and hallways, as she did every morning after breakfast. Vivienne started first, dusting each room, and then Belle followed behind with the broom. The first floor was so vast that it usually took her until noon to get just that task done. She started in on the second floor, picking the first two rooms in the east wing at random to scrub from top to bottom.

"Milady, I believe it's time for you to get ready. The guests will arrive within the hour," Lucien said to her with a bow from the doorway.

"Oh, wow. I guess I lost track of the time. Let me just finish up this room, and I'll hop in the shower."

Lucien paused, and when Belle turned to glance at him, she saw his arms crossed and a frown tugging at his features. "Surely you don't think you can get rid of me that easily. Vivienne can keep working, but you need to wash up. This is a grand occasion, and it was your idea."

"I know, I know. In my head, it sounded better than me making a fool of myself on the dance floor in front of Adam's closest friends. It's not like they're a big deal – only the Prince of Avondale and the Sleeping Beauty. Not intimidating at all."

Lucien scoffed at her insecurity, and then ambled over to her and tipped the broom from her hand. "You already know Prince Henry, and Rory's no one to worry yourself about."

Belle followed Lucien out the door and down the steps after Vivienne swooshed her feathers in Belle's face to get her moving, making her sneeze over and over until Belle forfeited her claim on the cleaning equipment.

Belle showered quickly. Each minute that passed by built her nerves up into a dam of anxiety. Thomas brushed her hair for her, taking his time with the chestnut tresses as he dried and curled them, fixing it all into an ornate bun atop her head. "Beautiful," he declared of his masterpiece.

Belle was too nervous to look in the mirror to confirm or deny his assessment. "The Chancellor's daughter, is she nice? I've only seen interviews with her."

"Rory is wonderful. If it weren't for her and Prince Henry, Adam would never have seen the sun. Their fight was hard on the master, though he would never admit that. Reuniting Adam with his oldest friend is the kindest thing you could've done for him, though I know it cost you your car."

Belle swallowed hard, wondering when she would have enough saved for a decent down-payment towards a gently used vehicle. She'd received the call that between the crash and the damage to the interior from the snow, her rickety vehicle would be better off totaled. "After I get a little more saved, then I can think about replacing my car. A couple months."

After a few minutes of fiddling with the hem of the slip Simone had made her, a knock drew her attention away from her current nervousness. She slid on the silk rose-hued robe and cinched it around her waist before opening the door.

Before she could stem her reaction, a gasp flew from

her lips. "Adam!" She'd never seen him in a tuxedo before, but knew she'd never forget the sight. He was dapper, and though his clean-shaven face would only last a few hours before his beard would grow back in, she drank in every inch of his features with unguarded appreciation.

It didn't even dawn on her that equal amounts of shock were radiating from him as his eyes combed over her form, which was clad only in silk. He clutched a folder in his hand, but seemed to forget its purpose. "You... I wanted to talk to you," he finally worked out, swallowing thickly.

"Sure. Make yourself at home." Then she grinned and mimed laughing at her own levity. "Get it? Because you already are at home."

"Indeed. I... There was something, but I can't seem to remember anything at all right now."

A demure smile lit Belle's face at the blatant compliment. "You're doing that tux all kinds of favors."

Adam's hand brushed down his abdomen, as if only just then realizing what he was wearing. "Is that so? I would say you should just wear that, but there's something alluring about me being the only man to see you in your robe."

Belle stepped back, ushering him into the room. "What is it you wanted to talk about?"

Adam's eyes narrowed at Thomas, who bowed and skittered out of the room, shutting the door behind him.

Simone did her amazing disappearing act, shutting her doors to give the two the illusion of privacy.

"Did Thomas see you naked?" Adam asked with a frown.

Belle grimaced. "No. I don't think so. I put on my slip in the bathroom."

"So he's seen you in your slip?" Adam shook his head and tried to focus on the folder in his fist. "It doesn't matter. I've been thinking about the woman with the red cloak. You were right. I didn't see it at first, but it was there. They were communicating. The white wolf acted separate from the pack and stayed with her. I want that. When I transition, I want to be able to stay here with the staff, and with you."

Belle sat on the edge of her bed while Adam took the chair and rested his folder on the desk. "I think that's great. Transitioning to the Lupine doesn't mean your life is over. It's just a new chapter. We can figure it out and make it work for you."

Adam nodded once. "I'm glad to hear you say that. Unfortunately, there are legal matters to address before I turn. I don't have any heirs, so the castle would be sold off, since the Lupine don't have rights and can't own property."

Belle hung her head, chiding herself for not thinking about that crucial detail. "Maybe you and the staff could move in with me and Papa in the West Village." She glanced around her long room and grimaced. "It'll be a bit tighter than what you're used to, but if you're okay sharing my bedroom, we can make it work."

Adam froze at the desk, watching her slight fidgets as she exposed her plan to help him. "You couldn't possibly mean that."

Her neck shrank, chagrinned. "I know it's small, but it's something. A step up from being out in the cold, for sure. You don't have to, but think it over before you say no." She shook her head, a look of angst pinching the bridge of her nose. "The thought of you living out in the woods all alone just kills me."

"You really think about that kind of thing? Of ways to save me?"

"Not well, obviously. I didn't think through the fact that you won't have legal rights. But if you need someone to make sure you have a roof over your head and a bed to sleep on at night, I can do that for you. I can keep you safe, Adam. Whatever you need."

Adam blinked at her, never more certain that he was making the right decision. "I may have a better plan, if you're up for it. I've been on the phone with my lawyer, and he drew up a few documents for me." He flipped open the folder and handed her several pieces of paper. "This first one is making you my Power of Attorney, so you can sign for things on my behalf when I'm considered not of sound body and mind when I turn." He paused for Belle's gasp, but then continued. "This one is willing you the deed to the castle and all of my personal assets. When people transition, it's considered a death, and their things are passed down or forfeited if there's no will. You'll be my sole beneficiary, with the understanding that you'll take care of the castle and everyone in it."

Belle clamped her hand over her mouth, dumbfounded. "Adam, you can't be serious!"

He lifted a third document, paying her shock no mind. "This is giving you my seat on the board of Fontaine Mortgage, and controlling shares of the company. Then this here gives you control of my smaller companies - the security business I acquired, a restaurant and a few others."

"I'm a nurse! I don't know anything about running a loans company, or one that... Adam, you're not thinking clearly!"

"I'm in the process of writing out step-by-step instructions, in case it takes us a few beats to figure out how to communicate after I turn. I can teach you all you need to know. And I assure you, the board is quite capable."

Belle stood and shook her head, her hand over her heart to stem the rapid syncopation that quickened her breath. "They're all going to think I swindled you into this! Can't you see that I'm underqualified? The stockholders will revolt."

Adam smirked at her. "They'll be stupid if they give up their shares, and we'll scoop them right up if they run. Fontaine Mortgage is the most profitable home loans company in the state. If you do things as I'm instructing you, then there won't be more than a few small bumps in the road."

He took in her skittish fear and reached his hand out to her, beckoning her toward him. They both exhaled when their palms touched – his fur against the silk of her skin.

"Adam, this is…"

"I can't let my family's legacy be stripped for parts. If anyone else gains control, they won't know what to do with it. They'll change the fundamentals that make the company great. Of all the things I cannot stand, that would be one of the worst. Please, Belle. I can't let my father down in this."

Belle ran her free hand over her face, her eyes wide and her head still spinning with confusion. "What about Henry? You trust him."

"I trust Henry to be my friend, but he can't hear the staff speak. He still thinks I'm mentally ill. He won't understand how to look after all of them with the same care you have."

Belle let Adam pull her down to sit on his thick thigh. She leaned into him and rested her head on his shoulder. "Okay, then yes to being your Power of Attorney, and yes to the house. I can keep things running and make sure you all have a safe place to stay."

Adam put the papers down and curved his arm around her hips, his other hand wrapping around her to trace his claws slowly up and down her arm. It was of great satisfaction to him that he could make goosebumps erupt on her skin. He loved how pliable she was in his arms. She trusted him, and what's more, what he discovered that morning as he started to put all the documents in motion with his attorney, is that he trusted her. "And what about the businesses? Can I put those in your hands, as well? It would pay you more than you'll need to provide a comfortable life for you and your father." He dangled the carrot, hoping she would take the offer.

Belle chewed on her lower lip, contemplating all she was signing up for. "You need this? You're sure I'm the one for the job? Adam, my degree is in nursing, not finance."

"I'll teach you all you need to know. I'll be with you every step of the way. You'd run it in name, but we'll be making decisions together."

She wrapped her arms around his thick neck. "Tell me that I won't be the person that breaks everything that's important to you. Tell me I won't wreck your great-grand-father's legacy."

Adam smiled, his cheek pressing to hers. "Does that mean you'll help me?"

Belle paused, steeling herself, but then finally nodded. "Yes. If this is what you need, then I'll help however I can."

Adam's gentle embrace bloomed into a full-blown hug of relief. "Thank you," he whispered. "I feel so much lighter, knowing the staff and myself will be taken care of after I turn. Thank you. I won't have to live in the woods without you."

"You love them."

"I do. They're only in this position because of me."

When the doorbell sounded through the house, Belle stiffened. "I'm not dressed yet!"

Adam gave her another squeeze before letting her go. "Take your time. It's only my attorney and a notary. They're going to make everything official. Henry and Rory are on their way, but it's a long drive for them both."

Belle stood and cinched her robed tighter, making sure she remained covered. "You want me to sign everything right now?"

"As soon as you're decent." He stood and, without thinking, pressed a kiss to the crook of her neck. They both reveled in Belle's shiver of longing, taking in the new advance that welcomed them to another level of their complicated relationship. "Thomas saw you in your slip?"

Belle closed her eyes, her cheek brushing his. "Only a little."

"Mm. I'll be waiting in the receiving room, wondering how undressed *I'm* allowed to see you."

Belle's intake of breath caused a seductive smirk to play on Adam's features. It had been so long since he'd been able to make a woman's body shiver for him. He stood and touched her hand before he left, leaving them both wanting more.

25

KEYS TO THE CASTLE

*B*elle made her way down the steps in a simple red dress that showed off her slender waist and belled at her hips, brushing her toes as she walked. Simone promised there were only a few more finishing touches that needed to be made to the ballgown, and that such extravagant things weren't for boring affairs like signing paperwork.

Adam stood when she entered the room. The lawyer and notary followed suit, glancing between Adam and Belle and taking note of the vast improvement in Adam's temperament in her presence. Introductions were made, papers were signed, and Belle wondered if things like this were always so quick, or if it was because Adam was who he was that guests wanted to make their visits brief.

They sat on the couch in the receiving room, his arm draped on the back while she blinked next to him, still floored at all that took place. "I can't believe all of that just happened. I mean, just like that, I'm permanently in your life."

"Just like that," Adam smiled, looking more relaxed than he'd been in ages. He reached into his breast pocket and pulled out a cell phone and a set of keys. "For you."

"What's for me?"

"Keys to the castle. You'll need them, since the deed will soon be in your name. There's a key to the silver Jag in the garage, too. I don't use it anymore, so it's yours."

"What?" Belle shook her head, as if that would force his words to make sense. "Adam, you can't just give me your car!"

"Why not?" he asked, unaffected. "Yours isn't salvageable, and you need a car." A frown tugged at the corners of his mouth. "Oh, you're right to protest. You shouldn't accept a hand-me-down gift. I'll buy you a new one that's just yours. One that no one else has ever sat in. I'm sorry. I wasn't thinking."

Belle's mouth hung open in shock. "Adam, of course I don't need anything new. I'm saying you can't give me your car because it's too expensive, and it's... You can't give me a car!"

When Adam understood the source of her consternation, his worry wrinkles ironed out with an easy smile. "Oh, is that all? You're funny when you get all worked up over something so small."

"It's not small. It's a car."

He shrugged. "To me, it's small. Your happiness and safety are big."

"Thank you, but I was saving up so I could buy one myself."

"Why bother? I haven't driven the silver Jag in ages. If you hadn't noticed, I have four cars and I rarely leave the castle. It's yours. Think of it was the company car, if you want. You're my caretaker, so eventually you'll need to drive me to the doctor's and whatnot."

Belle's eyebrow raised. "You'll let me take you to the doctor?"

"No," Adam admitted with a small smirk. "This is yours, too. Your phone was lost in the snow, so I got you a new one with all the numbers of the board, my attorney, and anyone else you'll need to contact when you take over the company. It's got the newest security features, too. My security company doesn't mess around when it comes to digital protection."

Belle jumped up and backed away from the keys and phone as if they were scorpions. "No! I don't want those things right now."

"You don't want keys to the house? I should've given you a set weeks ago."

"This feels wrong, like you're giving up that the curse might not come true. It's possible, isn't it? There's still hope." She started wringing her hands, anxiety coursing through her at the grand gestures. "Rory woke up from her curse. She beat Malaura!"

Adam pursed his lips, tilting his head to the side as he glanced up at her. "It's going to happen, Belle. I don't like it either, but make no mistake, Malaura always gets her way. Remus wasn't there the counter my curse, so it stuck. It's going to happen. I want you to be prepared."

Emotion was thick in Belle's voice, but she willed herself not to break down. "If I take those keys, somehow it all feels like there's no going back. You may have given up hope, but I haven't. There's... Maybe it won't work, but everyone knows what Remus Johnstone did for his niece. The only reason Rory had a chance at breaking Malaura's curse is because her uncle gave up a portion of his life to alter it."

Adam stilled, taking with caution the daring that flashed in her eyes. "Belle, you don't know what you're saying. Remus was reckless. Yes, it worked for them, but it cost Remus five years off his life!"

"Do you think it's every day I meet a man who reads to me by the fire?" she shouted, her eyes watering.

Adam was out of his chair, and in the next breath, he was gripping her biceps with an earnest plea she couldn't turn away from. "I won't come into your life only to shorten it. Besides, Remus performed the counter-curse within the hour that Malaura cursed Rory. The magic was still fresh, so it was more easily manipulated." He swallowed hard, picturing the memory as if it happened yesterday. "Besides, Audra and Lucien tried. Practically the entire staff offered themselves up and did their best to save me with a counter-curse the minute I was marked, but it didn't take." He motioned to his furry body. "Obviously. I've been living with this sword over my head for years. Trust me, Belle. There's nothing you can do."

"Or maybe it's something *only* I can do. I need to take a sample of your blood. Please, Adam!"

Adam crushed her to him, willing himself to hold onto his temper. "You're wrong. Everything about this is wrong. I won't let you give up five years of your life for the chance at saving a miserable man like me. It won't work, anyway."

"Then what's the harm?"

"You know the risks exactly as I do! If Remus had performed the counter-curse wrong, he could've died. He could've forfeited more than just the half a decade it's going to cost him off the back end to save his niece, and that's no small price to pay. And Remus is one of the most skilled people I've ever known. Thank goodness Audra and Lucien weren't all that powerful. They could have truly hurt themselves in their attempt. You're smart, and you're capable of many things, but Remus is smarter than both of us. He barely survived, and he still ended up giving away a portion of his life to save Rory!" He held her tight, not caring if he was laying too many cards out on the table. "Don't you dare try something so reckless, Belle. I won't hear of it. I was selfish and stupid, and Malaura cursed me for it. I won't be selfish with you." His claws dug into her back without cutting. "So help me, I won't let you do this."

"But Adam, I..."

"I know, and the fact that you entertained such desperate means to save me will stay with me and keep me by your side after I turn. That you would offer to cut yourself down that it might save me? Belle, I don't know what twist of fate landed me with you, but that's all the mercy I'll allow myself."

"I won't do nothing while you give up!"

"You don't think there's anything I wouldn't give to be able to stay with you another year? Another month?"

Belle let out a bleat of agony. "How much time do you have left? Weeks?"

Adam lowered his chin and shook his head.

"A week?"

His jaw tightened, and again he turned his head from side to side.

"Days?" she choked out as heartbreak shot through her. "No! Tell me you're lying! Tell me we have more time!"

"You are my torment, Belle. To know that if I hadn't been so foolish as a younger man, I might've been able to stay with you? It kills me. It's exactly the punishment I deserve, and you won't rob me of it." His tight grip loosened slightly, and his hand began to rub soothing circles into her back. "All I want is for you to stay with me – to remember the man I was to you when all that's left is the beast."

Belle remained in his arms, holding onto him while

the world rocked the small boat they'd taken solace in. "If that's what you want, I can do that."

She couldn't imagine forfeiting the feel of his massive chest, or the snuggly fur that poked out from his tuxedo shirt. There would be too much she would miss about him, and she wasn't ready to give it all up. For the moment, though, she let Adam believe that she had, and swayed in his arms as he rocked them from side to side while the chaos of the moment settled between them.

They didn't let go until the doorbell chimed.

26

FIRST IMPRESSIONS

*B*elle was nervous, not knowing what to make of Adam's friends. Prince Henry was boisterous and laughed loudly at the slightest provocation. "Tell me again about the cobwebs you found through this place. The spiders had to have been large as kittens."

Belle smiled politely and took his coat, hanging it on Thomas' arm. She was sad to see the coatrack stuck in an immobile prison, but tucked away her melancholy for the moment. "Slightly smaller than spiders, though not by much. It's good to see you again, your majesty," she said with a curtsey.

Henry put on formal airs to match hers, only he added a slightly snobbish stuffiness to his tone. "Ah, yes. Good to see you again, too, Lady Belle." When he took Belle's hand and pressed a kiss to the back of it, Adam snarled at his friend.

"Paw at your own date. Leave mine be."

Henry straightened at the threat, a wide, wicked smile claiming his face. "Your date, eh? And here I thought she was the housekeeper who transformed this crypt into a livable space."

"You're a housekeeper?" Henry's date asked, the corners of her mouth lifting with hope.

"I am," Belle said proudly, her chin lifting as Henry looked around at the vast difference in the castle since the last time he'd been over. "Belle. It's nice to meet you."

"Ella. This place is amazing." The blonde beauty with a heart-shaped face and delicate features blinked at Belle, her shyness keeping her tight to Henry's side.

"She's not the housekeeper," Adam argued, his brows lowering.

Belle turned her head to him, her lips pursed inquisitively. "I'm not?"

Adam huffed. "Well, I guess technically you are, but I don't like the way he said it."

Henry frowned. "And how did I say it?"

"Like she's... Stop doing this thing, and being your way. You've only been in the castle a minute, and it's already taxing." It wasn't until Belle touched the small of his back that Adam realized how caustic his words were. His shoulders slumped as his body angled toward her. "Maybe that was harsh."

Belle tilted her head up at him. "Maybe?"

"I think I might be nervous," Adam admitted.

Belle didn't scold him, but rubbed her hand in slow circles over the back of his hips, loosening his grip on his acerbic nature.

"Don't be nervous, old boy. I'm very handsome, but approachable. My PR people tell me so all the time." Henry didn't take offense, but offered Belle a wink. "This should be fun." He waggled his eyebrows at Ella to make her laugh.

Belle smiled at him, her hands clasped in front. "You're just as I remember you. Prince Charming, indeed."

"Yes, well, he farts every time he drinks beer, and he's a terrible driver," Adam groused.

"I was only joking, Adam. What use would I have with your date when I brought one of my own? This is my Ella."

The woman beside Henry was stunning. She had bright blue eyes and long, blonde lashes to match her wavy locks. While Henry looked as if he belonged with the rich and famous, his date's nervous expression looked like she was worried she might not belong in a setting like this. Though, she certainly looked the part. Her ballgown had a white bodice with a baby pink flowing skirt, boasting of expensive material that Ella wore like a model. There was one glaring problem – Ella was clutching a tissue and sneezed three times upon entry. Her eyes were lightly rimmed with pink, cluing Belle in to the fact that the woman wasn't quite recovered from a bad cold.

Belle smiled kindly at Ella. "Are you alright? I can make you some tea. Looks like you had an eventful week."

Ella's gaze locked in on Belle's with a hopefulness that someone understood that some things were too painful to examine up close. The woman didn't appear bothered by her cold, but seemed to have a greater cloud of doom behind her that wouldn't go away with a little over-the-counter medicine. "It was. I'm hoping to have fewer of those in the future. I'm fine, though. Thank you."

Though Belle didn't know the woman, she took a chance and stepped forward, foregoing a handshake and wrapping the stunned woman in a hug. "I hope that for you, too. I'm a nurse, if I can be of any help."

Ella's shock melted under Belle's sweetness, her chin resting on Belle's shoulder. There were a few beats where the girls exhaled their nerves without speaking of the things that were clawing at their insides. Finally, Ella pulled back with emotion sparkling in her eyes, but it refused to fully surface. "*Now* I'm glad I'm here. I think I was a little anxious before that," Ella admitted, her shoulders straightening.

Henry threw his arms in the air. "That's all it took? I could've hugged you."

Ella and Belle exchange a quiet smirk that bonded them quicker than either of them anticipated. Then Ella reached out her hand and shook Adam's with the hearty grip of the working class, and not the reserved featherlight touch of the upper-crust. "Amazing place you've got here. It's nice to meet you."

Belle shifted the red cloak Simone had made her,

moving the fur-lined cap back so it didn't tickle her neck. The heavy cloak concealed the dress she was to wear that night for dancing; she was too nervous to show it off. It was so fancy, so ornate. So very far above anything she could've afforded on her own. She kept the gown tucked inside the red velvet, hoping she could get away with wearing it the whole night.

Rory wanted in on the hugs and instant friendship the moment she stepped over the threshold. Though she was demure to the point of looking pale and frail, she greeted Belle with a hug and a kiss to both her cheeks. "I've so wanted to meet you. Anyone who can get Adam to..." She seemed to catch herself, and straightened, pulling out of the hug with a smile. "I'm so glad you're in his life, which means you're also in mine."

Belle let out a nervous breath. "Thank you." She shook Cordray's hand, noting his gloves. Though she knew Rory's husband was on the pill that muted his magic, he still wore black driving gloves just to keep his Lethal abilities in-check. "It's nice to meet you, sir. Congratulations on your wedding."

"Thanks." Cordray glanced around the foyer and whistled, scratching at his ebony forearm absentmindedly. "Wow. This is a far sight better than it was the last time I was here. It's like a whole different castle." He glanced over his shoulder twice, and then moved to the side, as if he was afraid someone might sneak up behind him. He shut and bolted the door, just in case.

Belle had read the paper and knew all about how Cordray Phillips had been abducted to keep him from waking Aurora Johnstone with true love's kiss. He'd been tortured, kept in isolation, and who knows what else by Malaura and her band of rogue Lethals. Though it had been almost a year, Belle wondered if a prisoner ever truly lost that dodgy, caged look after going through such trauma.

Adam took the rest of the coats from Belle and hung them on Thomas. "I hope you're hungry. Belle outdid herself."

Belle took the compliment with a slice of guilt, since she hadn't had a hand in preparing the night's dinner at all. Adam couldn't credit Chef Bouche, so Belle took the praise with a humble downward turn of her chin, making a mental note to pass along the kind words to the chef in the morning.

Rory's eyes were wide as she moved out of the foyer, her grand gray ballgown swishing behind her as she walked on her husband's arm toward the dining room. "I can't believe it. I mean, I've always known this place was stunning, but I guess I played down the details over the years. I barely remember the chandelier without all the cobwebs. I've been imagining it hot pink in my mind." She stared up at the elaborate fixture and shrugged. "I guess gold is better."

"You saw this place before Adam's curse?" Ella asked, causing Belle and Adam to stiffen. She drew to Adam's side, her arm looping through his as a sign of solidarity while the others walked ahead, listening to Henry and Rory tell the story of the last grand party that was held in the castle.

The four talked while Belle kept her steps measured next to Adam. "Please, Adam," she whispered. "Let me try to break your curse."

Adam patted her fingers that were latched to the crook of his elbow. "Not another word about it, Belle. I'm serious. Tonight, my curse doesn't exist. I don't want to be the beast. I just want to be the man in a tux who's lucky enough to have the most beautiful woman in the world on his arm."

Belle's frustration melted at the sweet compliment. "Thank you. But this conversation is not over."

He laughed through his nose. "That you think you're more stubborn than me is simply adorable." He smirked at her bristling. "That cloak is to wear outdoors, you know. Let me see your dress. Give a man something to rush through his meal for."

Belle shook her head, a slow smile spreading across her face. "Not a chance. It's too fancy. I feel like someone's going to think I stole it or something. Or worse, I'll spill something on it and Simone will murder me in my sleep."

Adam frowned down at her. "When will you understand that you deserve the finest things life has to offer?"

Belle shrugged, not noticing that the others had stopped talking, and were listening in on their hushed conversation. "When will you understand that the finer things mean nothing to me compared to you?"

Adam stroked the golden gloves that covered her hand. He'd specified to Simone that Belle should wear gloves, just in case Cordray forgot his. "Don't think I don't know what Simone is trying to do, dressing you in the red cloak. She's reminding us that there's hope. That after I turn, you'll remain with me. The girl in the red cloak, with her wolf by her side."

"You know I won't leave you. Stop breaking my heart with this kind of talk."

"It's only fair, since you've stolen mine."

At Rory's small intake of breath, Adam straightened, reminding himself that their conversation may not have been quiet enough to escape eavesdropping. It was the longest Henry had ever been silent.

When they entered the dining room, Belle was enraptured at the trouble the staff had gone to for the meal. The finest china had been broken out, polished and laid out with too many forks to indicate several courses to the meal. Lucien was standing in the center of the table, frozen, but able to take in every bit of conversation to dissect to the others later. Bosworth had set himself on the shelf in the corner, his face looking out at them so he didn't miss a detail. Belle inclined her head to them both as Adam escorted her to her place at the foot of the table.

Henry's eyes widened, and he glanced at Rory with barely contained glee when Adam pulled out Belle's chair for her, and slid it beneath her when she sat. They watched as he brushed her fingers before taking his place at the head of the table. He caught her gaze and winked, brushing a furious blush through her cheeks.

The salad course was served, and the six made polite chit-chat once Henry and Rory muscled through their utter shock.

"This place is magnificent in the fall," Henry told Ella as he ate. "Adam can actually enjoy his castle. You can explore the grounds and do whatever you like, unlike my palace, which has a full staff, guards, and far too many rules."

"It's beautiful," Ella agreed. "I bet cleaning it is a full-time job, though. Do you use one of those extenders on your duster for the ceilings? They're so much higher than a normal home." Then Ella clamped her mouth shut, as if she'd said something damning. Henry touched her arm, brushing his fingers across her palm to calm her nerves.

Belle shrugged. "Actually, the duster's got a double extender. Good eye." It was true. The castle did have one, but Vivienne did most of the areas she couldn't reach, so the extender hadn't been put to much use. "It's not so bad. Once I make my way through all the rooms, it'll just be upkeep, which is the usual dusting and sweeping and whatnot. I've already finished with the first floor."

"It's never looked so amazing," Rory offered with kind eyes. "You really outdid yourself. Henry mentioned that you're a nurse. Is that right?"

Belle nodded as she speared a tomato. "I was a house-keeper through nursing school. Then when I graduated, I did mostly in-home care. Adam's castle is a dream job."

When the doorbell chimed, Belle looked to Adam, who frowned. "Excuse me," he said as he stood. "I'm not sure I'm expecting anyone."

When he left the room, Cordray leaned toward Belle and talked with his fork. "Okay, what's Adam's deal? The last time I saw him, I had to electrocute him to keep him from attacking."

"That's not the whole truth, Cord. Jeez," Henry muttered. "We showed up with an unconscious Rory. Of course Adam flipped his lid. We handled the whole thing wrong."

"Still, did you see him push in her chair? Are you two..." Cordray made a crude gesture with his hands that Rory gasped at. She covered his fingers with hers and blurted out a string of apologies. "What? It's not like we all weren't thinking it. When was the last time you saw Adam so calm? He's doing something different, that's for sure."

Henry shook his head. "I'm trying to think back to the last time I saw him in anything other than pajamas. Did you finally get him to take his meds? We've been on him for years about it."

Belle took her time chewing the mushroom from her salad, hoping she could get away with not answering them at all. "I can't really discuss a patient's treatment with non-family members. Adam's doing great because he's a good man. He just needed a little push. He gets dressed every day now, and he's not as angry because there's less to be angry about." Belle hoped they would accept this as the whole truth.

Henry and Rory leaned in with a slight eagerness to their teasing tones. "You're sure there's no other reason he's done a complete one-eighty?" Henry asked, implying all sorts of things.

"You'll have to ask him about that." Belle kept her eyes on her plate, embarrassed that they could see her crush plain as day.

Henry whistled and then chuckled at Belle, pointing at her cheeks. "Look at that! She's blushing! Oh, there's definitely something there that wasn't there before. I see it. Deny it all you want, but I know Adam, and he's never played the role of the gentleman."

Belle straightened and tried to change the conversation. "So Ella, where are you from?"

"Out of town," she replied evasively.

"I'm from the West Village," Belle offered, knowing that her lowly zip code would soften the stigma that you had to be born with a fortune to be accepted around their table.

"I hear there's a fantastic ice cream shop there."

Belle nodded. "I'm glad you're here. You too, Rory. Adam's wonderful, but it's nice to have a couple of women in the castle. Brightens up the place." When Cordray and

Henry guffawed, feigning their affront, Belle smiled and amended, "You guys are lovely, too."

Henry shot Belle a sulky look. "Wouldn't hurt you to say it once in a while."

The five finished the salad course, and when Belle announced that she was going to bring out the soup course, Ella rose from her chair. "I'll help you."

"No," Henry ruled with sudden seriousness that was uncharacteristic on his usually playful features. "You are not the help here."

Belle raised her eyebrow, but said nothing to his odd statement. Ella's unpolished, short nails matched her own. She had the look of playing dress-up in her fine gown, with a quiet out-of-the-way demeanor that looked as though she was trying to fit in without raising any suspicion that she never would. When Ella made to help with serving dinner without being asked, Belle knew that Henry was dating a woman who was far below his station in life. The way he was attuned to her every movement, making concessions every time she shifted in her seat, told Belle that the prince was very taken with the sweet Ella.

Belle was giddy over the prospect of something incredible happening for Henry. He'd stuck by Adam for years when he'd been off the rails and lost in hermit-dom. That Henry was willing to risk the king's possible disapproval meant that Ella must be something special, and Belle reasoned that the prince deserved something special.

Belle served up the soup, still with no sign of Adam.

She wanted to excuse herself, but the lively conversation detailing Rory and Cordray's wedding was in full swing.

"Of course I was her Maid of Honor. Are you suggesting there's anyone more beautiful than me to strut down the aisle?" Henry said to Belle, tossing his imaginary locks over his shoulder. "Rory and Adam are my best friends. I would do anything for them."

When it was time to bring out the main course, Belle took a chance and jumped on the opportunity to talk to the girl in private, since Adam was till tending to the visitor. "Rory, would you help me in the kitchen?"

"Of course," she replied with a gracious smile.

"I can help, too," Ella offered.

Henry's smile fell and his jaw tightened. "No, you won't. For one night, Ella. Please. It's my turn to plan it all, and this is what I want."

"You want me to be unhelpful? You know that's not me."

"I want you to believe that you're good enough to sit at the table with me. I want you to know what it feels like to let other people be kind to you. Belle wants to be generous to us, so let her. Stay with me, Ella. Please."

Cordray shot his wife a look that was filled with a glimmer of sadness at things that might just be unfixable in Ella's interpretation of the world, to which Rory offered a bob of her head, and then went into the kitchen with Belle.

27

THE SERIOUS NATURE OF GIRLTALK

As soon as they were alone, Rory touched her forehead in confusion. "I don't know what's stranger – the fact that Adam's acting like a gentleman, or that Henry's finally seemed to have grown up. You and Ella both must have some deep-rooted magic in you." Rory commented as she leaned against the counter.

"If only it was as easy as murmuring a simple spell." She pulled a pan from the oven and set it on the stove, running her hand over the backsplash to let Chef Bouche know that just because he couldn't speak didn't mean she couldn't see him. "There's something about Ella that... I can't put my finger on it. Is she alright?" Belle's Pulse often imbibed her with a wave of Discernment without her meaning to call upon the gift.

"Ella was stuck in a rough situation, and she's in the tricky process of trying to get unstuck. But I think Henry's going to make it his business in life to ensure Ella never has to worry ever again. If anyone deserves a shot at that, it's her." Rory slapped her palms together and glanced around the kitchen. "What can I help with?"

"Honestly? I don't need help with dinner. I need to ask you for a favor." Belle didn't wait for a response beyond Rory's eyebrows lifting in surprise. "I was one of your scholarship students, you know. There's one granted to the West Village every year. Most people say it's a waste because nothing good comes from the West Village."

Rory straightened. "Nothing could be further from the truth. Every time we award that scholarship, it's the best decision the Johnstone Foundation makes. If you're born into rough circumstances, the people who rise to the top work that much harder. I didn't realize you were one of our scholarship recipients, but it makes sense. That you can get Adam to..." She shook her head, her eyes far away as if picturing a life long ago. "I'm amazed by you on a personal level. I can't imagine the giant you must be on an educational aspect."

Belle held Rory's gaze, a lump rising in her throat. "Thank you. You're kind of one of my heroes. All you've done for Avondale by the age of twenty-five? Most people don't make that much of an impact in their lifetime." Belle caught herself and waved her hand to get herself back on track, mildly flustered at the sincere compliment from the woman she revered. "But that's not what I meant to talk about. In my education, there was a gap that I was hoping to ask you about."

Rory quirked her eyebrow. "You want to ask me a question about magic? But I was a Deadpulse until this year."

Belle's eyebrows furrowed. "Just because your magic took longer to deliver doesn't mean you weren't a judicious student." She took in Rory's rolled back shoulders and the slightly mollified look in her eyes and wondered just how much condemnation the Chancellor's daughter threw at herself in self-loathing.

"Thank you. Not many people understand that. What's your question?"

"Your curse was countered by your uncle Remus. Remus Johnstone, correct?" Belle gripped the marble counter with tension enough to attempt to punish it.

Rory paused, blinking in confusion at the sudden shift in topic. "Yes."

"Adam seems to think that it only worked because Remus twisted the curse within the hour of Malaura doing her thing. Is that true?"

Rory frowned. "Well, there is a certain advantage to the curse being fresh, yes. It's more pliable when it's new. If it's had time to set in, it's far more difficult to bend, I would imagine, if not impossible. Why?"

Belle rolled her shoulders back, not caring if she sounded foolish. Though she knew Chef Bouche and Audra could hear her hairbrained scheme, Belle didn't back down. "Because I want to try my hand at breaking

Adam's curse. He's getting close to the transition, and I don't want him to turn. He's too important for the world to lose him. It's too harsh a punishment just because he was a brat after his parents died."

Rory gaped at Belle, the air going still around them. "Are you serious? You would give up half a decade of your life to save him?"

Belle nodded, unconcerned at the sacrifice. "I just need your uncle to show me how. I've been reading some of Adam's more obscure textbooks while he's been working, and I think I understand it well enough in theory, at least. It's just how they all come together that I'm having trouble understanding."

Rory's next words came out slowly. "And how does Adam feel about this?"

"He vetoed it, but he's wrong. Simple as that. If it's possible, it's happening. It's my life to do what I want with, and this is what I've decided."

Rory shook her head, her eyes wide with admiration. "I can see why you were chosen for the Foundation's scholarship. You're... I love seeing empowerment and determination in action. There's absolutely no more beautiful sight in the world." She crossed her arms as she thought through the secret plan. "How do you expect to get Adam's blood without raising suspicion? You realize taking his blood is part of the spell," she whispered, stepping closer to Belle. She frowned as she thought it through. "You'll need Adam's consent to get a sample of his blood. There's no way he'll let you do this. Had I been old enough to voice an opinion, I wouldn't have let Uncle Remus sacrifice himself for me like that."

"Well, Adam's not getting a choice, because he'll choose wrong. I want to save him. I just need your uncle's help. Please, Rory. You're his friend. I have to try!"

Rory touched her forehead, her eyes flicking from side to side as she processed the new information. "I suppose I can give you Uncle Remus' number. He can decide if Adam's worth saving, and if a counter-curse could even work this late in the game."

"Thank you," Belle breathed out in a gust.

Rory held up her hands. "Ho, no. Don't thank me. And if Adam asks, I didn't give you Uncle Remus' number, and we never had this conversation. My phone's in my purse. I'll text it to you later."

Though the woman looked on the frail side, and was far above Belle's station, Belle threw her arms around Rory, squeezing her tight. She made sure not to use her Pulse on Rory, so the Chancellor's daughter wouldn't get an extra shot of Discernment. If this was a bad idea, Belle didn't want to hear it.

Rory returned the hug the moment she overcame her surprise. "How is he holding up?"

"I don't know," Belle admitted. "He howled in his sleep last night. It's close. Too close, and this is the only way I can think of to stop it."

Rory chose her words carefully. "I've known Adam

since I was born. He's always been... difficult. I love him, of course, but how is it he's convinced someone like you to sacrifice so much for someone like him?"

Belle ran her tongue over her teeth, her hand resting on Chef Bouche. She pretended he was squeezing her fingers in support, and leaned on him as if he was more than an appliance. He was a person, and in that moment, she needed her friend to back her up. "Adam would do the same for me."

"Adam? Adam Fontaine? I admit, he seems different, but I can't picture him putting someone else's needs ahead of his own." Rory turned to leave, but paused on her way out. "If I hadn't seen the careful way he touches you, and the way he watches you when you're not looking, I'd say you were crazy to throw away so much for him. But seeing him smile at you? Maybe you're right. Maybe he's worth that kind of sacrifice." She placed her hand on the door. "But I don't think you'd advise anyone to risk their life on a 'maybe'. If done improperly, counter-curses can go very wrong."

When Rory exited the kitchen, Belle leaned against Chef Bouche, feeling a heaviness she couldn't shake. The stove came to life, the fixtures and knobs turning into eyes, nose and a mouth. "Do you think you can actually break the spell?"

Belle ran her fingers over the backsplash as if she was stroking his cheek. "I think I have to try."

AGENT MCNALLY

When Adam came into the kitchen, Belle had forgotten how dashing he looked in his tux and was taken aback all over again. "Is it wrong that I want you to wear that every day?"

Adam glanced down at himself, and then his eyes climbed back to her with a self-satisfied grin. "I'll wear it to bed tonight if I can just get a peek at your dress." He shook his head, remembering his reason for coming to find her in the first place. "It's the Department of Criminal Investigation agent I tipped off about Sheriff Gabe's illegal levies. I've given him the letters Gabe's sent you, but he wants a word with you before he goes in and unleashes government wrath. He's waiting for you in the receiving room. Shouldn't take more than a few minutes to get your statement."

Belle froze, but then came to herself, trying to hold her

head up. "Sure." Her hands felt suddenly clammy, so she took off her gloves and rested them atop the stool. She didn't want to talk to any authority figures, having lost her trust in the whole institution years ago. The last one she'd been too near had made unwelcome advances, and now stalked her.

She expected to face the agent alone, but leaned into Adam when his arm coiled around her hips. "You don't have to come. You have guests."

"They can wait. I'm not leaving you alone to drudge up all your painful memories. Besides, I know you don't trust law enforcement."

Belle balked at him. "I never said that."

"You didn't have to. I know you."

It was a simple statement, almost off the cuff, but the two stopped and stared at each other, mulling over the shift in their relationship. It had started out contentious, but now their bond so important to them both that they didn't like to be away from each other. Belle reached up and touched his lips. "You can't say things like that and not let me kiss you."

Longing that tangled with pain flared in Adam's green eyes as he took hold of her hand and pressed her palm to his cheek. "You shouldn't kiss me. I might cut you with my fangs. You know that. Did I tell you what happened when I tried to wake Rory? I sliced her lip."

Belle's heart yearned to share a kiss with Adam, but

she lowered her hand and continued walking with him through the hallways.

He escorted Belle into the receiving room, where the agent was already standing to greet her with a firm handshake. "Belle," he greeted her with a bob of his head. "I'm Agent McNally." He had a military haircut paired with a no-nonsense charcoal suit. His jerky movements communicated that he wasn't one for wasting time on rudimentary chit-chat, which Belle appreciated. "I just have a few questions for you."

The next twenty minutes passed with Belle seated on the settee next to Adam, his arm around her while she forced out the details of crimes she'd rather forget. She'd never told Adam all the ways Gabe had tormented her over the years. His hand never moved from hers as she confessed all the sordid elements that slowly chipped away at her smile.

The visit ended with another firm handshake, and a promise from Agent McNally that they had all the information they needed to move quickly and arrest Sheriff Aston.

"I thought you'd be relieved," Adam admitted after he escorted the agent out and locked the door. "He believed you, and he's moving on the information. An arrest is a great outcome, Belle."

"I know. I am relieved, I think. I'm too wary to get my hopes up. I've gone through this song and dance before, you know. The sheriff in the East Village didn't believe me, and even told Gabe that I was spreading rumors about him." Nervousness multiplied in her eyes as she looked at Adam, who was leaning against the heavy front door. "If all of that happens again, I can still stay here? If it turns out Agent McNally doesn't believe me, I can still stay with you?"

Adam softened, disappointed that the agent wasn't ringing him a minute after his departure to confirm that he had the foul sheriff in custody. "Don't you know? You can stay with me forever." He opened his arms to her, exhaling with his eyes closed when her body folded into his invitation. "Stay right here. Exactly here. In my home, and in my arms. My rescuer in red."

Belle's lashes fluttered as his claws teased the small curls at the base of her head. Her hand moved to his chest, stroking over the heart that only she knew was still there. "I couldn't rescue myself," she admitted, giving small voice to the defeat that gnawed at her insides. "I tried so hard to get anyone to help, but no one would go up against Gabe. You're the one who rescued me."

"Oh, Belle. You rescued me long ago. I'm still trying to catch up." His other hand moved up and down slowly over her spine, while his chin rested atop her head. His facial hair was already growing back in, but he hoped he still looked more man than beast. "The first day you came here was the first time I'd breathed in years."

It was Henry who interrupted their moment of vulnerability, causing them to pull apart with matching frowns at the distance between them. "Hello, children. Anything I can assist with out here? I couldn't help but overhear, mostly because I was snooping and eavesdropping. Why's a Department of Criminal Investigation Agent stopping by?"

Adam straightened and brushed a few errant pieces of fur from his sleeves. "I'm trying to put an end to the levies Sheriff Aston is burdening the people with in the West Village."

"Are you, now? The West Village, eh? Isn't that where you're from, Belle?" Henry's knowing smile caused Adam to look away and move toward the dining room, but he didn't get farther than a foot from Belle, needing to feel her close to him.

"It is. I'm sorry we kept you waiting. I'll go grab the next course."

"I'll help," Adam offered.

Henry's grin stood no chance at fading in the presence of the gentleness Adam exuded. It could only emanate from a man in love. "Take your time, kids."

29

POLITICS OVER COCKTAILS

The dinner was seven courses, and by the end everyone was too full to dance. Cocktails were served in the parlor on the second floor, where there were high glass walls for them to view the castle grounds. There was still that heavy peppering of snow falling, but from inside the castle, everything seemed peaceful, if not whimsical.

They talked about the silly and the serious, even venturing into polite debates that Henry never shied away from. "Then the budget for that isn't large enough," Cordray challenged Henry, who sat in his light gray suit with his legs crossed, and his hands clasped over his knee.

Henry wore a calm smile of veiled delight at the challenge. "The government already allots a sizeable sum towards further development of the pill. How do you think it came about in the first place? Progress will evolve as time, and funds, come."

Cordray leaned forward on his chair next to his wife's. "You can't honestly tell me you believe the pill is fine as is. It mutes our Lethal abilities, yes, but it also leaves us without any magic. I should be able to perform charms first graders can." At this, he froze, his shoulders tightening as if he'd said something offensive.

It was widely known that the Chancellor's daughter had been a DeadPulse for most of her life, and had never been able to perform the simplest of spells.

Belle had never seen anyone with such composure. Rory's posture was straight, but not rigid – like a ballerina's. The social scale of praise or bane was largely linked to one's ability to perform spells. Everyone knew that Rory had been given a seat on the council only because of her birthright, and not because the magical community saw her as being of any use to the world at large. When she was awakened by Cordray's kiss, her Pulse finally surfaced, bringing Peace to everyone she chose to dole out her gift upon.

Cordray lowered his chin and leaned his head toward hers. "I'm sorry, Rory. I didn't mean it like that."

Rory reached over and rested her hand atop his ebony wrist. "Go on."

Henry reached over to mimic the familiar gesture with Ella, but as soon as his hand touched down on hers, she retracted it, looking away as if she was trying to remain invisible. Henry's jaw tightened, but he focused on Cordray. "I agree with you. The pill has a long way to go. However, I fail to see how the nuances are the government's responsibility. There are privately-funded labs that are well-equipped to handle such things."

"Yes, and they'll do what they like with it when they make their alterations. They could force us to register, collect all sorts of data on us that can be used against us if the wrong person is at the helm. They could enact all kinds of rules and make hoops for us to jump through. Then the government will have to intervene during a much bigger crisis than a simple discussion of budgetary allocations."

Henry gave Cordray his best bedroom eyes. "I love when you say things like 'budgetary allocations' to me. Rory, is that the kind of saucy bedroom talk he uses on you? Because I must say, it's working its charm on me right now."

Cordray shot Henry an eye-roll to show that their friendship was good-natured enough to weather a little political tension. "It sounds like you're saying you feel you're owed a vote in how it's distributed, and that matters like this shouldn't be left to the council."

"I think that's a right everyone should have, since Lethals affect the entire community."

Henry nodded. "That's exactly why anything beyond the standard pill can't be government-funded, and why the vote can't be public. The nuances to a new pill will have qualities that not everyone will agree on. The throne will take the heat, and the fall, if anything should go wrong in the experimentation phase. When everything surrounding the welfare of Lethals is a fight the whole way, the government can only involve itself in the most basic of ways. That's why we're considering allowing privately-funded companies permission to attempt improvements to the pill."

Cordray shifted next to his wife. "They'll make a mess of things. It's too important a tool to be played with by just anybody. So much could go wrong."

"Agreed, which is why the basic pill that's available now will still be available to anyone who wants it. If they want the variant, though, which might come with perks and unknown cons, we're leaning toward outsourcing that social responsibility to private companies. We simple don't have the funds for such things."

"Listen to what you're saying. You're expecting private companies to behave responsibly. What obligation do they have to us?"

Henry let out a sigh and ran his hand over his face. "You're thinking of you, which is good. My father and I have to think of the entire country, and the faith in the throne that needs to stay steady. The risks far outweigh the benefits right now." Henry glanced up at the ceiling. "Is there never a camera around when I have a valid point? What's in this whiskey, Adam? It's making me brilliant."

"Arsenic," Adam replied glibly, bored that this was

what his friends considered interesting after-dinner conversation.

Henry smacked his lips. "Delightful."

Cordray sat back with a frown. "You didn't win."

Henry shrugged. "It'll be put to a vote, which I don't expect will be an easy road. However, that's the way of democracy under an aristocracy. Sometimes you love me and want to jump into bed with me, but other times you can't understand a thing I do. Actually, I think that's how it goes with any type of government. Would it help if I took my shirt off? People usually like me better that way."

Rory covered her mouth to stem her amusement, knowing Henry's politics better than most. He played the charming cutie to the public, but he was well-educated on the issues.

Cordray frowned as he downed the rest of his drink. "So the government is washing its hands of the pill because there might be a fallout?"

"Of course not. We offer the basic pill with all of its advantages and dysfunctions, and we always will. It's free of charge, since the Lethals who take it are helping keep the world safer by muting their abilities." He uncrossed his legs and leaned forward. "Rory, don't let him make me the bad guy."

Belle could tell Rory was caught in a tight spot. She had to think and vote as both the future Chancellor of Avondale, and as a wife of a Lethal. "Our duty is to give the world a chance, not bend over backwards so we can levitate teacups. The details after that are just that – details."

Henry's eyes widened as Cordray harrumphed at his wife. "Oh! Watch this. I haven't done this with a drink in me in ages." Then he let go of his crystal high-ball glass, drawing Belle's eyes as it floated in the air. He clapped for himself, clearly amused as he elbowed Ella. "Are you seeing this? I'm incredible! With a drink and a half in me, at that!"

"Show-off," Cordray grumbled, but that seemed to be the end of his frustration.

Ella snatched his glass out of the air and downed the fiery liquid, shrugging at his affront. "See that? Henry missed out on the important thing – the whiskey – because he was focused on magic. He just doesn't want the same thing to happen with the pill issue."

Henry threw his hands up. "Did that truly need a visual demonstration?"

"Nope," Ella replied with a light snigger.

Henry smirked at her gall, and then shifted next to her, hooking his arm around her shoulders to bring her tighter to his side as he turned back to Cordray's issue. "Millions of dollars and possible negative side effects to you aren't worth that parlor trick, Cord."

With a little levity and whiskey in her, Ella's tongue loosened. "Your taxes should go to things that are desperately needed. Life and death come before innovations for mere comfort."

Cordray scoffed and looked over at Adam. "Where do you land on the issue?"

Adam shrugged. "I only know your last name because it's now Rory's. You can imagine how much less I care about your magical dysfunctions."

Belle scoffed at Adam and batted at his arm. "Be nice."

Adam raised an eyebrow at Belle. "Was that not nice? Sorry. Cordray Phillips, do accept my apologies. It's just that as I'm about to turn into a wolf and join the Lupine in less than a week's time, I find it hard to care about things that don't matter."

"Adam!" Rory was out of her chair, as if that might make the time he had left slow down. Belle could see Rory mentally tabulating her calendar and realizing that Adam's thirtieth birthday was sooner than she remembered. Her hand went over her mouth to stifle the horrified gasp. "I'm a terrible friend!"

Henry turned his chin away and closed his eyes. Ella reached out to the prince, her hand atop his thigh to comfort him over the impending loss of his friend.

Belle's heart raced at mention of the ticking clock. Adam knew the date was just around the corner, and he'd made a joke about it.

Adam regretted his blasé retort when he saw Belle's eyes start to mist over – half-sad and half-angry. "Belle, I'm sorry," he mumbled. "I shouldn't have said it like that. I'm sure I have more time than that."

It was a lie, and they both knew it. But he'd lied for her comfort, which was a true pledge of loyalty between them.

No one spoke for nearly a minute; there were too many things to say. When Belle leaned in, Adam pressed his forehead to hers, and their eyes closed in unison. "Lie to me," she begged. "Tell me we have years."

Adam couldn't give her the lie she needed, so he remained quiet. He breathed in and out, dragging the scent of her skin into his lungs as if he meant to memorize every detail of what made her the only woman to captivate him so thoroughly. He wanted to savor her and be near her so the storm inside of him might have a chance at calming.

Belle shivered, since her seat was nearest the window. Without a thought, Adam removed his tuxedo jacket and wrapped it around her slight shoulders, swallowing her frame in the black material that had been tailored for his broader body. He rubbed warmth into her shoulders.

"Thank you. You didn't have to do that."

"You'll never again be cold in my presence. That was my promise to you."

Adam didn't break his focus from Belle until he heard the sound of Rory sniffling. He turned his head to quirk his eyebrow at his friend, wondering what he'd missed. Whenever Belle spoke, his entire focus was on her. Whole worlds could've collided, and he wouldn't have batted an eye if Belle was near.

"I'm sorry," Rory said, dabbing at her eyes with her

handkerchief. "It's just that I've never seen you like this. I mean, our whole lives you've been... And now to hear you say such beautiful things to someone? I can't tell if I'm crying because I'm proud of you, or because this whole thing is breaking my heart." She leaned into Cordray, who wrapped his arm around her and kissed her temple.

Adam cast a conspiratorial eyeroll at Henry, but the prince was equally stunned, his mouth popped open in shock at the sweetness he no doubt never expected to witness in his oldest friend.

Adam wiped his palms off on his pants and stood. "Quit staring. I had to watch the two of you fawn over who knows how many dates through the years. This is a drop in the bucket." He extended his hand to Belle. "I believe you promised me a dance."

Belle ignored the stares and the tears. She ignored for the moment her plans to give up five years of her life for the possibility of a couple decades with him. She ignored her nerves, her fears, and the millions of questions that might never have an answer. She took his hand and rose, knowing this first dance just might be their last.

30

A BALL FOR SIX

The ballroom was decadent with the overhead lights turned on, but when Lucien had taken the liberty of lighting candles in all one hundred of the candelabras on the walls the atmosphere was dripping with the heat of a night to remember. Music sounded through speakers that had been built into the gold-covered walls. They were trimmed with ornately etched blue baseboards and flying buttresses, giving everything the look of wealth passed down from an age where the finer elements actually meant something. The swirled etchings on the crown moldings two stories above made Belle feel as if she'd been transported to a time when the nobles convened for no reason other than to entertain themselves with how decadent they could shine after the sun went down. There was a stage in the corner, but for this night, the ghosts of musicians past filled the ballroom with melodies that made Belle's heart race.

Rory's tears didn't stop at the sight, speechless as she took her husband's hand at the top of the red-carpeted steps and slowly moved down with him. She looked every bit the royal she'd been raised to be – dainty yet somehow strong in the way she carried herself with her chin raised. She showed off her tears to the ballroom without shame, letting the violin music fill the nearly empty ballroom as if announcing her presence to thousands.

Henry, who had been so self-assured, stumbled over the edge of the carpet when he walked with Ella on his arm. It was as if the very act of being together in front of witnesses was a scandal, though Belle couldn't understand why. Ella was perfectly kind. If she was below his station, Belle couldn't imagine how much something so silly could really matter when there were so many more harrowing things going on.

Henry led Ella to the top of the steps and bowed, swallowing thickly as he righted himself. There was a nervousness to his jerky movements, as if he was the one beneath her, having to prove himself. Ella glanced around and, confirming that there was no one besides the six of them there, curtsied, and then took Henry's hand. Belle watched Ella's fingers sliding into Henry's and thought that it was the way their hands were meant to be, and every day their fingers had been separate was a crime they'd been forced to endure. The way they walked was devoid of pretention, though they were both dressed lavishly. Their hands swung when they moved together, and Belle thought they looked like two teenagers with a secret.

When Henry and Ella began to dance together a few yards from Rory and Cordray, there was a simplicity to their steps. The waltz was without the dips and turns that might compromise the eye contact they were locked in, which seemed steeped in too many unspoken emotions.

Belle shrugged out of Adam's tuxedo jacket and handed it back to him. She sucked in her stomach as she mentally prepared herself for taking off her red cloak. Adam buttoned his jacket, but his fingers forgot their purpose when Belle's cloak slid from her shoulders and was folded over the railing of the second-story balcony.

The gold material was unlike anything Adam had ever seen. It looked like actual buried treasure, but had the softness of silk to it. The skirt was large enough to capture everyone's eyes, but not so wide that Adam couldn't see himself twirling her around on the marble dance floor just to show off her smile. The corset clung to her slender frame, with the top leaving enough exposed to give a man something to rally for, but not so much as to give her away completely. She was missing her gloves, but that only meant he got to feel the slight tremble in her fingers that put his own nerves at ease. If she was anxious, he would be a calming presence to her, as she'd done for him so many times.

Belle was beautiful in scrubs, even covered in years-old

dust. On this night, however, she left him with only his vulnerability intact. "You are perfect," Adam breathed with a note of rapture to his low voice. "It was worth inviting them over and sitting through seven courses of the longest dinner of my life to see you in this."

Belle looked down, smoothing out the many layers that each added some new detail to the look of the dress – decadent, off-center, lovely, laced, crimped, draped – all of it without apology for the spectacle the dress made.

Belle curtseyed, fanning out the skirt and dropping the edges when she stood upright again. "I'm nervous," she admitted.

Before Adam could stop himself, "I'm yours," tumbled out of his mouth.

Belle's demure smile teased her features, brushing a sweetness across her cheeks that drew him in. "And I'm yours."

Adam's heart was racing as he bowed to her, and then looped her hand through the crook of his arm, calming slightly when he felt her side brush his. If she was near, life was manageable. Love was possible.

He led her down the steps and onto the polished floor, where Cordray was spinning Rory around with a flourish that made Belle anxious. She chewed on her lower lip before her confession rushed out. "So here's the thing; I don't know how to dance like that."

Adam's shoulders rolled back with a confidence that

came from years of good breeding. "My parents used to send me to the palace to take lessons with Henry. The king and queen thought that if I was there, Henry wouldn't seduce his instructors."

"And how did that work out?"

"It didn't. But I did learn a lot about dancing that year while Henry learned the art of French kissing." He gripped Belle's hand and held it out to the side, his other one touching on the small of her back with a firm command that her body would move to his rhythm. He swayed slowly at first, taking in her cagey glances and stiff movements. "Do you trust me?"

Belle frowned up at him. "That's a heck of a question to ask me right now. I have no idea what I'm doing!"

Adam sniggered at her fretting. Ella moved gracefully only because Henry chose simple steps. Rory had been born into a life filled with ballrooms and men in line to ask for her hand to take a trip around the dance floor, and Cordray had apparently been educated on what it meant to marry into such an elite class.

Adam pressed his chest to Belle's, smirking as her eyes widened. He leaned in to speak, but the curve of her ear distracted him. Though he wouldn't let her kiss his mouth, his lips acted on impulse and brushed against her earlobe, his body strung like a live wire as his hips moved with hers. Her body always teased him, covered as she kept herself. Now that her cleavage was on display, parts of him awakened, yearning for her in ways he couldn't bring himself to apologize for.

Belle's throaty gasp and fluttering lashes at his sensual caress would've embarrassed her, were not the other two couples lost in their own lovestruck waltzes. She gripped his bicep and hand as her knees trembled. "Okay, you can't do that if you want me to actually get through an entire song."

"Why not?" he asked, his lips teasing her earlobe again. This time, he drew it into his mouth and sucked, as if she was the most delicious candy treat.

"Oh," she moaned, biting down on her lower lip. "It feels too good."

"Don't you want to feel good?" He indulged her in a slow twirl, but then brought her firmly to his front. "Belle?" His whisper was just low enough to provoke a shiver out of her. "I want to Pulse you. Just a little bit." He recalled the last time he'd Pulsed a woman in this very ballroom. He didn't even remember her name, but he could visualize the naïve eye candy up on the stage, taking off her top and throwing it into the crowd. His parents' reputation of upper-class civility had long since been shattered after he'd buried them and indulged in a stretch of debauchery.

Adam didn't want Belle to lose herself so completely. In truth, he hadn't meant for the girl on the stage to go so far. He never knew how close to the edge people were until he Pulsed them. For some, his gift made them come out of their shell so they could have face-to-face conversations, when before they'd been previously lost to their introverted tendencies. For others, they were already contemplating a wilder life, and needed the smallest of urgings to fling themselves over the edge. Still, the man he was now knew he should've asked if she wanted his Pulse. He wouldn't push Belle forward unless it was what she wanted.

Belle looked up at him curiously. "I think I'll leave that up to you. Take some of my Discernment, and then decide." Her hand snaked up his bicep and slid over to palm his heart to give him a direct hit. "I trust you."

A flood of caution over pulsing her too hard mingled with an overwhelming urge to kiss her as Belle's Pulse battled with his desires. Oh, how he wanted to taste her lips. There were so many things he wanted to do with Belle, and it even seemed as if the wave of Discernment was giving him the green light. Still, he hesitated. If he scraped her with his fangs, she might not look at him with that adoring expression he'd grown to crave.

His right hand palmed her tailbone and Pulsed a low-level dose through her to strip away a thin layer of her inhibitions. He frowned down at her, his mouth drawing to the side. "I must be losing my touch. It didn't work. You were supposed to be tearing off my clothes and making love to me on the floor by now."

"Ha, ha."

Belle's limbs loosened just enough to where he could

start to turn them as they danced, his chest beaming with pride that she trusted him so. She wasn't adept in the art enough to waltz, but he didn't need her to be. He needed her to be in his arms and to trust him enough to let go, which finally, was beginning to happen.

When she laughed as he dipped her near the end of one of the livelier songs, the sound of her unfettered joy was pure honey coating his heart, bringing him to life again and again. An hour passed, and then another, but Adam never tired of watching Belle truly let go. She'd cared for her father, then protected herself against a cruel sheriff. Now her life was to look after him. He wanted so much more for her – a lifetime of dancing.

Adam brought them to a slow side-to-side as he pondered the unselfish nature of her life.

She tilted her head up at him, a look of mild concern tainting her smile. "You went somewhere in your head just now. What's wrong?"

"After I turn, I want you to travel."

"Travel? Do you need me to deliver something?"

He let out a groan of frustration. "You can't even be hypothetically selfish. No. Travel for fun. I'll put aside some money. Anywhere you want to go."

Belle pondered the offer before outright rejecting it. "Why don't we go somewhere together before you turn? We could pack up and go up north."

Adam rolled his eyes. "I meant travel that involves a

plane ticket and faking your way through a foreign language."

Belle stilled, bringing their dance to a halt. "Okay. Then let's go. You and me. Let's leave tomorrow."

Adam's mouth was tight in a firm line. "You know I can't do that. Imagine the looks we would get. A beautiful woman and her beast."

Belle wanted to argue. Oh, she had buckets of things to say to counter his harsh assessment of himself. But she kept them locked inside, because she knew her valid points wouldn't do any good. "I want so many memories with you that I forget the details. I want to look back at our life and see a series of blurry smiles."

Adam's chin lowered at the one thing he couldn't give her. "Belle, I wish I..." Then he stopped, gripping her hand with sudden excitement. "Maybe I *can* give you memories of us."

Belle's eyebrows lifted with anticipation. "Please, Adam. Let's go."

Adam glanced around and saw only Henry and Ella still dancing. "Where did Rory and Cordray go?"

Henry smirked at his friend, finally tearing his eyes from Elle's lovely face. "They're probably making babies in her bedroom upstairs. If they conceive on your mattress, you could probably get a pretty penny for it on auction."

Adam blanched, and then led Belle up the stairs toward the second floor. "Stay as long as you like, but you're on your own for the rest of the night. Don't fall for his charms, Ella. Make him beg for it!"

"Where are we going?" Belle laughed as she ran up the steps with Adam, her hand in his and her other fist bunched in her skirts to lift the silk so she didn't trip.

Adam's reply came with a hearty, barking laugh of his own. "Vacation!"

31

SEEING THE WORLD

The parlor on the second floor where they'd enjoyed their cocktails looked different at night. Lucien came in and lit a few dozen candles for them, dimming the overhead lights for optimum romance. Adam sat Belle on the ornate light blue velvet couch and dashed back out of the room, returning a few minutes later with a cedar display case. His breathless look of achievement made Belle giggle at how worked up he was over something he still hadn't explained.

"I can give you a glimpse of us anywhere in the world. I can give you a glimpse of anything, really." He sat down beside her and carefully unlatched the chest, which was about the size of a briefcase.

Belle's nose crinkled in confusion when she peered inside, finding something unexpected resting on the red cushiony fabric. "I thought you didn't like mirrors in the house."

Adam's lips tightened. "I don't, but this one is special. Do you remember the story of Queen Snow?"

"Of course. The princess who overthrew her mother, Queen Vanessa, who tried to kill her because her daughter was prettier than she was." Belle shook her head. "What a stupid reason to try to get someone killed. Glad it backfired. Queen Snow had a good reign after that."

"That's right. Every morning, Queen Vanessa would look into her magic mirror and say..."

"'Mirror, Mirror on the wall. Who is fairest of them all?'"

"Exactly. Queen Vanessa was Henry's great-grandmother. When she was overthrown, Queen Snow auctioned off a bunch of her stuff. The magic mirror was broken into parts and sold off. My grandfather bought one of the pieces." He looked down into the mirror with excitement, seeing Belle's flabbergast. "If you ask it, this mirror can show you anything you like, even if it hasn't happened yet."

Belle was afraid to touch the briefcase, for fear of shattering the national treasure. "Are you serious? I can't believe you have this! You hate mirrors!"

"Ah, but I love obscure bits of history." Then he cleared his throat, looking into the mirror with Belle. "Mirror, Mirror in my case, show us Belle and me in Helensville."

Belle's mouth fell open as she peered into the glass

with Adam's furry cheek pressed to hers. For a moment, it was a normal mirror, and Belle saw what they looked like side-by-side. He was hairy, and his fangs weren't all that easy to hide, but there they were – Beauty and her Beast.

Adam shut his eyes against the image and burrowed his nose into her cheek, as if that might erase the grand divide that was obvious upon first glance.

"I like the look of us," Belle whispered.

Before Adam could protest, Belle's gasp drew his eyes back to the mirror. The solid reflection began to flex, as if it was suddenly under water. The rippling surface twisted the background of the light blue and brass-bedecked walls and swirled them until new bits of color emerged, and the spinning slowed. As if the paint of a portrait had been flung with centrifugal force and then somehow perpetrated into a new design, Belle began to see shapes that kept molding themselves into more recognizable forms. "That's me!"

"And there I am," Adam said with disdain. "I'm sure the Helenvillians will be pointing with horror at any moment."

"Show me the Broadsmith Tower," she said, breathless as the mirror focused in, transposing their bodies just underneath the iron webs that made up the enormous landmark. Belle reached forward to touch it, but retracted, remembering that it wasn't real. "The Arc of Julien," she whispered, and the image shifted again.

Over and over she switched the pictures, seeing the

two of them at all the places she'd read about and had desperately wanted to visit. The two sat there for hours, long after the sun went down, traveling the world from the comfort of their couch. There they were, smiling at all the great wonders, holding hands and brushing their noses against each other's with unmasked affection.

"Where next?" Adam asked, transfixed at the sight. After he'd muscled past the knee-jerk revulsion at his own appearance, he slowly began to look forward to seeing them in the next setting she chose, and the next.

"Somewhere completely exotic," she replied with a wild tint to her voice.

"Mount Carenina? You should really go in person. The sights are only half the fun there. I'm putting it on the list."

"Not overseas." She leaned in and said to the mirror, "Show me my papa's home in the West Village. Show me what it looks like right now." Before the image shifted, she glanced over at Adam with a slight hint of embarrassment. "My house isn't nice like this, but I like it. I miss Papa. I think if you two had met under different circumstances, maybe you would've liked each other."

"I've spoken to him a few times on the phone. We get along just fine."

Belle quirked her eyebrow at him. "When have you been talking to my papa?"

Adam smirked at her. "He worries about you, especially after your car accident in the snow. I've been calling him every few days to let him know you're alright, and make sure Sheriff Aston's not being a problem. Helps us both sleep better at night."

Belle's mouth fell open, a tender expression tenting her eyebrows. "You call my papa just to make sure he can sleep better? You check up on him just to be kind?"

Adam narrowed his eyes at her. "Don't say it like that. Obviously I do it for you. If anything happened to him, I know you would be destroyed."

Belle's gaze fell to his lips. "Why am I never allowed to kiss you?"

Adam swallowed hard, remembering his promise not to be selfish with her. How he wanted to kiss her, but he knew the possibility of cutting her soft lips was too great a risk. Instead, he traced her plump lower lip with his thumb, telling himself touching it was just as good as tasting. "Because it matters if I hurt you. I regret many things, but if I did that? It would be the crime I couldn't stomach."

It was several beats of longing before either of them looked away. Belle turned her attention back to the mirror, but as the picture focused, their shared looks of desire vanished. "What... This isn't right." She shifted on the couch, her eyebrows pinched together in consternation at the sight. It was her home, but not. The eviction notice was back up, and a squad car was parked rudely on the front lawn, a tire toppling the hedge near the mailbox. "Mirror, Mirror, please show me my home in the West Village as you see it tonight."

The image didn't change, but Belle's heartrate did. Her

breath began to syncopate when the front door opened, and none other than Sheriff Aston himself marched out with her elderly father, holding him by the scruff of his nightshirt. He had bare feet and wore his long johns, calling out for help to neighbors who were too frightened of the cops to do anything but shut their drapes and pretend they weren't home.

Adam was on his feet, resting the briefcase on the floor. He pulled out his phone and barked into the receiver. "When you assured me you would deal with Sheriff Aston as soon as you took Belle's statement, did you mean that metaphorically or literally? Because the old man is literally being dragged out of his home by that criminal right now, barefoot in the dead of night."

The agent's groggy voice only angered Adam. He shouted into the phone about not wanting to hear excuses about the team assembling to make the arrest first thing in the morning.

Belle was already out the door. She ran to her bedroom, stripping off the gown as quick as she could and flinging open the doors to the wardrobe. "Simone, I need travelling clothes. It's freezing out, and I need to run now!"

Simone came to life and asked all sorts of questions, but beyond producing a pair of gray slacks, socks and a lavender sweater for Belle, there wasn't another exchange between the two. Belle threw on boots Adam had bought her and ran out the door, tears marring her vision, but not slowing her down.

"Belle, wait! Agent McNally is sending his people to your house right now to retrieve your father."

She fisted the door's handle, but paused her escape. "Not good enough! I should never have left him alone this long! I didn't check on him! I only called once a day, Adam! What kind of a terrible daughter am I?"

"The wonderful kind. I don't want you going after him. It's snowing out, and the sheriff isn't going to see you and let you go. He's only taking your father to draw you out!"

"You don't think I know that? I have to try, Adam. I can't let him..." She screamed into her hand, terrified at all the sordid options that ran through her head.

Belle's cell phone rang from her pocket, and she answered it after she saw it was her father on the Caller ID. "Papa, thank goodness. Are you alright?"

Belle's blood ran cold when Gabe's voice answered her. "Well, well. It's good to hear such concern. I was beginning to think you didn't care for me at all. Though I prefer you call me 'Daddy'."

"Gabe? Leave my father alone!" She gripped Adam's arm, balling her toes inside her boots as her muscles all tightened at once.

Adam ripped the phone from her hand, put the call on speaker and punched a few buttons, showing her that the call was now being recorded, courtesy of the features installed in her higher security-enabled phone from his company.

"Of course, of course. I'm sure it's just one of the paperwork mix-ups. Those happen all the time. Kind of like the photo I saw of you cozying up to the beast."

Belle shook her head. "What photo? What are you blabbering about? Give me back my father!"

"The photo they printed in the paper. It's not every day the beast leaves his cave. In fact, an unnamed witness is coming forward tonight, pressing charges against your new boyfriend."

"Pressing charges against Adam for what?"

As if on cue, the doorbell rang. "It seems he was out earlier this evening and exposed himself to some children. Of course, he was so hairy, they could barely tell what it was, but it's the principle of the matter, you see. Flashing is against the law."

Adam answered the door and ushered in two police-men, a grim look on his face as he waved for Belle to exit the area. Belle could barely keep up, but she gripped the phone with a desperate edge to her voice. "You know Adam's innocent. Leave him out of this. What do you want with my father?"

"Isn't it obvious? You, Belle. I've always wanted you. The one girl too pure and wholesome for me. The only girl to ever turn me down."

"Fine. I'll meet with you. Release my father, and I'll come have coffee with you at Lou's Diner."

"Not good enough. See, I think your father is worth more than a cup of coffee. I think he's worth an early honeymoon, during which you're very, very grateful."

Bile rose in Belle's throat. She closed her eyes and clenched her fist as she uttered the words she hated herself for. "Tell me where to meet you. Even trade – my papa for me."

Gabe chuckled, and the low sound made her skin crawl. "That's my good, good girl. I'll meet you at your home."

"Papa would murder you if you took me under his roof. I'll meet you at the station, and my father will be sitting comfortably at my house long before then."

"Whatever you say, tasty cakes."

Belle blanched, but steeled herself as she hung up the phone. She moved as if in a daze to the foyer, where Adam was arguing with the policemen. "I was in my house all night. I haven't left my home in days. There's my statement."

"Can anyone corroborate that?"

"I can," Belle offered, her mouth dry.

The policeman on the right cast her a baleful look. "I'm sorry, but if someone other than his girlfriend could vouch for him, that would be helpful."

Belle recoiled at the acerbic blow-off. She'd been so isolated in the castle, but now wondered what that article could've possibly said.

"How about the Prince of Avondale?" Henry said, rounding the corner. His gray suit was slightly wrinkled, and his blond hair was sticking up in the back, but he was no less commanding.

The policemen both visibly shrank, knowing that they didn't have a cause to arrest Adam that could trump the crowned prince's testimony.

Quietly, Belle said to Adam, "Gabe's agreed to let Papa go. He's dropping him back at the house."

"Good." Adam reached out and gripped Belle's hand. "This might take a while. Grab the mirror, take your car and go pick up your dad the second Gabe's gone. Bring your father here. He can stay as long as he likes."

Belle pressed her forehead to his shoulder, marveling at the unselfish generosity that rolled off him without a second thought. "Thank you."

"If it's not safe to go in and get him, hang back and wait for Agent McNally. Promise me."

Belle looked up at him as her heart broke in her chest at the thought of leaving Adam. She wished she could put his mind at ease, but knew his mind was most tranquil when she was there to chase his darkness and demons away. She lifted herself up onto her toes and blessed his cheek with a kiss, trying to communicate all the things he was to her. "I'll be back soon."

Only she knew she wouldn't be back. If Gabe had his way, she would never come back.

A RACE TO BELLE'S FATHER

Belle's mad dash down the freeway was taken at fifteen miles over the speed limit, but the car barely registered the additional exercise. Adam demanded only the best, and the car he'd given her was no exception. The roads had been plowed and salted, making for a speedy race to her father. The briefcase was open on the seat next to her, and she glanced at it to make sure Gabe was keeping his word.

All the things she'd never said to her father passed through her mind in quick succession, each one more important than the last. She knew he'd heard her say that she loved him, but did he understand all the ways she adored him for who he was and all he'd done in raising her by himself? Belle bit down on her lower lip, gripping the leather steering wheel as the barrage of things she wished she'd thanked him for beat her conscience, stripping away her solace until she was a trembling mess.

Glancing at the mirror, Belle cringed when she saw Gabe throw her father into the drunk tank at the precinct. Her heart hammered with betrayal when she realized Gabe never had any intention of following through on his end.

To be fair, neither had she.

"Show me my home," she said to the mirror. In a flash, the castle came into view, warming her heart despite the cold. The mirror was never wrong, and this was no exception. Somewhere between fear of the unknown and adoration of the man she now knew more than most, the castle had become her home – in legal deed and in her heart. "I meant my papa's home in the West Village."

The mirror flashed again, revealing to Belle three squad cars parked in front of her father's house. She snarled when she recognized the squat and portly Deputy LeFeu. They were waiting for her, staked outside her address to bring her in on whatever grounds they felt like making up, in case she did what she was trying to do – rescue her father and ditch Gabe.

"Show me Sheriff Aston," she commanded the mirror. Errantly, she was disappointed in the wicked Queen Vanessa who'd ruled before Queen Snow. To have such a powerful tool and waste its use by asking who was the fairest to look at? Belle shook her head, grateful she didn't have to live under the rule of a queen like that. King

Hubert was fair, and though not everyone agreed with his policies one hundred percent of the time, Belle knew such a thing was a pipedream, and that the kingdom was fortunate to have someone so wise and balanced as King Hubert.

The mirror showed Gabe checking his gun and thumbing his handcuffs as he leaned on his desk. His widow's peak was always exaggerated, but he ran his fingers through the coif a few times to make his full head of black hair stand even higher. His biceps were large, complimented by the fact that he wore a uniform that was meant for men far smaller than him. It looked as if he was so muscular that he was bulging out of his button-down. It worked on some of the women in town who were impressed by things like badges and bodybuilders, but that had never been Belle. At least, not when the badge was so tarnished, and the bodybuilder used his stature for selfish gain. He yelled something over his shoulder to her father, who shuddered – either from the residual cold aching his bare feet, or from the disgusting venom always dripping from Gabe's words.

Belle picked up her phone and dialed Agent McNally, not bothering with greetings when he picked up. "Sheriff Aston's got my father locked in the drunk tank. He told me he won't let him go unless I..."

"Belle? Hold tight. We're assembling a team now."

"He won't let my father go unless I trade myself for him!"

"You'll do no such thing. Go back to the castle or tell me where you are, and I'll have one of my people pick you up."

Belle ended the call and bit down on her bottom lip, taking a second to think her half-a-plan through. She'd gotten away from Gabe the first time he'd attacked her because she Pulsed an exorbitant amount of Discernment into him and had her hunting knife stashed in her glovebox. She didn't count on getting the same advantage this time. She saw him playing with his government-issued handcuffs and shuddered. She guessed the handcuffs might be used this time to keep her from being able to touch him, thus inflicting a shred of conscience into his evil heart.

She pulled the car over onto the shoulder, thinking through her actions. In every book and movie, the girl who goes into the villain's den with no backup rarely comes out alive. She shook her head, knowing she had to consider the long game, and not just her father's momentary escape. If she died, there would be no one to come to her father's aid the next time Gabe acted on his baser instincts.

As if knowing she was thinking about not coming to him, her father's name on her Caller ID lit up her phone. She rolled her shoulders back, a wave of the bigger picture washing through her, gifting her with a dose of clarity. She answered with shaking fingers, hoping her voice sounded in-control. "You'd think I'd be shocked that you're not a man of your word, but I've always known what a snake you are. Let my papa out."

"I returned your father to your home, as promised."

"He's in your drunk tank, Gabe. I'm not an idiot." Though for a few moments, she'd veered toward the unwise choice of going in alone. She breathed through her impulses and tried to center herself. "And what a nice collection of cop cars in front of my house. Almost as lovely as a bouquet of roses, but I know you've never been a traditionalist."

Gabe paused, but then let loose his wicked laugh. "I'll let your father go when I see you walk through the precinct doors."

"You took him without his shoes, and the entire precinct is empty. Who's going to drive my father home, dummy?"

She glanced at the shard of mirror, pursing her lips defiantly when she watched him look around wildly for signs of her. "Where are you, Belle? Are you watching me?"

"I'm everywhere," she chuckled darkly, relishing the feeling of finally being the one with a little bit of power that made him squirm with discomfort. "Do you really think there's a move you make that I'm not seeing right now?"

Gabe glanced up at a security camera with frustration, pulled over a chair and taped a piece of paper over it to block the view.

"Guess again, buttercup. You try to get me kicked out of my house, then you go after my papa, dragging him out of bed in the middle of the night?" She tsked him as if he was a misbehaving schoolboy. "I'm disappointed in you."

"You won't be so haughty after I get through with you."

"That's the thing. You can't get to me anymore. I think your time on the force is up, Gabe."

She watched his face sour. "It's the beast who's in your bed, isn't it. Does he know how to satisfy you like I can?"

Belle scoffed. "Adam is kind and gentle. He's generous, and doesn't leave me wanting for a single thing." She let her words hang with all the intimate implications, just to drive Gabe crazy. "And forgive me, but what girl was lying through her teeth when she told you that you could ever satisfy a woman?"

"Do you love him? You honestly love this monster? That's who you've become? Mrs. Beast?"

Indignation rose in her whenever Adam was attacked. He'd been through enough, and didn't have much time left. "He's not a monster, Gabe. You are!"

There was a deadly quiet, and then Belle watched him finger his keys and march out the door. "Maybe it's time we see who the bigger man is, then. If he's talked himself out of the arrest I still haven't seen come through the wire, then maybe it's time he was taken out. Funny thing about people attacking officers. We can defend ourselves, you know. When a civilian dies in an altercation with an offi-cer, it's a boatload of paperwork, but I'm willing to wade through the extra headache for you. It's time your beast was put down."

Belle's blood felt cold in her veins. "Leave Adam out of this!"

"In fact, I think this is a matter that needs the backup of the entire force. I can't believe the beast has been holding you in his castle against your will."

"He has not! Gabe, stop this!"

"Of course he has. It's what everyone will believe, because there's no other logical explanation that would make you stay with him over coming back to me!"

"Leave him alone!"

But Gabe didn't back down. The last thing Belle heard before Gabe hung up was his squad car roaring to life.

HELP FROM REMUS JOHNSTONE

*B*elle was in tears when she called Adam, leaving him a voicemail. She checked the presets, but Henry's number wasn't in there. Rory's text with her Uncle's phone number had come through, so she called the Chancellor's daughter as the bushes on the side of the freeway passed by in a haze. Belle cursed when Rory didn't pick up, and tossed the phone into the case with the mirror. Too many emotions ran through her, clouding her thoughts until finally, one lucid idea rose to the surface.

Her fretful angst began to clear by the smallest of degrees as a plan started to form in her mind. Once the decision was made, her fingers lost their tremble and her mind latched onto the last vestige of hope with a steadiness that relaxed her shoulders and lifted her chin. Her breathing evened out to an almost meditative state as she reached for the phone again, calling the number Rory had texted her.

Rousing the great Remus Johnstone in the middle of the night was the only thing Belle would apologize for. With command in her voice she usually only reserved for troubled patients, Belle laid out her plan to the widely-respected stranger. The Chancellor's brother was well-known and beloved for his sacrifice that saved his niece. Belle knew he had a handle on magic she would never dream of understanding. Yet as the conversation trudged on, he took the time to explain the ins and outs of the complicated spell he'd used to protect the treasured Aurora Johnstone.

"Then I was right. I have everything I need, except a few drops of his blood."

Remus' voice was huskier than she'd heard him sound in his interviews on TV, due to the late nature of the call. "Very good. Now repeat the charm to me. Pronunciation matters, so don't hold back on your diction. Each syllable must be overly crisp."

Belle obeyed, opening her mouth wider than usual to get in the entire spell that Remus had set to the tune of "Happy Birthday" to get her to remember.

"That's exactly right. Do it just like that. But Belle, you have to understand that there are certain advantages to performing a counter-curse when the curse is fresh. It's more pliable within the first hour, and hardens into place over time. To undo a curse that's nearly a decade old?" His pause was telling that he was working up to something grave. "I'm not sure it's possible to break it at this point, but I won't begrudge you a try. If you follow my instructions to the letter, you won't accidentally harm yourself in the transaction, other than the five years that will come off your life if it actually works, which is no small thing to consider."

"Thank you. Thank you so much. I have to try."

"Love," Remus said with a firmness to his voice. "Malaura never understood love, so her curses aren't set up to maneuver it. If you love Adam, hold that firmly in your heart. It's your strongest weapon against her evil."

Belle nodded, though she knew he couldn't see her on the phone. "That shouldn't be a problem. I wouldn't be calling you right now if I didn't love him."

Remus' next piece came out slowly, as if he didn't want to put a voice to the worries that were beginning to surface. "Are you certain Adam is worth the sacrifice?"

"Was Rory worth yours?"

"Family always is. I don't regret what I did to save her. But make no mistake, five years taken off your life is a hard pill to swallow. I want you to really think this through."

Belle's lips tightened in a firm line as she pictured herself without Adam's teasing, without his barking laughter, and without the gentle way he reached for her. She thought back to her life in the West Village, which seemed ages ago. Before Adam had come into her life, there was duty, imagination, and familial love, but not much more. Adam had enhanced all of those things, and gave her so much beyond that. She couldn't stomach her life without their quiet reading time by the fire. She couldn't fathom going to sleep without him to curl her body around. "It's worth it. He would be wasted with the Lupine."

"Then you know what to do. You'll know he's down to only days left when he starts howling in his sleep," Remus offered sagely.

Belle nearly veered off the road. "He howled in his sleep earlier this week, Remus!"

There was a telling silence, and then the gavel of doom. "Then do it now, if it's not already too late. And Belle?"

"Yes?"

"I want you to keep an open mind. The laws of magic aren't as concrete as we assume. It's often our assumptions that life can only be what it is that keep us from achieving our goals."

Belle drew in a steadying breath. "Are you saying that you think this could work?"

"I'm saying it matters that you *know* it will work. For the next twenty-four hours, concentrate on breaking the rules. It's your only chance to make this happen."

It was with no thought of her own safety that she sped down the freeway, and again it was an unselfish desire that drove her feet to pound through the snow to the house and fling open the front door. "Adam! Adam, I'm home!"

"Belle, we were so worried!" Thomas fretted, closing the door behind her.

"Bolt that shut!" she ordered, realizing that Henry, Ella, Rory, Cordray and the police must've left, if the household was coming back to life. "In fact, barricade it." When Thomas backed up in confusion, she pointed to the front door, ignoring the rest of the staff that ambled in to greet her. "I'm serious, Thomas. The sheriff is on his way to try and arrest Adam. When Adam resists, Gabe is going to shoot him and call it self-defense. But if he can't get in, that's one point for us. All the doors, all the windows, lock them now." She glanced around at the staff, who were gaping at her with fear in their eyes. "Hurry!"

Bosworth took charge and clapped his hands. "Alright, troops! You two take the second floor, you never know if they can climb up the trellises. You four, secure the doors and lock all the windows on the first floor, then report back to me. I'll see what we can do about reinforcing the glass." Then he puffed out his chest and shouted, "If this will be our final hour, then we'll go into the next phase intact." His voice rose further, warbling slightly with emotion that caused Belle's heart to swell. "They will not break us!"

For all his usual bravado, Bosworth was built for taking control in dire situations like this. Belle appreciated him anew, and bent down to speak directly to him, once the staff scattered to their posts. "Where's Adam?"

"He's in the West wing, milady. You shouldn't disturb him."

Belle ignored the warning as she stood. She ran for the stairs, but paused on the third step. "Bosworth, what did you mean, your 'final hour'?"

Bosworth met her eyes and saluted her slowly with a grave look on his face. "The last petal will fall before the sun rises. Then Adam will turn into a wolf, and we will remain inanimate household objects forever."

Belle gripped the railing as a noise of angst and terror escaped her lips. "No!" She turned and bolted up the steps, taking them two at a time as her heart raced.

She knew she wasn't allowed in the West wing, but she didn't care about the rules anymore. She didn't care if he yelled, or if the world knew she was sharing sheets with her boss. She cared about Adam, and needed to see his face.

"Adam!" she shouted when she threw open the doors to his study. She glanced around wildly, but didn't see him anywhere.

Panicking, she screamed loud enough for her voice to carry through the entire wing. "Adam!"

She heard a commotion from his bedroom and bolted down the hall. She ran into the messy room she'd only been in once before, unsurprised to find it in the same state of disarray.

Sitting at the desk where the rose was floating in the glass vase, there was Adam, a highball of whiskey in his fist. He turned to face her, light rising in his red-rimmed eyes when he took in the sight of her filling his doorway. "Belle? You came back?"

"Of course I did! Why didn't you tell me how little time there actually was? I thought we had more." She tried to hold back her tears, but when her feet started to move her toward him, a few slid down her cheeks. She arrested the glass from his hand, noting how feeble his grip was. "You're drunk."

He took in her face as if she was an angel, come to escort him into his next phase of existence. "You came back for me."

"Adam, listen carefully. There's not much time. Gabe's on his way, and he's going to try and arrest you. He's counting on you resisting, so he can murder you and call it self-defense." When no shred of indignation rose up in him, Belle's shoulders deflated. "You're not getting a word of this, huh."

"You're the lady of the house," he said with a slowness to his cadence. He reached for her hand and pulled her down to sit on his thick thigh.

Belle softened as she took in the sadness that was obvious, and etched in deep beneath his full, furry beard. "Oh, honey. I don't want you hurting like this."

"It always hurts," he admitted. "But I don't feel it so much when you're here. Stay," he rasped, touching his nose to her shoulder so he could inhale a deep drag of her natural scent.

"Of course, I'll stay with you." With tears in her eyes, Belle stretched out her arm and felt around on the desk for the letter opener that lie in the mishmash of papers. She wrapped her arms around him and thumbed the sharp end, hoping he wouldn't even feel the prick.

The commotion downstairs made her stiffen, and she knew they had only a minute together before it all broke loose. It was too much to ask the household objects to lock down the castle, trinkets as they were. Adam hadn't enacted the various security measures, so all there was to hold the madness at bay were a few deadbolts. The staff were no match for a corrupt police force, and their boss was three sheets to the wind.

Belle turned Adam's chin so he could look into her eyes. "You should've told me the last petal was about to fall. Now, hold still. This might pinch a little bit."

"What?"

"It's your turn to trust me," she said softly to him, kissing his cheek before she jabbed the letter opener half an inch into the firm muscle of his forearm.

His sharp intake of breath told her that he wasn't completely without his senses. "What was that?"

"It's my turn to protect you. Do you trust me?"

"Trust?" Adam repeated with a frown as he tilted his head at her. "Love, Belle. I love you."

More tears fell, though she knew this wasn't the time. She nodded and touched the wound, gathering up a few drops of his blood and touching them to her tongue. "Then let me do this for you."

"Do what?"

Belle closed her eyes and pressed her forehead to his, tasting the rust of his blood on her tongue. She savored the flavor of him, but didn't swallow. Remus had instructed her that she had to get through the entire incantation before she swallowed, which would seal the counter-curse. Her heart pounded as she began the soft tune of "Happy Birthday", using the words that were a string of Latin and Greek in hopes that she could keep him a little while longer.

Adam shook his head, confused, but trying to hold onto the moment as best he could. "No, Belle. No. You can't do this. I won't let you give up five years of your life for mine! It won't work anyway!"

Belle ignored him and soldiered on through the song, gripping his collar when he tried to slide her off his leg.

She was only halfway through the verse when the door burst open.

"Belle! Get away from the beast!" Gabe ordered in a booming voice.

Adam's head jerked over to the source of the disturbance, his lips pulling back to reveal his fangs. He snarled at Gabe, standing slowly and moving Belle behind him to shield her. "Get out."

"Now, now. I don't think civilians get to make demands

of officers. Stand down, or I'll be forced to draw my weapon."

Adam's fists clenched, his neck straining forward as he opened his mouth to tell Gabe once again to get lost. But instead of a sharp retort, a frightening howl erupted from somewhere deep in his diaphragm, shaking the windows and rattling Belle's teeth.

Belle held onto Adam's hips from behind, hugging him through the beginning of the transformation that frightened them both.

His bravado cast aside, Gabe let out a whimper of distress. "Is it really happening? Right now?

"Go, Gabe!" Belle shouted, furious that an interruption from the man she hated might make her too late to save the man she loved.

Gabe found enough pieces of foolhardy candor to puff out his chest and extend his arm to her from the doorway. "Come with me, Belle! He's going to turn, and when he does, he'll attack you!"

"He won't hurt me; Adam loves me! I won't leave him!"

Adam dropped down onto all fours, his hair thickening and spreading out to cover his hands completely. The chestnut fur seemed to blow as if a breeze was bending it, spreading the follicles down his legs and over his feet.

Belle sank to her knees and wrapped her arms around his ribs, promising him over and over that it wasn't too late, and that she would find a way to fix this.

The safety cocking back from the firearm was the one sound that snapped Adam back to the present. He growled at the intruder, who was now being joined by his colleagues in crime. He leaned back on his haunches like a slingshot ready to launch, and then lunged forward with a roar.

Everything blurred in Belle's vision when multiple shots fired. Fury formed a tornado in her gut, and everything in her swirled with a vengeance that made her teeth vibrate. Though she knew she couldn't wrestle Gabe's gun from her vantage point across the room, she clung to Remus' sage advice to view the laws of magic as breakable.

All the noise of the chaos floated away, leaving her with a shell-shocked sensation of somehow rising above the cacophony. Her hand lifted, and with an anger she couldn't put a cap on, she summoned the nearest cop's gun right out of his hand.

In school as a girl, she'd learned the basics – how to use her Pulse, how to levitate objects, how to slightly alter their color, and innocuous things of that nature. It was the elite that could rip an object from a person's hand. Some of her professors hadn't even been able to perform such a task.

The gun didn't come all the way to her, but it leapt out of its owner's grip and flopped on the floor.

That was all the encouragement she needed to give herself over to Remus' words of wisdom. At once, she believed in the impossible with all her heart, and refused to look on Adam's plight as something that wasn't mendable.

Belle summoned the gun again, and this time the object slid to her unfettered, laying at her feet like an obedient pet.

When her gaze climbed to the fray that was partially in the room and partially out in the hall, she gasped. More shocking than the handful of downed cops that were all bleeding out on the hardwood floor was the antique clock that hopped atop one of the men and stabbed him through with a kitchen knife.

"Bosworth?" she called, though she couldn't hear her own voice. Too many shots rang out. Too many men cussed out of both fear and pain. Belle didn't understand how the curse was beginning to crumble, allowing the staff to animate in front of outsiders, but she took the advantage without questioning it. She charged forward with nothing but a letter opener in her fist and jammed it through the jugular of one of the crooked cops who'd tried to take away everything that was precious to her. She fought without reservation or conscience, throwing her oath of "do no harm" out the window. Not one of them had stood up to the sheriff, so Belle didn't hold back in her tirade to rid the intruders from castle. The magic mirror had dubbed it as her home, and she defended it as such.

Vivienne flew in, using her handle to jab the men in the eyes, cackling with abandon that she was freed from her constrictions enough to fight for her home.

Lucien's usually joyful laugh turned wicked as he blew into his thumbs to turn his candles up to full blast. Fire shot out three feet in the air, lighting a few of their polyester uniforms ablaze.

The fight was mostly out in the hall now, except for Adam, who dragged Gabe back into the bedroom, his deadly claws sinking into the meat of the sheriff's shoulder. He was hunched, his nose elongating and looking more like a wolf's than a man's. His legs were furrier, but still human, so Belle held onto hope as she ran toward them.

Adam was limping, a trail of blood coming from his right leg, but his gaze burned with determination to finish off the man who'd stalked the woman he loved. If his last human moments were spent ridding the world of Sheriff Aston's evil, it would be counted as a victory.

34

THE FINAL BATTLE

Gabe Aston's blood-soaked fingers were shaking as he cocked his gun, shouting in agony as he twisted in Adam's fanged grip to aim his weapon at the beast.

"No!" Belle screamed, reaching him just before the shot went off. She kicked his hands, and the bullet missed its mark as the gun fell from Gabe's grip. The bullet shattered the tall glass door that led to the balcony, introducing a gust of freezing air to the castle.

Belle didn't have time to shudder at the cold; she wanted Gabe finished.

Adam was just as determined to defend the lady of the house to the death. He dragged Gabe over the glass, cutting his own hands in the process as he heaved the sheriff out onto the stone balcony. There were two gargoyles perched on either end of the terrace, each staring out at the world, silently asking it how everything had spun so out of control.

Belle watched as Adam dropped his grip on Gabe, wound up and let his fist fly across Gabe's dimpled jaw over and over again. The punishment was unforgiving, and meant to be a wound the crooked sheriff wouldn't easily recover from.

Belle stiffened, and Adam paused his second punch when they heard a band of wolves calling out in the night.

"It's time," he growled to Belle, falling back to sit on his butt, exhausted.

Belle kicked Gabe in the temple with her boot on her way over to Adam, falling down at her love's side. "No! No! I won't let this happen!"

"It's too late." He clutched his chest and screwed up his face, letting out a roar as he fell backward, lying supine on the balcony. His torso twisted violently, and his legs kicked out as they prepared to change into those of a wolf. Belle tried to hold eye contact, but the pain of the transition made his words come out choked as his lashes fluttered. "At least I got to see you one last time."

Belle's hands fluttered over his chest, her vision clouding as tears fell down on his shirt. "This isn't how this ends! I can fix all of it!"

She didn't expect Gabe to stumble around her, nor for him to have the wherewithal to clutch a shard of glass with steadiness enough to ram it into Adam's side. He stood with a weary triumph at Adam's guttural howl, but stumbled under the weight of the many blows he'd sustained.

Fury flooded Belle from head to toe. She was tired of the constant bullying by Gabe, and even the wolves who came by to howl at night and remind Adam of his doom. For all the weaponry and shattered glass strewn about, Belle didn't bother with any of it. She leapt over Adam's body with a cry that resounded from the very depths of her soul. It wasn't a call for help or even mercy. It was a thunderous pronouncement that she would endure the tyranny no more.

It was as simple as a push to his chest, but that was all it took. Gabe screamed as he toppled over the railing on the stone balcony, managing to catch himself on the ledge. The howls from the Lupine below widened his eyes in fear. "Belle! Belle! Help me up!"

Belle glared down at him, her resolve feeling colder than the snow that cascaded around her. "Beg me, tasty cakes." Then before he could get in another word, Belle kicked at his fingers, releasing him from the ledge.

Gabe fell three stories, landing with an unnatural thud on the frozen earth. He didn't move – couldn't move – as the Lupine closed in on the fresh kill they hadn't had to work for. One of them howled up at her in thanks while the others made quick work of tearing flesh from bone.

35

ADAM'S TRANSITION

Belle staggered back, falling down on her butt as the shock of the horrible deeds she was capable of rocked her core beliefs about how to be a good person in the world. The snow drifted without hurry, unperturbed that Belle had once held certain truths in high regard, but now had forsaken even the most basic rules.

She'd killed a man and fed his body to the wolves. Belle was frozen in her shock, wondering how it was she'd fallen so far from the woman she'd dreamed she'd become when she was just a girl.

Adam's ragged breathing snapped her back to herself, and she turned to crawl to his side. "It's okay. I'm here. You're safe now because we're together."

"I should've kissed you," he choked out, a tear sliding

down his face that was slowly mutating, the fur on his cheeks thickening and moving in closer to his eyes.

Though his fangs were long and frightening now, Belle longed to taste his lips. There were so many things she owed to Adam, and the gratitude swelled inside of her, making her wish for lifetimes of memories with him.

"I love you," she whispered, combing her fingers through his hair, and lifting his head slightly.

She laid him back when his body started to tremble to the pitch of almost a seizure. Dread coursed through her when she realized how little time there was left – if any. Even if the counter-curse wouldn't work because he was mid-transition, she had to try.

"Go, Belle. I don't want you to see this!" Adam growled through the pain as his legs began to jerk. The bones cracked to re-form into something far less human, ripping a fresh howl from Adam's throat.

Belle gathered up a smear of blood from his side and painted it on her tongue. Leaning over his body, she covered him in a hug so he knew that no matter what, he wouldn't be alone. She didn't let go as he yelled into her bosom. She didn't let go when he gripped her hard, gritting his teeth through the agony as his bones continued to break.

She didn't let go as she started to chant the spell Remus had taught her. Though she was scared, she kept her words even and her diction overly crisp, willing the love she had for Adam to be enough to break something as uncrushable as a decade-old curse. Malaura's magic was strong, but Belle knew the love she had for Adam was stronger. Remus had explained that Malaura never understood love, so her curses weren't set up to counter it.

The transition seemed to slow while she uttered the ancient words, coming to a halt when she worked through the last sentence with a shout of determination. She nearly screamed her frustration before she reached the end.

It was then that she noticed the smallest movement that held the greatest impact. Inside the glass case on the desk in the center of the study, the final petal drifted off the stem, landing with great irrevocability as she shouted the last syllable into the night. She made sure she kept her love for Adam in the forefront of her mind, keeping an image of him laughing at one of her jokes locked tight in her heart.

She expected... something. Lightning striking perhaps. Rainbows and moonbeams coming from his skin to signify that yes, love did save the day, and their connection could conquer all.

But nothing happened. Adam was unconscious in her arms, motionless and stuck mid-transformation. His mouth was partially elongated, and his legs were still human, but bent and broken in dreadful angles. His fur was thick now, and covered his entire body. His claws were long and sharp to match his fangs.

Belle looked up, taking in the empty study. The cops

had fled when the trinkets came to life and began talking and attacking, but she only just noticed the silence that meant the fight was over. She heard the wolves munching below, but as her hearing began to come back to her, she listened in for other sounds.

"Lucien?" she called quietly through her tears. "Audra?"

She could see the candelabra and the teapot sitting in the study on the floor, but they didn't come to life to speak to her. They were trinkets – useless objects that brought no life or laughter to the castle. She would've given anything to hear Bosworth's bravado, but the one time she wished he would speak for hours, he remained utterly silent.

Belle held Adam in her arms, checking his heartrate with shaking fingers and coming up empty. Death could've been caused by anything, really. The gunshot wound to his shoulder, the glass stabbed into his side, the mess of the brawl, or the agony of his broken bones that marked the transition he hadn't made it through.

Belle swallowed the last of his blood that had coated her tongue, holding him to her chest as her tears peppered his motionless face. She touched her trembling lips to his, wishing more than anything that their first kiss wasn't also their last. Then she whispered the resounding truth of her heart. "I love you."

Belle wept for all she'd lost, holding him tight to her breast as the snow slowly floated down around them.

Then there was silence. A complete and utter nothing that floated down and blanketed the castle with her heartbreak. The quietness in the castle was quite the opposite of the war that had broken out on her insides, mourning, crying and wailing in her heart for the loss she knew she would never survive.

She couldn't let go of him, motionless though he was. Part of him had belonged to her, and even now, she refused to give up her hold on all that they were to each other.

The wind warned her of the cold night that might never leave her now, but she paid the iciness no mind. The cold inside her chest felt set in deep, taking up residence where the glow from Adam's warmth should've been.

A breath broke the void, shaking Belle's very existence. Fear and wonder crackled through her when Adam's lips parted with purpose, as if he meant to say something. She cried out in shock when Adam's chest began to move on its own.

She paid no attention to the boots she heard tromping up down the hallway. She saw only Adam, felt only his body as real heat began to spread through his core.

When his eyes opened, Belle nearly fainted. "Adam? Adam?" she called his name, slapping his cheek, and then combing her fingers through the fur that had taken over the area.

"Get back!" came a loud voice from inside the study. It

wasn't until solid arms pulled her away from balcony that she fully grasped someone else was in the castle.

Prince Henry righted her and stumbled several feet back, bringing her into the bedroom just as beams of light shot out from Adam's chest, erupting a silent cry from his mouth that shook Belle to her very core.

36

MAGIC AT WORK

*P*rince Henry held tight to Belle amid the destroyed bedroom, while a man she didn't immediately recognize stood in front of them like a shield, his arms extended. "What happened?" Henry shouted as the castle walls started to shake.

"I performed the counter-curse, but Adam died before I could finish. Then he came back to life! Let me go, Henry! Adam needs me!"

"Stay back," ordered the mid-forties man in front of them. He wore gray slacks and a pink dress shirt, his black hair cropped in a clean, modern cut. "Adam's body needs space to figure out what it's going to do."

When the man turned his head to the side, Belle finally recognized him from photos in the paper. It was the great Remus Johnstone, in the flesh. He was the only one who'd been able to successfully pull off the counter-curse before – Malaura's student coming out to storm the master.

Belle was astonished he'd come to see it all play out. Remus' arms were raised toward Adam, and he began to mutter a string of Latin that Belle could only pick out bits and pieces of.

Pure light emanated from Adam as his body lifted and turned, so that he was vertical in the air. It was as if Remus was making him levitate – a thing that was far beyond a person's abilities. At most, Belle had seen someone at a traveling show that came to her school levitate a bowling ball. It was so impressive, the entire school cheered the accomplishment. To levitate a whole person, much less someone as large as Adam, was an impossibility Belle couldn't wrap her mind around. She began to understand Remus' advice about ignoring the traditional rules of magic.

A harsh breeze that seemed to exist only around his body whipped in a swirl. The concentrated wind grew at an alarming velocity. It blew his fur so hard that a peppering of hair ripped off his skin and was caught up in the growing tornado that was rapidly gaining momentum.

Henry let out a noise of distress when Adam shouted through the pain of his bones going through yet more breaking, his body contorting midair. Adam's eyes weren't closed due to unconsciousness, but instead scrunched in agony, his mouth open through his distress.

Belle wanted to get to him, to ease his pain somehow,

but as the tornado encased the man she loved, she knew this was lightyears beyond her level of study. All the schooling she'd undergone for both nursing and magic felt like a joke as she drank in things she'd never before witnessed, or even heard of.

Wolves were howling below, some scattering and leaving the fresh kill behind at the sight of the tornado. In the backdrop, far enough away from the scene to be part of it, Belle's gaze caught on a flash of red. Her eyes widened at the sight of the woman in the red cape.

The woman seemed to say a great many things without even opening her mouth as she took in Adam's agony. Next to her was the enormous pure white wolf, who was almost invisible, surrounded by snow as he was. Her hand rested atop his head, not to pet him, but as if to unite herself with him as they studied the rare bit of magic.

Belle held tight to Henry, whose fingers were digging deep into her ribs. He'd started out holding her back from the chaos, but now it was him who needed someone to hold him through his best friend's pain.

Belle watched Adam as his body started to slowly turn as if on a spit, moving in conjunction with Remus' rotating hand motions. Adam's fur flung off in chunks, carried away by the wind, who seemed to know what it was doing. Nature had a plan for Adam, but Belle was still teetering on the edge of betting whether nature would be kind or cruel.

Remus' arm reached behind him so he could tug Belle

forward. "This is your magic at work, Belle. Hold your hands out and repeat after me."

Belle found herself standing in between Remus' outstretched arms, her back pressed to his chest. He was one of the elite – the Chancellor's brother whose extensive understanding of magic saved Rory. He had a seat on the council and was the successful CFO of the Foundation that had granted Belle her scholarship.

Belle swallowed hard and tried to make-believe she belonged on the playground with the big kids, swinging for the homerun as if she knew what she was doing.

Belle held her head high, extended her arms to press against the inside of Remus' reach so he could guide her. She held her love for Adam tight in her breast as she repeated the string of syllables as crisply as she could manage. Without meaning to, the last few words welled up inside of her and came out with a ferocious punch that echoed out across the castle grounds, as if the words had been waiting for her to set them free. "Caritas est fortior!"

Belle felt suddenly weak with a sensation of carbonation popping over her skin and fizzling in her esophagus until it bubbled and snapped in her chest. Her left knee buckled, but she didn't fall.

Remus was silent for a few beats, and then let out a gust of relief when light shot out of Adam's body like a beam of hope. The inches of fur that made Adam look like the beast he'd feared he would become dropped from his skin completely, whipping away, due to the kindness of the tornado.

Remus' voice was tense, but relieved. "That was brilliant, Miss Belle. You did it."

Belle shook her head, confused at the storm that was brewing in her belly as the carbonation in her chest moved downward. A fierce battle waged inside of her, begging to be unleashed. "There's something more!" she told Remus, not holding back the uncertainty and fear in her voice.

Remus paused, but then moved his hand to her abdomen, palming her stomach as if to feel for the source of her magical dilemma. "Let it out," he urged her, pressing into her stomach to encourage the last vestiges of the spell to birth from her – creating what textbooks had never captured. It was the next evolution of magic, and Remus was prudent enough to see the miracle for what it was. "Open your mouth and unleash it all!"

Belle didn't have time to give in to her fright, but listened to the words of her impromptu professor. The voice that erupted from her didn't sound like her own, but carried with it a baritone quality that almost made her shut her mouth. She closed her eyes and trusted her instinct that the universe wanted good things for the magic that danced about in the world. She trusted her intuition, though she had no explanation for the hunch.

Finally, she trusted in the love she had for Adam – that it was stronger than any curse Malaura could've dreamed up. Belle's head tilted back, and to the sky she shouted, "Et cum hoc mundo liberari a malo!"

A gust of something pure and new erupted from Belle's lips and shot out into the air toward Adam, leaving her limp in Remus' arms.

The lavender glittering cloud that emanated from her seemed to operate outside of nature, ignoring the tornado as if it was a hyperactive puppy that could be brushed aside. The whirlwind slowly died down, lowering Adam to the stone balcony like a lover carrying its weary mate to bed. The wind returned to a slight winter's breeze, giving the lavender cloud space to dissipate and spread out into the world, infiltrating the air with something entirely other.

A smattering of the lavender puff remained, hovering over Adam's flaccid, supine body like a blanket. After a few beats, the glittery cloud sank into Adam's skin, mending abrasions and setting his crooked legs straight again – only this time, without the agony of rebreaking his bones.

Remus hadn't seen Adam's true face without the fur and slight mutations in a decade, but suddenly there he was – the boy who'd come over to play with Rory and Henry, aged passed the young man who'd lost his way when his parents died without nature's permission.

Remus hoisted Belle up in his arms like a bride and carried her over the rubble, making sure the glass had been blown away by the tornado before he laid her body next to Adam's. He leaned over and tested Adam's heartrate, pressed his ear to Adam's stomach, and then listened to Belle's, taking mental notes to explain the uncharted magic, and predict any possible ramifications.

Belle remained still, too stunned to speak. She was the perfect patient while Remus poked and prodded them both, jotting things down on the paper that Henry brought him upon request.

Prince Henry knelt at Adam's side, willing his oldest friend to open his eyes. Adam's heart was beating, but he was locked in a deep sleep.

"It's the same as Rory." Henry swallowed hard as the memory played clearly in his haunted gaze. "I tried to wake her. I do love her, but I've never been *in* love with her, so my kiss did nothing." His eyes moved to Belle, whose body felt like jelly after the new magic had birthed from her. "It's you. You're the cure." Then Henry moved over to Belle's side and helped her to sit up, allowing her to lean back against his chest while she fought to steady herself. "Only Cordray could wake Rory, because he's her true love."

Remus nodded. "That's exactly right. When I got here and saw the chaos, I wasn't sure Adam's body would be okay. My contribution tonight was the same thing I did for Rory – putting her in a deep sleep until true love's kiss could wake her." He pried open one of Adam's eyes to check his pupils. "But it doesn't seem like that was necessary. You did it all far beyond what I thought possible. He's... I only thought you might be able to stop the mutations, but he's actually restored as if it never happened!" He slapped Adam's cleanshaven cheek, but the patient didn't stir. "Miss Belle, this is incredible." His eyes drifted from Adam back to her, taking in her heavy breathing and languid demeanor as she rested against Henry. "I should like to work with you. I've been Rory's tutor since she was a small girl, and I work with other exceptional students on occasion. I think Rory might enjoy having you sit in on her lessons."

Belle's mouth fell open. "Remus Johnstone? You want to tutor me? You're like, way up here." She tried to motion with her hand a level above her head, but her palm flopped back onto her knee. "And I'm way down there."

Remus smiled, his eyes locking on hers with a promise. "You didn't just stop Malaura's curse, you reversed it. Even I couldn't do that."

"Sure you did, saving Rory like that."

"Adam's curse was far more complicated. Death is one action, but a mutation is a series of steps that are far more complex. Never in my wildest... Say you'll let me tutor you."

Belle stammered through her response, but eventually landed on a humble, "I'd be honored."

Henry squeezed her biceps and shoulders, rubbing sensation back into her body so she could sit up on her own. "Expect an obnoxiously large gift from me, once I process all I just saw."

Belle laughed through her nose. "He really won't wake

up unless I..." She didn't want to say the words out loud in front of the Great Remus Johnstone, but in that moment, there was nothing she wanted to do more.

Henry started making kissing noises. "Would you like me to sing a love song to set the mood?" Then before Belle could answer, he belted out a few lines of the sappiest song to hit the top of the charts that year.

Belle clamped her hand over the prince's mouth and giggled, wondering when it was that she'd become comfortable enough around the prince of Avondale to pal around with him as if he was a ridiculous brother. "Give me some space for this. We've never... This would be only our second time... Just turn around or something. I can't do this with an audience."

Henry scoffed, affronted. "I can't believe you don't want me here to sing for you. What a grand story that would make for your grandkids. 'The Prince of Avondale sang while I kissed grandpa back to life.' The press release practically writes itself."

"Come on, you." Remus hefted Henry up, and the two stepped over the broken doorframe to give Belle her moment.

When she was finally alone with Adam, Belle's eyes fixed on him. He'd been in agony a handful of minutes ago, but now he looked peaceful, if not totally foreign to her. "I've never seen you without your fur in person." Though she knew he couldn't see her, she took her time drinking in his features, weighing how strange it would be to kiss a face she wasn't totally familiar with.

She pushed the strands of hair that had come loose from her bun behind her ear. Though Adam was unconscious, she was suddenly nervous. He was far more handsome than the pictures of him she'd seen in the papers. Of course, he'd been only twenty back then. In slumber, the childishness seemed groomed out of him, replaced with a maturity she couldn't tear her eyes from.

In a word, Adam was beautiful. Still, she wondered if she would one day eventually prefer this vast improvement to the fur-lined face she'd grown to love.

She knew she should complete the breaking of the curse and kiss him, but she was transfixed, inching closer so she could study the crevices and angles of his features that had been previously concealed. He had a strong jaw, with a slight dimple in the center of his chin, though it wasn't overly pronounced, like Gabe's had been. Before she could stop herself, she reached out and traced the hard line of his jaw, acquainting herself with the feel of his skin. It was smooth and untarnished by life, and a little foreign.

There were slight crinkles on the outsides of his eyes, making her desperately wish she could see him smile. She'd only ever seen his mouth covered with his thick beard. Belle studied his lips, running her finger over the plump bottom to test its silkiness.

That was all the hesitance her body allowed her. Belle

curled her forearm under his head, lifting him slightly so she could cradle him as if he was her most precious thing. Belle could have stared at his handsome face forever, but the urge to see him open his eyes again drove her to lower her lips to his, and placed upon them the first kiss of the rest of their lives.

37

A MIRACLE

Though she'd been hoping for it to happen, when Adam's eyes fluttered open, Belle got spooked and nearly dropped his head. She scrambled to lower him gently, peppering his face with small kisses as she stroked his cheek.

The moment Adam's arms realized their strength, the only thing they wanted to do was wrap around the woman who'd brought him back to life. His lashes swept shut again as his knee lifted. He tugged Belle closer, holding her face as if he was afraid to let go. Over and over they kissed, sealing the demise of Malaura's curse as Belle lifted him to sit up, so they could better hold each other.

The kiss broke only when Adam tasted her tears and realized she was shivering. "Inside," he ruled, running his hands over her arms. "I promised you'd never be cold while I'm around. I'm here now."

Henry and Remus helped the two up, and the men each draped one of Adam's arms around their shoulders. Adam stumbled over broken glass and felled chairs on his way to the settee on the other side of the room. The men lowered Adam to the cushion and patted his shoulders as Belle took the seat beside him, still gaping at his transformation.

"How did..." Adam began, but his question caught in his throat. "Lucien!"

Belle's eyes tore from his face and looked to where he was pointing. The motionless candelabra shook as sparks began to fly from the brass. Adam cried out, but Belle merely gasped when the candelabra she adored stretched rapidly to the height of a man, the thin poles of brass expanding and shifting until, in the next breath, a man in his early forties stood in the center of the room.

Henry swore, his hands scrubbing his eyes to make sure they weren't playing tricks on him. "I don't... Lucien? How did... It's..." He turned to Adam in shock. "You weren't seeing things?"

Adam threw his hands up, finally vindicated. "I tried to make you understand in the beginning, but after a while it was easier to just let you all assume I was delusional." Adam leaned on Belle, who helped him stand to greet his butler. "Lucien, old friend." He didn't bother with a handshake, but rather hugged the man who'd been even more trapped than Adam by the curse.

The look of rapture on Lucien's surprised face brought tears to everyone's eyes. "Master, it's a miracle!"

Remus shouted when Audra, Bosworth, Thomas, Sultan the dog, and Vivienne were no longer inanimate objects, but were transformed into whole people. They each stood trembling in the study with expressions that ranged from flabbergast to out-and-out weeping.

Adam stumbled to each of them with the glow of a new man who'd been given a chance at redemption. He scooped each of them in a hug, welcoming Simone and Chef Bouche into the fold with a hearty kiss to both their cheeks.

Belle's love had filled the entire castle, redeeming things that were broken, and breathing life into mere objects, making them purely human again.

Agent McNally had a hard time keeping up when he had to step over the pile of dead bodies to reach the scene of the many crimes and miracles. After taking everyone's statements, the agents still couldn't explain everything they'd written in their reports when the sun finally rose.

Belle's father had been promptly released. The moment he had shoes on his feet, drove to the castle and scooped his daughter in a hug. His love broke the brave face she was trying to put on for everyone. Belle sobbed on her father's shoulder, confessing how scared she'd been when Gabe had thrown him in the drunk tank. She told Fabrice the entire story that had kept her from coming to him, and how devastated she'd been when she'd thought Adam gone forever.

"There, there. It's nothing a good pot of tea can't fix." His cheek brushed against hers as he held tight to his only daughter. "I'm so proud of you. I knew you could solve it all. You're the smartest person I know."

She chuckled through her tears. "I love you, Papa. I was so scared when I found out Gabe had taken you."

"Now, now. I'm alright, aren't I? I feel most sorry for those poor Lupine. Foulest meal they've ever had, I'm sure."

It was a grim joke, but Henry loved it, and clapped Belle's father on the shoulder with a tired laugh. Of course, he was loopy from not having slept, but he was in high spirits. Everyone had a reason to celebrate, including Rory, who couldn't stop apologizing from the moment she received the call. It was a stream of debasement every time she was near Adam from that day forward, humbling herself for not believing him about the staff all these years.

"Story, it's okay," Cordray finally said to his wife. "It was uncharted magic. Adam forgives you, I'm sure," he said with a hint of a threat at the former beast.

Adam had been attached to Belle all through the morning, but now that she was in her father's arms, he permitted Rory the hug she'd been craving. His dainty friend who'd stuck by him through too many dark days shook in his arms as all the pent-up grief over his curse finally crested. "It's alright, Rory."

"I just... I haven't seen your face in years!"

Prince Henry encircled the two of them in his arms. "And it's such a letdown that you're weeping? Poor girl. Adam, Adam, frightening the sensitive ones, as always."

Adam's chest vibrated as he removed one of his arms from Rory to shove Henry. "I'm back, Rory. I'm back, and I'm me again."

"How I've missed you," she whispered, and then planted a kiss to his soft cheek, marveling at the smoothness of his skin as she touched his face with her delicate fingers.

After a tearful goodbye and a promise to visit the next day when Adam and the staff had been permitted some time to settle down after all the changes, Cordray escorted his wife out of the castle.

Audra and Bosworth were talking to Adam, overjoyed at being able to move about freely and speak to whomever they wished. But Adam had eyes only for Belle, who was still confiding her fears to her father. He was anxious without her, though he knew he was being silly. She was in the same room, only a few feet away. Still, he longed to be nearer. All the uncertainty, the pain of his long-time isolation, and the confusion of the night melted away the moment she touched him. Without her by his side, he felt restless and on the edge of agitation.

"Of course, Audra, take whatever room you like. You won't exactly be sleeping in the cupboard anymore," Adam answered while still gazing at Belle.

Bosworth rubbed his round belly and adjusted his spectacles. "I was thinking I would set up in my old bedroom, but Lucien and Vivienne are coupling so loudly in the next room that I think I might prefer something down the hall."

Adam finally tore his eyes from the back of Belle's head to look at the two. "I'm glad you're all going to stay on. I can't imagine this place without you."

Audra smooched Adam's cheek, the same way she'd done when he'd been young. "I could never leave you, my beautiful boy."

Adam chuckled and scrubbed at his cheek, looking every bit the child she'd helped raise into adulthood. It was nearly noon, and the agents, coroners and crime scene specialists were finally starting to clear out. With the officials and dead bodies gone, it was easier to imagine what the next chapter of his life might look like. He couldn't stomach the idea of his home without Audra to keep him in line, Bosworth to organize the household, Lucien to see to the details, Chef Bouche to keep him away from dog food, Thomas to greet his guests and see to the upkeep of his cars, Simone to make sure he got dressed every morning, and Vivienne to keep the place clean.

Adam had big plans to relieve Belle of her housekeeping and nursing duties the moment the dust settled.

It was the longest Belle had been out of Adam's reach in hours. The moment her father released her from their embrace, she returned like a magnet to Adam's outstretched arms. He'd clung to her as if he'd been waiting to pull in a full breath, but couldn't unless she was by his side. His eyes closed contentedly as he rested his chin atop her head. "That's better."

Audra kissed Belle's cheek, and pinched it just to seal her role as the matronly figure in the home. "Let me draw you a bath, sweetheart. It looks like the two of you could use a nap after you wash up."

Belle nodded into Adam's chest, which for months had been one of her favorite places to rest her head. She worried it might feel different without the soft fur, but it turns out it was the solid nature of who he was to her that made his chest her home. "That sounds nice."

Remus put his coat on, a yawn doing nothing to hide the sleepiness in his eyes. He ran his hand over his shirt a few times, changing the buttons from white to blue, and then to yellow, almost as if he performed rudimentary magic subconsciously. "Miss Belle, I look forward to starting our lessons. I'll give you a week to let things settle around here, and then you can expect my call."

"Yes, Mr. Johnstone. Thank you." Belle didn't have any tears left in her, but if she did, she would have shed a few in gratitude for all Remus had done to see them through the trauma of the night. "I don't know what I would've done if you hadn't..."

Remus held up his hand to stop her with a kind smile. "This was entirely you." He extended his hand to Adam, knowing the man wouldn't want to be parted from Belle even a few inches. The two shook hands as men who understood how cruel the twists of Malaura's magic could be. "Adam, always a pleasure to see your face. Can I expect you'll come to Miss Belle's lessons?"

"You can expect that wherever she goes, I'll be right beside her."

Remus nodded, as if needing to hear the confirmation that Adam truly did understand how to love, and that he wasn't holding back anymore. "Excellent. I look forward to pushing you both to your limits."

Before Adam could do more than raise his eyebrow, Remus turned and exited, leaving Adam with questions, and Belle with concerns. She'd been top of her class in the West Village, but that was largely because of the low value put on any sort of education. She hoped she would be able to keep up.

The hustle and bustle of the household fell into a comfortable rhythm, but Adam and Belle remained locked in their embrace while the world continued to spin around them. They breathed in unison, unwilling to let the smallest of changes pry them away from each other for the rest of their lives.

38

ANYWHERE AND EVERYWHERE

Three months wasn't enough to undo the social stigma Adam had built up over the years by holing himself up inside his castle, but slowly people began to accept his presence in public. The white linens on the tables were set with the finest crystal as a pianist played light and feathery songs to the enjoyment of Avondale's upper crust. The finest restaurant nearest the palace served salmon that people from miles around made reservations for, but Adam, Rory and Henry's fame was such that they weren't subjected to the formalities of waiting.

Belle still felt strange being included in the tight-knit group of the elite, but Adam's thumb slowly teasing her side put her at ease. Still, she stiffened whenever someone took their picture and asked Adam for an interview.

"You want an interview with the beast? Fine. You can write in your papers that I survived for years by feasting on the blood of unicorns and journalists. The reporters I ate turned out to be pure poison." Adam frowned at the pushy woman. "You can clearly see I'm with my girlfriend. Get lost."

Henry's camera-ready smile was always locked and loaded, and Rory's posture was perfect as ever. Cordray had a naturally commanding presence, so he looked the part well enough. But Adam felt no such need to perform for the public's approval. He wanted Belle to be pleased with him, and the list of opinions he concerned himself with ended there.

Henry forced out a laugh to cover over Adam's surly nature, which no amount of healing magic could cure completely. "You'll have to forgive Adam; he's had to cut back on devouring reporters. He gets a bit crabby when he's hungry."

"The people deserve to know the truth about your curse!" the red-headed journalist insisted, leaning over Belle to smile at Adam with a flirty look that left nothing to the imagination. "I was hoping to get an exclusive." Now that he was handsome, it seemed everyone was quick to overlook his days of being the beast.

Belle stiffened, and carefully moved the woman's breasts out of her face, Pulsing Discernment into her. "Leave him alone. You didn't want his story when he was desperate for anyone to believe him that he hadn't killed his household. Where was your exclusive then?"

The journalist's focus shifted to Belle as she pulled

back, a cat's evil gleam in her eyes as she shook off Belle's Pulse. "You're the one who broke his curse, yes? Tell me, Adam. Have you always been attracted to the plain sort, or has she bewitched you somehow?" Though the reporter muscled through her sass, the Discernment twisted her confident expression to a grimace of distaste as her conscience flared.

Rory gasped and scolded the reporter, while Cordray motioned for the waiter to bring over the manager.

Belle's mouth dropped open, but Henry was the one who intervened as Adam stood and threw his napkin down on the table, his chair scraping against the polished floor and drawing every diner's eye. Henry understood that just because Adam had been cured didn't mean that he was completely devoid of the beast who could snap on a dime.

Henry placed his hand on the woman's elbow after pressing a text to his guard. "Now, now. Is that any way to treat my fiancée?" he asked, making the reporter gasp with a greedy gleam of a good story in her eye.

"You've moved in on your best mate's girl?"

"Are you truly that surprised?" Henry grinned at Adam's scowl. "I'll fight you for her, I will!" he challenged Adam, drawing a make-believe sword and swishing it through the air. "Belle is mine! We've had a secret affair for months, but we didn't know how to tell you. I was waiting for the right moment, which just so happened to be when a reporter stopped by in front of all these witnesses."

Adam rolled his eyes. "Maybe Cordray will let you hump his wife, but you can keep your hands off Belle."

Cordray scoffed, and Rory held up her hands. "Ho, no. Don't you bring me into this again. I swear to you, Henry. If you propose, I'll make sure to hide Cord's pill, so he can really teach you a lesson."

Cordray stood and clapped his hand on Henry's shoulder. "I don't think I need to use magic for that. You want us to give them a real show? Hit on my wife again, and we'll earn front page headlines after I break your nose for sniffing around Rory."

Henry threw his hands in the air. "Finally! Someone who understands good production value. Pop me one right here for slipping it to your girl while you're out. Do it quick before... Oh, for crying out loud. My guard's here. The fun is over, I guess." Henry handed the reporter over to his guard with a nod. "I so wanted you to get a good story. I was just about to announce that I'm pregnant, but it's a tossup over which of these two lovelies knocked me up." He made a show of arching his back to stick out his stomach, and smoothed his hand over the bump lovingly.

Belle was crimson from head to toe at the attention. She buried her face in Adam's chest when he resumed his seat after giving the manager a firm talking to. He made it very clear about the kind of dining experience he would tolerate, and the interruptions he would not. His arm wound around Belle, his other hand weaving through her hair that Audra had done in a knot of braids for their weekly friend brunch. "I'm sorry, Belle. Maybe we should go home."

"No." Belle was firm that they wouldn't be hermits. "It's good for us to get out. The more they see us, the sooner the story will get old."

"You're not plain," Adam growled with a protective irritation, holding her tight as if to shield her from mild insults.

The restaurant was the nicest in Avondale, and due to its close proximity to the palace, it attracted notable officials and prominent public figures. Every diner watched the young royals surreptitiously.

Rory giggled and shook her head. "Of course she's not. If she was, women wouldn't have to try so hard to run her down. Belle's made of tough stuff, Adam. Man, you apologize so easily now. It's strange to see."

Henry flopped back in his chair. "I hate this, being the fifth wheel. Cord and Rory have always been adorably annoying, but you two," Henry motioned between Belle and Adam with a look of feigned disgust. "You rarely have an inch of space between you two. Come on, Adam. How am I to make improper advances on your woman with you hovering all the time?"

Adam narrowed an eye at Henry as he speared his salad with his free hand. The other remained securely wrapped around Belle, with her hand resting on his thigh. "You're not, that's how. Find your own girl. Or a scratching post or a chew toy or something."

"What ever happened to Ella?" Belle asked. "I liked her."

Henry shot Rory a cagey look as he shifted in his seat. "She's got a busy schedule. Can't sneak away all that often. Her stepmum's something else."

Rory reached over and patted Henry's hand. "I think she's worth pursuing. She's the only woman who's ever twisted you up this much."

"That's the thing. It's complicated, and she made it clear that won't change. I wish she would give us more of a chance." The melancholy didn't suit Henry, so he shook it off and donned a charming smile, his eyes fixing on Belle. "Plus, I'm still hung up on this one. When can we run away and get married?" He spoke loudly, so his proposition would carry to the nearest tables.

Belle chuckled at his theatrics, grateful that Henry had never given up on Adam through the years, though their personalities were polar opposites. "Just as soon as I finish my meal. Where you are whisking me off to today?"

"Anywhere and everywhere." Henry's eyes stayed on his salad as he spoke. "Ella wants to go hiking in the mountains someday. She thinks the flowers up there will be prettier, because they're closer to the sun, and there aren't as many people around them to muck nature up too much."

Rory and Belle exchanged knowing smiles, but said nothing. Every now and then, Henry would bring Ella up in conversation for no reason, other than that his head and heart were constantly filled with glimpses of her.

Adam had slightly less tact. "What is it about this girl that's got your head in the clouds? She didn't strike me as anyone to lose your mind over."

Henry's eyes sharpened at Adam, his spine stiffening. "Ella is the kindest, gentlest, most beautiful woman I've ever met. There's nothing she can't learn, nothing she can't do. The woman is pure magic. If you knew the first thing about her, you'd know that she is lightyears above every other female in the kingdom." Then his eyes cast to the women at the table. "Present company excluded."

Adam's jaw dropped, while Cordray chuckled. "I don't think you understand how deep you're in it, man." Cord's arm draped lazily around his wife's chair.

Henry seemed to come back to himself, his neck shrinking with chagrin. He waved his fork as if to clear the room of a bad smell. "Don't pay attention to me. I don't know what I'm saying."

Cordray cleared his throat to steer the conversation away from the lull. "We're supposed to be talking about how we're going to vote on Proposition 7."

"Right," Adam commented, placing a kiss to Belle's cheek. It seemed he couldn't go two minutes without stroking her arm or lavishing affection on her, and she never tired of it. He was always overly gentle with her, speaking softly and anticipating any need that might occur. It was a struggle to turn his attention to the world around him, but he made the attempt for his few friends. "I think we should let you take the lead on this one, Cordray, since it affects you the most."

Henry shook his head. "It affects me just as much, as Father and I are to come up with room in the budget if it's approved, as well as take any heat if experiments on the pill that our scientists make have any negative effects."

Adam inclined his head to Henry. "Fair enough."

Rory pulled out a piece of paper from her purse and began reading. "If passed, Proposition 7 promises to make production of the pill public, and turn the recipe over to privately-funded companies to explore different mutations of the drug as they wish for the good of the people, and sell for profit. The original pill will still be given to those who need it free of charge by the government."

Cordray nodded, lightly bopping his fist atop the table to seal his vote. "I say yes. I don't see the harm in it. I want full use of my magic back without fear of harming my wife."

Adam nodded, but didn't speak. Belle lightly dragged her fingernails across his toned stomach, which was one of his favorite things she did while cuddled up in his nook. He leaned back in his chair and kept his eyes on his salad as he spoke. "It's the 'all who need it' part. I mean, I admit that you need it, Cordray. I've no doubt it's the best thing that's ever happened to you, aside from Rory here giving you a second look. Still, *you* decided you needed it. If the government had come along and forced the pill on you, you'd be singing a different song."

Cordray's nose crinkled. "From what I've seen, the throne is stable and wouldn't do that to us."

Adam tilted his chin to the side. "Ah, but Malaura was in power before King Hubert, and she would've taken all sorts of liberties with a bill like that. You have to think long-term."

Henry nodded. "Plus, we're just assuming the mutations the other companies might come up with are all good. We assume they'll try to get the Lethal abilities to go away while bringing back your other magic. I've seen too much to put that kind of faith in people. This isn't the kind of thing we should leave to trial and error. I'm voting we leave well enough alone, and keep the pill as is."

Adam's arm tightened around Belle. "Fine with me."

Belle spoke up, her voice brushed with contentment. "Henry, you might want to have your father look at that last line. It's a broad use of the word 'need'. The government shouldn't decide who needs the pill. That's a recipe for dictatorial control and fuel for a possible registering of all Lethals. That's a whole other set of arguments."

"Change it," Cordray cut in without apology. "I didn't think of it like that, but she's right."

Henry ran his hand over his face. "I'll talk to my father and see what he can do. But this isn't his bill; it's the Baron who wrote it up. I'm not sure how much my father can do this late in the game. I mean, the bill is set to go to vote before the end of the year."

Rory's chin lowered, her expression grave. "The world is going to change, then. And soon."

The silence that fell over the table was laced with tension that slowly began to dissipate as they sipped their tea.

"Would a fart joke help break us out of this funk?" Henry offered.

Rory rolled her eyes. "Pass."

Belle reached across the table and placed her hand atop Cordray's ungloved knuckles. Adam stiffened at her touching a Lethal, but didn't intervene. There was nothing but compassion in her eyes as she spoke to Cordray. "I love that you love Rory, and that you take the pill to keep her safe. I think you're a good man. We just have to keep thinking of a better way to go about it all. Not everyone is as upstanding as you."

Cordray thumbed Belle's fingernails, his lips drawing to the side in appreciation. "I really wanted this bill to be the ticket."

"And maybe it will be, but not in its current state. A better world is possible. Last year, I never would've dreamed my life could be like this, but now here I am, living with the most wonderful man I've ever known. A lot can change in a year. Give it time, otherwise you'll jump at the wrong chance. Then it won't be just you who falls, but Rory, as well. We can't have that."

Rory inclined her head to Belle, but it was Adam who couldn't stop staring at her. "You really think that about me?"

Belle shifted next to him as she placed her hands in her lap. "Of course. You're incredible. Every day I get to spend working by your side at your companies is exactly where I want to be. All day, all night, it's you I want to be with."

"*Our* companies," Adam reminded her. "They belong to both of us now."

Henry motioned to Belle, who was contentedly snuggled into Adam's side. "See? That's what I want. Only I can't have what I want because of... complications." He frowned at his crystal goblet. "Best lock this one down, Adam. When the woman of your dreams can actually be with you, you jump on it. I'm telling you, if you don't ask this one to marry you soon, I will."

Belle balked at Henry. "It's only been a few months since the curse was broken! You're being ridiculous."

Henry tucked away his melancholy for the moment and donned a playful expression. "It's been far too long since I've proposed to anyone. I'm starting to miss the thrill of it." He glanced around. "Where is that dreadful reporter? There's no point in proposing to you again if the whole world can't see your embarrassment."

Belle held up her finger while Rory sniggered. "You need a hobby, Henry. Proposing to me last week in the middle of the parade? I was mortified!"

Henry waved off her complaint. "You were the talk of the festival. After that little media boost, I bet you had no trouble securing investors for the education for mental health you started building into your Foundation."

Belle's mouth fell open. "That's why you did that?"

Henry shrugged. "That, and I was bored."

Rory shook her head at her friend. "Two of the best reasons to propose to someone, I'm sure."

Adam had been quiet through the levity, but then nodded, seeming to have decided something important. He reached into his jacket pocket and pulled out a velvet box. "Henry, when you're right, you're right." He stood up, only to walk around to Belle's other side and sink down on one knee.

Every eye in the restaurant zoned in on Adam on bended knee before the woman who'd stolen his heart.

"Adam, what are you..." Belle's throat went dry as she gaped at him.

"I've had this ring for months, but didn't want to spook you by asking too soon. But if Henry can propose to you and you don't get scared off, then I think I've got a shot. If not, I'll be asking you again in a month, and every month after that until you say yes. If Henry can survive you turning him down, then I suppose I can muscle through your possible rejection as well, if there's a chance you might say yes." Then he closed his eyes. "Don't say no."

Rory squealed, her hand over her mouth. Cordray

clapped and hooted his approval. Henry swore in astonishment at his friend's humble body language.

Belle was utterly taken by the insecure look burning in Adam's eyes, not to mention the sparkle of the largest diamond she'd ever seen when the box flipped open. "Adam?" was all she could croak out.

The clanking of silverware around them and dull conversations went silent as everyone leaned in to witness the proposal in action.

Adam swallowed hard. He'd been carrying around the ring for too long, the diamond burning a hole in his pocket. Every moment had felt like it might be the right one, but he'd been afraid of her answer. Though she seemed taken with him, most days he still couldn't believe his good fortune. Though he now held the adoration of many women throughout the land, thanks to his good looks being restored, his former haughtiness had dissipated. He had eyes only for Belle, and could scarcely comprehend all she'd done to save him.

They'd moved up to his bedroom in the West wing and cleaned it out together, making his castle one that belonged to the two of them, and not just him. Every morning that he woke up to the glow of her in his arms brought the words closer to the surface. Still, he'd held back, not wanting to risk moving too fast for her, and spooking away the best thing that had ever happened to him.

He'd wanted to ask her the moment her father had

given him his blessing. He'd wanted to ask her over breakfast last week when she'd had a smear of strawberries on her top lip, looking positively adorable. He'd wanted to ask her every time she stared at him as if he was something amazing. Beast or man, she loved him the same.

Still, he'd held himself back, for fear of possibly pushing her too fast. The media was such that she couldn't go to the grocery store without reporters following her through each aisle. News companies had started a bidding war over who would get rights to Belle's baby pictures, which her father still refused to give up.

Belle's mouth was open in an "O" of pure flabbergast as she took in the man on his knees in the middle of the restaurant. Her eyes were glistening with a sheen of adoration for him, showing no signs of flight.

He didn't realize he'd been utterly silent until Rory screeched, "You have to actually ask her, you fool!"

Adam fumbled with the ring, recalling the speech he'd rehearsed over and over again, whispering it to her after she'd fallen asleep in his arms. He'd practiced it on Audra and Vivienne, who'd said "yes" every time. He cleared his throat as cameras and phones clicked around them, cataloging each facial expression shared between them. "I love you, Belle. I want to spend every day of the rest of my life with you. I promise to love you and take care of us as long as I live." He dug in deeper, worrying he hadn't put enough on the table for her to say "yes" to. "I paid off your father's mortgage, so he'll be taken care of. But if you want him to move into the castle, that's fine too. Whatever I need to do to make sure you stay with me, I'll do it. Only please, please marry me."

The tears were falling like raindrops of pure sunshine and love as Belle gasped and covered her mouth. She hung her head, overwhelmed that he knew her so well. Only the perfect man for her would make sure he could take care of her father before asking if he could take her away. Adam understood how important her father was to her, and that small note tipped over any reservations she might have had that they were moving too fast, or that they hadn't known each other a full year. The gift was grand, but then again, Adam's love always swept her away.

There wasn't a drop of hesitation in her heart when she nodded, gulping through her choked response. "Yes, Adam. Of course I'll marry you."

Relief flooded through Adam in waves, slumping his shoulders as he slid the ring onto her finger with a gust of contentment. The knot that had felt permanently lodged in his chest loosened whenever she was near, permitting him to breathe easier. The ring looked right on her finger, like her hand was the only place meant to display such beauty. She owned the warm and the icy parts of him, which reflected in the diamond for the world to see.

When a tear came to Adam's eye, he leaned forward to bury his head in her lap, offering up his raw emotion only to her as a pledge of intimacy he wouldn't share with anyone else. He didn't care that the internet would be buzzing with photos of him so debased, kneeling before a woman with his arms wrapped around her hips in supplication for a better existence. He only cared that his ring stayed on her finger for the rest of their lives, sealing their future with the unending magic only true love could bring.

Through the highs and the cruelty of life's lows, they would never let each other go. For better or worse, the beast had found his beauty.

The End.

Love the book?

Leave a review.

39

BEAUTY'S CURSED PRINCE

*E*njoy a free preview of *Beauty's Cursed Prince*, book three in the *Cursed Beauty* series.

HENRY STARED AT HIS PHONE, HIS FACE A WASH OF indignation. Since he had no audience, he spoke to his phone as if it was his best friend's stubborn face. "The nerve! You can't hang up on me just because I check in on you, Rory. You married a man whose Pulse had to be taken away, it was so deadly. I'm not overreacting."

Henry wanted to say more, but slid his phone into his pocket. He tried not to let the frustration affect him, but that seemed to be a losing battle.

Rory Johnstone had married a Lethal, which meant Henry felt no shame in calling her more often than usual. He'd felt a mild pang of chagrin when he interrupted her honeymoon, and even permitted her new husband, Cordray, to chew him out for a good five minutes before he'd agreed to back off. That, of course, meant only one phone call per day, as opposed to nearly a dozen. As her best friend, Henry felt it was his duty to make sure Rory was, at the very least, alive.

Henry ran his hand through his blond hair, glancing around the foyer of the palace before his eyes landed on his father's raised eyebrows. "Oh, I didn't see you there."

The King of Avondale was known and beloved for many things, and rarely spoke out of turn. He closed the leather-bound day-planner he was holding and tucked it under his arm, adjusting his tie. "How is our dear Rory doing? Settling into married life well, I hope?"

Henry took in a long breath through his nose before he answered. "She's fine. I'm fine. We're fine. I'm glad she's happy and all; I just didn't expect her to settle down with a Lethal. I'm worrying more than I was expecting to."

The king smoothed his hand over the buttons on his pressed shirt, looking every bit the part of the professional. Since they were on the main floor of the palace, important officials were permitted to walk through with the escort of a guard. King Hubert's hair, angular jaw, high cheekbones and easy smile matched his son's perfectly. The only difference was that the king had a few wrinkles around the corners of his pale blue eyes, and his chest was slightly less barreled than the late-twenties prince. "Cordray is still on the pill, yes? His magic is muted?"

Henry nodded. "He can't hurt Rory by accidentally Pulsing his deadly electricity into her with a stray touch. I get that." He shook his head at himself, his shoulders slumping. "The whole thing is throwing me, is all."

"Did you wish your betrothal to Rory had held? Is that what's really bothering you?"

Henry's eyes widened as he leaned back against the closed front double doors, glancing up at the elaborate crystal chandelier. He recalled running around the palace with Rory and Adam when they were children. They'd chosen the ornately tiled circle under this chandelier as the safety zone when playing tag.

How he wished for a safety zone now, one where he could tell his oldest friend anything, and she'd truly hear his heart. Henry studied the golden loops and twists above, wondering where things had fallen so far off the track that he couldn't make himself understood to the one woman who'd always known his mind. "No, I don't want to marry Rory. She's like a sister to me. It's that she just barely woke from her coma, and now she's diving headfirst into what could be a dangerous situation."

The king nodded sagely. "Ah. The papers are still printing pictures of the kingdom's Sleeping Beauty. Her wedding was months ago, Henry. Perhaps you should let her go a bit."

Henry snorted at the name the press had given her. Before, they'd called her "the Chancellor's daughter," or the snarkier papers, "the Chancellor's shamed Deadpulse daughter." When true love's kiss had woken her from her coma, Rory's magic was finally awakened. She could perform all the spells she'd failed at before, and finally won the respect that should've been hers all along.

When her father passes away someday, she would sit in the Chancellor's chair as head of the council. When Henry's father passes someday, he would rule Avondale. The two got along better than most President and Vice President pairings did.

Henry shoved his hands into the pockets of his khakis. "What if Cordray forgets to take his pill? What if he rolls over in bed one night and electrocutes her by accident? I like him and all, but this whole thing is going to give me an ulcer."

The king chuckled at his son's consternation, letting his folder go and floating it in the air at his side, so he could reach down and tug at his sock that had slipped to discomfort. "I guess I know how you'll be voting on Proposition 7," the king said as he stood. He looked every bit like his son, only with brushes of silver lining his temples. While his glory days playing rugby were far behind him, he was still almost as imposing as his tall, broad-shouldered son, especially when he went head-to-head with members of the council who occasionally got out of hand.

Henry shrugged. "I had my opinions before, but now I don't know. I keep going back and forth."

"Forfeiting all of one's magic to mute one's Lethal abilities is a steep price to pay, but that's the only option I can offer them. The pill has its shortcomings, but it took so long to get it where it is now. It's a viable option if you want to keep your loved ones safe when your Pulse is deadly. I've invested all I care to in the project. The Baron thinks privately-funded companies might be able to take the pill to the next level—muting the deadlier aspects, while still allowing Lethals to perform perfunctory magic."

"And what do you think?"

The king met his son's gaze with a tight smile. "Henry, it's the Baron's idea. When have I ever not trusted the Baron?"

The two shared a loaded chuckle. The Baron was a snide, sniveling weasel who was always vying for more power. It had been the Chancellor's seat he'd had his eyes on for too long, but now it seemed the Baron had moved on to wanting control over the pill. "Fair point. So you're saying I shouldn't vote yes on Proposal 7?"

The king shrugged, a wizened look softening his eyes, making them crinkle around the edges. "I'm saying I have faith in your decision-making process. I know you'll steer the country well someday." He glanced at the watch on his wrist. "The guests will be arriving soon. Remind me again why I host these dinners?"

Henry gripped his father's shoulders, looking him in the eye as if he were a football coach. "Dinners for the Elite are important rituals for the council and other officials to get together in a non-political setting. They're supposed to use the opportunity to make friends with people who have opposing views, and not talk politics, so we have a more unified nation, even when we disagree."

"Right. That sounds exactly like something I'd say—wise but taxing. Tell me that each day only holds twenty-four hours, and this one won't drag on beyond it."

"This evening will feel like an eternity, but it's worthwhile. This is a good thing you're doing—encouraging the leaders to see beyond their own agendas."

"Yes, I'm very smart. One day when the throne is yours, I hope you have a son of your own who can talk you through each of the brilliant ideas you hate." King Hubert and Henry shared a smirk as Henry slapped his father hard on the shoulder twice. The king checked his watch. "See that you make it to the dining hall before the Baron, otherwise I'll be forced to sit next to him. He's been taking garlic pills." He shuddered, and then grabbed his folder out of the air and tucked it back under his arm, kissing his son's cheek before leaving for his study.

Henry deflated against the doors the moment his father left. He always hated when his father made comments like that, bringing to attention that the adored king might not always be around. Many people in Henry's position would be happy to inch closer to the crown, but that would only mean his father wouldn't be there—a concept that sat heavy in his stomach. He knew that when the time came, he would rise to the occasion. But no one seemed to realize that the day he put on the crown would mean that his father was no more.

Henry couldn't think of a worse thing.

His secondary cell phone buzzed with a text from his date last night. He thumbed the nude photo she sent him to entice him into another night out, at which he merely chuckled. That was far beyond his level of commitment. No matter how much fun they'd had during their night together, a second date felt like a marriage, which made him itch to delete her from his contacts.

His primary cell phone rang, and he answered immediately. Only his family, the palace staff and his small circle of true friends had his real cell phone number. "I'm sorry, Rory. I was overbearing."

Rory's gentle voice came out in a rush. "I don't like it when we fight. Let's be sorry and forgiving, and forget it ever happened."

A lazy grin swept over Henry's handsome face. "Darling, telling the kingdom I'm amazing in bed means never having to say you're sorry."

Rory giggled through her nose at the innocuous flirtation. They'd never slept together, though the tabloids had entertained the masses with many stories countering the truth. "I'll be careful. Cordray doesn't have a problem taking the pill. We both have alarms set to make sure we don't forget."

"For what day? I'll set one, too. Then you'll only get a

territorial overprotective phone call from me once a month."

"I can't imagine you'll show that much restraint." Henry could hear the smile in Rory's voice. "First of the month. But if you're not barking at me about things I'm already on top of, then I'll miss out on all of your fantastic apologies. I'm not sure it's worth the trade-off."

"I miss you," Henry admitted. "Tell me you're almost here."

"I am. Be nice to Cord."

"Fine. I'll offer to make out with him first, and then you second, so he'll feel all important."

"What a gentlemanly proposition."

"Pass!" Henry heard Cordray shout in the background.

Henry sighed as he walked through the walls of the palace that were outlined with gold-painted wainscoting and baseboards. He passed the portrait of his deceased mother on the wall and blew her a kiss, as he always did whenever he happened by it.

"That was our longest fight yet," he commented. "I didn't care for it. In fact, I wrote whole oceans of sappy poetry in the two minutes we were at odds. Would you like to hear some of it?"

Rory groaned good-naturedly. "Not even if it's in song form."

"Of course it's in song. How else does one apologize to a fine lady like yourself?"

"You're too much," Rory chuckled.

"You're exactly the right amount of everything. Tell your husband the second he drops the ball, I'll be marking my territory, peeing all over you to tell the world you're mine."

Cordray sounded bored, if not mildly irritated when he chimed in. "You realize I can hear you, right?"

"Oh, Cord. Don't be jealous. I can pee on you, as well. I had no idea you were so fond of such things." Making Rory laugh was easy enough for him to accomplish but it was satisfying every time. "See you soon, sweetheart. You too, Rory."

"Please don't pee on me when you do," she requested through her laughter.

"I make no promises." Henry ended the call and moved into the kitchen, pinching Carlotta's pudgy waist just to make her jump and shriek with indignation. She'd burped him as a baby, but didn't hesitate to get out the dish towel and whap at the prince's caddish grin.

"Henry, I swear! I'm putting the finishing touches on the rolls. What if I'd messed up the Baron's?"

"Which one is the Baron's? I'll rub it under my armpits for good luck."

Carlotta narrowed her eyes, her flour-covered hands on her generous hips. "I swear, you make me crazy some days." The doorbell rang, and her eyes widened. "They're already arriving! Move out of the way. I have to get these in the oven."

"You have to relax, otherwise people are going to think

we run too tight a ship around here. Dinner will be served when it's ready. You're looking at this all wrong. The stuffy officials don't hold the power; you do."

"Said the stuffy official himself."

Henry scoffed, his hand over his heart. "Dad and I adore you. Dinner is served when you get to it, and we're grateful every time."

Carlotta shoved the rolls in the oven and sighed. "I know. I love you, too, you sweet boy. It's not you; it's the others. The Baron's date has called three times with different specifications on how her meal is to be served. I'm half-tempted to rub her portion in the dirt."

Henry's eyes danced with mischief. "Which one is hers? Come on, let me mess with it."

Carlotta's round face was red with sweat, but she grinned for the boy she'd always adored. "You can mess with her all you like, but not her food. That will come back and bite me, for certain."

"Did you make me a pre-meal snack?"

"Only because I know you'll dig into the meal early if I don't. Top shelf of the fridge, sweet pea. But if the guests are arriving, you should go out and greet them with your father."

"I will, I will. But a growing boy needs nourishment."

Carlotta blew a raspberry and waved her hand at the jar of preserves, so it screwed itself on without her having to touch it while she busied herself in the cupboard.

"You're nearly thirty! The only way you're going to grow is wider if you keep eating two dinners."

Henry rubbed his toned abdomen as he pulled down a bowl of cut-up fruit and tossed the lid into the sink. "Just more of me to love. From Avondale's sexiest bachelor, to Avondale's sexiest Santa. The tabloids will eat up every glorious ounce of me."

Carlotta tossed her dish rag in his face, shaking her head at him with a smile as the cloth fell to the counter. "At least take that food out back. Don't eat it in front of your father's guests."

"Alright, alright." Though the air had the chill of fall to it, Henry didn't bother with a jacket if it meant he could put off the stuffy formalities for a few more minutes. It had been his father's idea to get the notable officials together every other month to have social niceties, so every interaction wasn't always about furthering an agenda. It was a good system, but Henry grew tired of the many occasions that required him to be on his best behavior.

The kitchen door on the side of the palace led to a small gazebo that was visible from the long, winding driveway. Henry didn't mind if the chauffeurs saw him, and sat and ate his bowl of berries while he waited for Rory's driver.

His phone buzzed with a text from Adam, his other best friend. The three had been inseparable from childhood, but recently Rory and Adam endured a falling out, in which she'd needed Adam, and he'd remained a hermit, stalwart in his resolve to seclude himself while the world still turned, often in need of his intervention.

"What have you done to me? You've stuck me with a cyborg. This woman you hired never sleeps. I swear, I got up this morning, and she'd shined all my shoes in the night. What am I supposed to do with that?"

Henry chuckled and typed in his response. *"Why yes, I believe I did see some wires sticking out from her hair. She's working out alright?"*

Henry loved his friends as they were, but every now and then, he found that they needed a little push. Rory had needed a push with Cordray in the beginning, and Adam needed someone to make sure...

Henry swallowed hard, the strawberries losing all flavor. He didn't like thinking of one of his best friends holed up alone in his castle, secluded from the world. The nurse and housekeeper Henry had hired to look after Adam seemed capable of handling Adam's prickly nature, which, Henry reasoned, perhaps did make her part-cyborg.

He could hear Adam's acerbic nature coming out in his text. *"Belle's fine, I guess. The next time you go hiring someone to work for me, make sure I actually need the help, which I don't. I can shine my own shoes."*

But you won't, Henry thought, pain twisting his handsome features. He summoned up his courage and spoke the truth to his friend. *"You haven't showered or gotten dressed in who knows how long. You wear that bathrobe like it's a uniform. Belle stays."*

Adam wasn't labeled "the beast" by the media for no reason. He'd been cursed by Malaura nearly ten years prior. On his next birthday, Adam was destined to turn into a wolf and go off to join the Lupine. The curse deformed him and made fur sprout all over. Adam didn't go out of the castle much anymore—only when Henry and Rory forced him outside.

Henry knew Adam wouldn't respond to the hard truth, so he tucked his phone back in his pocket.

His attention was drawn from Adam's predicament when a car backfired up on the winding driveway. He didn't think much of it until smoke started spilling out of the hood. While most of the vehicles were sleek and waxed town cars, this sedan was a bit older, though not decrepit just yet. Henry put down his bowl of fruit on the bench in the gazebo and trotted up the embankment toward the car. "Can I help you out? That didn't sound all that great."

He expected a suited man in his fifties to come out of the driver's side, since that was the norm for these types of events. Henry's eyebrows rose when a flash of golden curls caught his eye, a look of determination pinching her button nose as she emerged. "I've got it. Thanks. Stupid carburetor. Does this all the time."

Henry was fascinated with her preoccupation, utterly transfixed by her frown. Usually women got within ten feet of him and lost their minds with the excitement of stardom. Her informal attire made him wonder whose driver she was. It seemed none of the more notable officials' staff got out of bed in anything short of a full business suit.

None of the other drivers offered to help until they saw the stunning woman in jeans and a white button-down inspecting the contents of the engine. Then suddenly everyone was a car expert, getting out of their vehicles to lend a hand.

Henry waved them off. "I think we've got it, gentlemen. As you were." Then to the woman, he offered a smile through the autumn chill that stung the nape of his neck. "I take it you're in need of a mechanic?"

She peered into the mess of wires as if frustrated with the puzzle she knew how to fix, but somehow couldn't. "Actually, just a wrench would do the trick for now." Her eyes closed in frustration. "But my tools are at home."

"You can use ours. Though, I confess, I don't know much about fixing carburetors."

"Thank you." She glanced around to the line of town cars, and waved them to pull around, mildly embarrassed. "Is it okay if I leave the car here like this while we go get some tools?"

Henry smirked at her, though she hadn't even looked up at him yet. "I'd wager we don't have much choice. The garage is just over there." He proffered his elbow to her, but she didn't take it.

Instead, she held up her hands and finally met his eyes with a sheepish note of apology. "I don't want to stain your shirt. But thanks for the gentlemanly escort."

She was stunning in a way that made him wish he could study her features for far too long. Her deep blue eyes were more vibrant than his. Her heart-shaped face was utterly captivating – complete with naturally pink and plump lips, rosy cheeks and a sweetness to her smile that made him want to lean a little closer.

Henry walked beside her, shoving his hands in his pockets to keep from fidgeting. "I'm Henry."

"Nice to meet you. Do you get many cars breaking down in the driveaway of the royal palace, or am I just the luckiest of all the girls?" She grinned over at him, revealing deep dimples that didn't disappear when her smile faded to a pleasant expression.

"The fortune's all mine." Henry blanched the moment the words hit the air. He'd wanted to come across as his usual charming self, but he sounded like some stuffy royal. He wanted to say something funny just so he could see her smile again, but he was coming up empty. "That sounded stupid. My name's Henry."

The woman sniggered, but covered her mouth out of politeness. "You said that already."

He cringed. "This would be the part where you tell me your name."

"My name is also Henry," she deadpanned, her hands in her pockets.

He narrowed his left eye at her. Most women were too nervous around him to poke fun, or they came onto him like cats in heat. "Hilarious."

"That's what they call me. Hilarious Henry who can't go on the freeway without overworking her carburetor." Her smile drifted away, but the wells in her cheeks remained, transfixing Henry as they walked. He wanted to touch them, but guessed that wouldn't be appropriate. "I'm not a fan of unreliable cars, but that seems to be the way of things."

"To be fair, you're relying on one that's probably more than half your age."

When they reached the garage, Henry cursed himself for not spending more time learning how to fix cars. He'd had a driver since he was born. Though he had his license and drove himself occasionally, he didn't know the first thing about vehicle maintenance.

He cast around for a toolbox, relieved when he opened the third tall white cabinet on the side of the sixteen-car garage and found one. "Here you are, Henry," he said with that same squinty eye.

"Why, thank you, Henry." When she glanced up at him, he was treated to a fresh view of her loveliness. Her blonde waves were swept back, fashioned with two crossed pencils that allowed a handful of ringlets to escape and tickle the nape of her neck. "You're the prince, then?" She shot him a look that bore a small bit of hesitance, as if needing it confirmed how far out of her world he was.

Henry flashed a bright smile that always dazzled his dates. "It seems a little showy to introduce myself with my title." He reached into his pocket. "Let me call Maximus. He services our cars, and he can give yours a look."

The woman waved her hand, gripping the toolbox with the other. "No need. Unless he's got a new carburetor up his sleeve, I can handle it." When Henry's face fell at not having a reason to stick around her, a small smile pulled her mouth to the side. "Feel like learning how to do a poor man's fix on an old engine? Being that we've got the same name and all, I figure you'd be good with your hands. All Henrys are."

The prince's face lit up at her slight teasing. "Only if I can carry the toolbox. It'll make it more believable when I tell my dad I helped fix a car with my bare hands."

The two chuckled together as they walked back up the embankment. With every step they took, Henry realized when he bantered with her, the fall breeze wasn't quite so chilly anymore.

Read *Beauty's Cursed Prince* today!

ABOUT THE AUTHOR

USA Today bestselling author Mary E. Twomey lives in Michigan with her three adorable children. She enjoys reading, writing, vegetarian cooking, and telling her children fantastic stories about wombats.

While she loves writing fantasy, dystopian, and paranormal tales for her readers, Mary also writes romance under the name Tuesday Embers, and cozy mysteries under the name Molly Maple.

Visit her online at www.maryetwomey.com, and sign up for her newsletter, so you never miss a new release.

* 9 781088 183069 *